The Other Stolen Generations

The Other Stolen Generations

David Adams

Published by David Adams, 2022.

This is a work of fiction. Similarities to real people, places, or events are entirely coincidental.

THE OTHER STOLEN GENERATIONS

First edition. December 5, 2022.

Copyright © 2022 David Adams.

ISBN: 978-0645361148

Written by David Adams.

I dedicate this book to all the victims and those affected by child abuse throughout the generations.

DAVID ADAMS

ABOUT THE AUTHOR

David Adams served his last two years in the A.D.F as a Platoon Commander Military Police. This exposure to law enforcement lead him to work closely with his civilian counterparts in the Queensland Police Service. He has participated in Under Cover Operations within the Queensland Police Service.

His civilian career saw him working with the Commission for Children and later as a contractor with the Department of Child Safety, now named the Department of Children, Youth Justice and Multicultural Affairs.

Author's Notes.

I hate writing an Author's Note, however the level of authenticity and the powerful and emotive nature of this evil topic demands it.

The statistics noted on the front cover come the Australian Government, The Australian Institute of Health and Welfare. It is an acknowledged fact that a significant number of abuse cases are never reported so this number may be understated and serves to demonstrate the devastating impact this evil has on society.

1. While this book is a work of fiction it is inspired by real abuse cases, known paedophiles and Police procedures deployed in the on-going battle against this growing evil. The latter part of my professional career saw me work in the Child Safety sector. This provides me and now you the Reader with both authentic cases and insight and experiences. Naturally, I have changed names, places and some details to avoid identifying all parties, and causing any further pain to the victims and their families.

2. I mention there is an orchestrated well funded and world wide push to change our way of thinking about what is deviant or heinous. The rights of an individual have in recent decades eclipsed those of the community and it's laws and mores. What is ignored in this, is that this is often at the cost of another individual. Those usually those less powerful and therefore more vulnerable, the young, elderly or disabled. The rights of an adult whose sexual choices involve a child is being aligned with all the other preferences, and as being normal. Clearly, the child lacks the maturity and experience, or the opportunity to choose to be involved. This imbalance of power turns the adult into the Abuser, and the child the unwilling Victim.

It is not the purpose of this book to preach about this, however the vast majority will not be aware of this paid lobbying and subtle exposure to manipulating changes in attitude that wears down a moral society's natural resistance and eventually leads to acceptance.

3. After much internal struggling I have provided the Reader a 'behind the scenes' tour of the Paedophile's mind. I have done this because the normal human being raised in a mature society, possibly a loving nurturing family can not comprehend the world of selfish, driven depravity that some men and a small group of women live in.

Having said that, Paedophiles can come from any level of society, education. At times the cause of the individual's choice seems blatantly obvious, such as being a victim themselves, while on other occasions most unlikely. We all know that not all those abused become abusers. However research shows that the jails are full of angry men and women who came from abusive homes.

4. I am in no way endorsing, condoning or suggesting that any vigilante, or vigilante group should take the law into their own hands and harm a known paedophile. If the laws and courts don't reflect society's expectations then politically society must protect the innocent. This can be demanded by voting and commenting when the courts and systems fail to protect the babies and children of our communities.

5. The insights into paedophile's strategies and tricks are present in a similar way to forensic TV shows, or any crime show, be assured that the criminals are fully aware of these already. Thankfully so are the Police.

6. Even though one could say that in some instances the abuser is a victim as well, children must be protected as a priority. The paedophile must be contained and isolated as it has been proven in the vast majority of cases recidivism is likely.

7. The following is an extract from the Australian Government, The Australian Institute of Health and Welfare report. Emphasising the life long negative effects of abuse on the victim as an adult.

Child abuse and neglect can have a wide range of significant adverse impacts on a child's development and later outcomes, including but not limited to:

- reduced social skills
- poor school performance
- impaired language ability
- higher likelihood of criminal offending
- negative physical health outcomes
- mental health issues such as eating disorders, substance abuse, depression and suicide (ABS 2019; AIFS 2014).

PROLOGUE

Factual Quote from a famous Holocaust Survivor and Nazi Hunter Simon Wiesenthal:

"I have talked with other 'victims' and they want to do the same thing to the abusers (execute them), take away from them what they took away from us.

But no we will not be like them. We will use the law. If we kill them the world never learn what they did. They will be pitied and seen as victims.

There must be an accounting. There must be testimony in court, a record for history.

The plan worked. When I saw him arrested I felt the excitement of triumph, not any personal achievement but for the fact that justice knows no limits in time."

Quote from the book's fictional character Detective-Sergeant Ben McQueen of the Child Protection & Investigation Unit.
All I can say is: **"I wish I was as good a man as he, but I'm not."**

Not all those abused become criminals. However, many crimes especially those of violence are directly related to childhood abuse.

Not all abusers become paedophiles abusing others. However, many manifest the impact of this abuse becoming violent towards wives, children and others. Their anger white hot.

I have named this book because I have personally observed the negative and devastating impact abuse has on the victims, their families and even the families of the abuser. A child's ability to learn, relate and love is in many cases stolen forever.

A STOLEN CHILDHOOD = HURTING GENERATIONS PRESENT AND FUTURE, ROBBED OF IT'S POTENTIAL.

CHAPTER 1

"But whosoever shall offend one of these little [children] which believe in me, it were better for him that a **millstone** were hanged about his neck, and that he were drowned in the depth of the sea" (Matthew 18:6; Mark 9:42; Luke.17:2)

High pitched screams shattered the serenity of the idyllic beach-side park. Every adult automatically turned towards the source imagining some terrible event that had just injured some hapless child. The majority of the men or women in the park could not control that most basic reaction of an adult when a child screams. Although, strangely, not one of the men sitting around the coffee shop table even looked up. All the other patrons at the coffee shop looked up expectantly. Then all sighing in relief that there was no tragedy, smiled as one. Enjoying the children's energy and fun they returned to their coffees, newspapers and phones. Kids in swimsuits scream again as a sudden but highly anticipated jet of water springs up from the flat concrete water playground. However, control is what has kept this group safe for over a decade, self control when in public scrutiny. It is simply a group of men sharing a morning coffee and the free papers. There are seven members of this group, and they are not remarkable in any sense. They meet every morning and always sit at this table away from the other patrons and the children's water play area. But not too far away.

Still not looking towards the water park Paul the oldest of the group; plump, balding, laughed quietly. "Funny, that water playground has always been fun to watch. Whatever your preference, boy/girl any age even Robert's preference, his pre-teenagers love those water jets hitting them in the nether regions."

Robert looked up, at least the group assumed he had as his head moved. His eyes were permanently hidden behind aviator sun glasses, even on rainy days. Responding with a light sort of Canadian accent that the other group members firmly believed he had picked up from TV.

"Firstly, if they're old enough to bleed they are ready to butcher. Secondly, if I take them out to eat somewhere at least they can read the menu." He paused to appreciate his own humour.

"But back to the water feature the real irony is there's probably more coppers hanging around there than perves. They're always down there looking for single males, idiots taking photos, all the amateurs who keep the boys in blue busy." He concluded.

Paul continued. "Yep, you're right Rob, if they had any brains at all they'd do what I always do."

"What's that Einstein?" Robbie asked, emphasising the 'Einstein'.

Paul looking irritated by Robert's sarcasm responded."Well Robby I carry a kid's pair of pink sparkly runners. I sit them beside me while I enjoy watching all those those littlies and slightly bigger versions playing in their tiny swim suits and guess what? Everyone thinks isn't that cute Grandpa is looking after his grand kid's shoes while they play on the swings or in the water fountains. It works so well other parents come up and start talking to me."

Sitting at the end of the table a Courier Mail that was lowered exposing a red headed man in his thirties the 'baby' of the group. Damien was different to most of these men, he was well dressed, well educated and was always analysing what was being said. Even though, or perhaps because he had served in the Military he was highly analytical. He was the hard man of the group.

"Speaking of the good work being done by Queensland's finest I'm just reading about their internet campaign against paedophiles." Damo started to read from the paper in front of him.

'This morning the Minister for Police and Corrective Services Joseph Wright MP joined the Queensland Police Service to deliver an important message to all parents, caregivers and educators as part of Safer Internet Day. The investigators within Queensland Police Service's Argos and child protection officers across the state do a job not many of us could." "Boo fuckin hoo!" , he inserted as he read from the newspaper, and then continued. "They investigate internet facilitated crimes against children." Minister Wright said. This was met with smiles and subdued laughter by the entire group.

Charlie, or Charles as he demanded to be called by the men seated around him smiled. He was the unofficial leader. He asserted this by waiting, because he knew that every morning a topic would surface that he could and would hijack. Never failed. These may have been long term associates, sharing a common need but still diverse interest. But with the possible exception of Damo, they were pretty much an uneducated bunch. And maybe Richard who seldom spoke and thereby maintained an aura of intelligence, yet to be confirmed.

Charles continued. "Now the way I see it you've got three porn groups."

Paul holding his head as if suffering from a headache. "Oh, I can feel another half assed theory comin on and all we're only drinking fuckin lattes."

Charles glared at Paul but ignoring his disrespectful sarcasm continued. "Yeah, yeah, anyway, ordinary punter starts with something mild and works their way in deeper. Some of them aren't looking for any young stuff but ordinary adult straight websites trap them. In amongst the straight adult women, surprise surprise photos of some girl of indeterminable age dressed up in school uniform. Something they've been pushing down since puberty, when they were inexperienced but that age too. The dragon shows a glimpse of it's tail rising. And that dragon either wins or looses."

They all hated his dramatic descriptions, dragons what next?

He continued. "If the dragon looses a quick click and the schoolgirls are replaced with naked adult women of every colour and size type. But all grown ups, mostly from Russia, all looking bored staring out at them disinterestedly with drug glazed eyes."

Annoyingly for Charles, Robert interrupts his speech. "Yeah, and if it's a win the other group clicks on the Asian school girl next, click once, click twice more. Then as their pulse rockets they click off, feeling guilty and promising never to look at that 'filth' again."

Richard mutters to himself. "And most of them keep that promise don't they?"

Charles needs to discourage any potential challenge veiled as an intelligent comment. "Sure, the good little boys suppress it all again. But there's another group right? These just like Tricky Dickey just said keep following the links and clicks until all the photos and live cams are models are, or at least look very under-age."

Pausing for effect, to drain his chai latte, Charles finally got to the point. "This is where these virgin child porn fans are always getting caught. These coppers have laid some baits, some links to their fake websites. Dumb ass punters head down dick firmly in hand follow the breadcrumb trail all the way into the trap." Bang his hand bounced off the table rattling the cups and mugs either side of him. He regrets this dramatic act as a young couple at the opposite end of the outside eating area look over.

Lowering his voice even further he continued. "He's screwed, cops are knocking on his door the next morning. Pats on the back all round for the coppers, and off course the celebratory press release from our esteemed Premier. The pigs might even make out they are a kid and lure the sucker into a meeting and get 'em on more that just kiddie porn."

A man in his sixties with dark thinning hair and a 1960s moustache called Mike joined in, his high voice not matching his Mexican appearance.

"And we could nearly feel sorry for them except once again they keep the heat off us. Thank God for the Dark Web hey? Although I'm sure God doesn't have a lot to do with it."

Maroochydore Police Headquarters

"So how did Detective-Sergeant McQueen do in court?" Smiling, my boss, Superintendent Barry Fisher a tall and wide shouldered ex Military Policeman whose shaved head made him even more intimidating than he had been when he had hair.

I laugh at his formal use of my rank. "Yeah good Sir, it always worries me when you call me Detective-Sergeant McQueen I always feel like I'm in trouble again. Got the absolute max fourteen years, no parole for ten. Friggin awesome, for once the law backed us up full strength." I answered smiling as I checked my phone messages that had piled up in my absence.

"Only fair, a real hero father of the year, bashin his own four month old son for God's sake he nearly killed him." .

As a Detective-Sergeant in the Child Protection Investigation Unit Queensland I had seen it all and understood the policies and court findings we operated under were driven by politics, budget cuts and their constant companion fear.

These in turn are driven by the media's agendas usually ill-informed and uncaring seeking only to gouge a dramatic story from a broken child or family. I had seen so many child abusers get off lightly this recent result was rare indeed. My first year in the Child Protection had taught me that abuse came in more varieties than ice cream. Selfish parents who couldn't control their tempers when they disciplined. Bashing their own kids, angry at something else. Some spent money on drugs instead of food or medicine. Most of these were left to Child Safety or the local coppers. The repeat offenders, the physical abusers like today's came to us. Of course there was always good old uncle Jack the family member/ sexual abuser. This type came under our section's purview. Along with family members abuse there were strangers ready to abuse both boys or girls of any age. These were normally the habitual paedophiles, the expert or professional abusers. Lastly, there was a group not interested in children sexually but dedicated to the money they could make from the children suffering abuse either live or via the net.

Many of this group worked with children, teachers, leaders in various groups trusted to teach and support children. Sadly, as history had demonstrated some were politicians, carers, police and any other profession or work. However, they all shared an obsession, a habit that until they were caught was seldom suspected by their families or colleagues. This group because of their knowledge, network and professional approach were seldom caught by the police. When they were arrested the system under pressure from their family and prisoner rights groups granted them early release even though they represented the worst recidivism of any offender group.

The boss interrupted my thoughts. "Ben when you've caught up on your messages come and see me we just got another out at Fernygrove."

Most of the messages were routine so I made four calls left two messages and made a coffee.

"So what cesspit do you want me to look into now boss?"

Superintendent Fisher looked up from his desk and picked up a manilla file marked ACTION.

"Ben, just near the railway station at Fernygrove, a ten year old girl, attempted abduction. Witness saw it, single male in a white Toyota Hilux. It's all in the file here." He handed the folder to me.

"Thanks boss, I'll read up on it and let you know."

"Oh. Ben if you think it's worth a try, I'm happy to get media to ask for public assistance every ones got a friggin dash-cam these days."

"Not me, but yeah might be a good idea, thanks I'll let you know."

I read the File, and hit the road. One of the hardest parts of the job. I turn up, some strange man rehashing a painful memory asking a ten year old girl in tears the same questions her mum and three other coppers had already asked. But the perve must have either been stupid or like a lot of these failed abductions he had tried it on the spur of the moment thinking with another part of his body. As the file had said a ten year old girl was walking to school, when a guy passed her in his ute and then pulled up. He made out he was checking something in the tray and grabbed at her when she got beside the vehicle. He then attempted to drag her into the front of the pick up. She'd put up a hell of a struggle, and as another vehicle approached the scene he let her go. Then he ran to the driver's side, got in and took off spinning the wheels as he went.

After I interviewed the girl, her mother saw me to the door and although clearly shaken by what had happened was putting on a brave front. "Thank you Detective-Sergeant McQueen, I appreciate how gentle you were with Lea. Please find this man before he tries again with some one else's daughter."

"Thank you Mrs Fogarty we will certainly do all we can." I said confidently.

This guy was clearly no genius trying this near a Railway Station, these days everyone knows that all government buildings pretty well have CCTV security. A quick visit to the Train Station and a call to Queensland Rail Security Service and I had permission to get a copy of that mornings CCTV. There he was and unusually for security video, in colour. A white ute, probably a Toyota Hilux, to be confirmed under magnification, and maybe if I was lucky some registration plate as well. The man was Caucasian in appearance wearing a long bill black cap, in his early 20s and had a proportionate build. He was wearing a light blue sweatshirt, running shoes and black shorts. When I got back to the office I watched the video again and zoomed in on the plate, but couldn't see a single letter or digit. I phoned Superintendent Fisher and reported what I'd found and requested permission to take it to Media Liaison with the video, of course he was fine with that.

"Get straight down there and you'll be in time for the six pm News."

"Roger that Sir, I'll let you know how I go."

All the news outlets ran the story; "Detectives have released a video of a vehicle of interest and it's driver who attempted to abduct a ten year old girl in Fernygrove this morning." Followed by some more details, and a request for witnesses, information and any dash-cam video. No less than two of his neighbours and the car owner that had unwittingly spooked him phoned in with information including his name and address. The would be abductor was in custody by eight thirty that night. But it's not always that easy.

Chapter 2

Robert looked around at the others and asked. "Did you guys see the TV last night. Like the Six o'clock news this idiot tries to get some kid into his car. Dumb as a bag full of hammers, hasn't he heard of CCTV s? Anyway, a full on colour vid of this clown and his white ute. What a goose."

Damo chips in. "Not to mention all the kids know about stranger danger right? Like it's not taught in every school these days. Dickhead."

Charles smirks. "Yeah, shows poor planning, no intelligence and in the long run a lack of commitment." He states as though commenting on failed business or even a football player.

Robert makes out he's going to raise his sunnies and then changes his mind, or maybe he was just playing with the group who had yet to see his eyes. "Real abductions are few and far between but a woman who is into it, you know willing to help that must make it so easy man. Kids don't think twice about getting a car with a woman in it."

Charles voice is even more condescending than usual. "Yeah, well like you said, very few women will help do that they are all too motherly and protective. And besides just another variable that can go wrong, another dog who can turn on you. You can't trust women once they grow up." The group laugh.

A young waiter arrives with a tray of various coffees, all conversation hits the pause button. "Thanks Stan, great work as usual." Charles speaks for the entire table. As the waiter walks away with the empty tray he thinks about the abrupt silence that his arriving always seemed to initiate like a switch. Common enough if it was a couple whispering sweet nothings, but this group were always the same. Very careful, they sat as far away as possible, always stopped chatting whenever anyone approached their table. Not for the first time as he walked into the kitchen the young waiter asked. "Boss, who do you think those wankers are?" Pointing over his shoulders as though they could see the group of men he had just served.

The overworked coffee shop owner straightened his tired back and slightly irritated by the young man's questioning responded."Stuffed if I know Stan, but I don't care either, they spend money here every single day so I love 'em."

"Yeah I know but there's somethin not right about them." The young waiter said doggedly.

After quietly slurping from his flat white double shot Charles continues as if someone had really paused the group like a video."Meeting out in plain sight has it's advantages guys, no one's going to notice all of us traipsing in and out of one of our houses. And of course no listening devices, but we have survived by being cautious so we must continue that way."

Paul being the senior member had always resented Charles constant claim on the leadership of the group, took an opportunity to usurp him. "Yes, yes Charlie we all know why we must put up with this daily penance suffering your theories. Can we get on with the business?"

Nods all round the table caused Charles to nod as well even though he hated the way Paul had if only for a moment taken informal control of the group. Charles regrouped quickly.

"Alright gentlemen, I suppose if we not to be like the idiot we just discussed we should start planning. Robert where are we re Thailand?"

Robert was once a Sergeant at Arms with an outlaw Bikie group based in Sydney. That was until he had been stripped of his colours and expelled from the gang. He had kept his preference for girls of ten but not older than thirteen hidden from his fellow club members but through an unfortunate turn of events his secret was exposed. Bikies had few moral boundaries but his tastes pushed them too far, after a bashing he still bore the scars from he was thrown out knowing he would be executed if he ever returned. Even so, this had made him a natural choice to liaise between this motley group this Grub Club and the Hunters Outlaw Motorcycle Club located on the Gold Coast hinterland. His mind returned to that beating and for the moment he was oblivious to his surroundings and Charles' voice.

"Robert, Robert earth to Robert." Charles was laughing at his colleague's lack of reaction.

Reaching out he took Robert's forearm and gently shook it, causing Robert to start and look around like he had just woken. Recovering quickly he responded to Charles' request.

Refocusing he responded."Sorry guys, yeah the trial order's been placed they want six units by the fifteenth of next month. The friggin hypocrites they kill peds like it's a sport but they don't mind makin money on it."

Paul knew Robert's story and understood his comments so he was gentle. "Robbie, mate that's great work. How are we going to fill that order?"

The rest of the meeting saw all the members work through the logistics and roles each would play in achieving their business plan.

Up to now he hadn't spoken much, Damo sensing the meeting was drawing to a close felt he should contribute. "Don't you love a cashless society hey, how good is that? Those Bikies are the smart ones though. The Gold Coast club make a huge profit on-selling the units they get from us. It's no coincidence that their ex President just so happens to be the proud owner of a hotel and bar in Bangkok. Not just any hotel this one has hot and cold running kids of every age and type. No money trail no fear, and us with an all expenses paid holiday. Paid for by our collecting and passing on a batch of kids. I don't know about you guys but I love Thailand and everything about it."

Charles ever the wet blanket felt duty bound to remind the group of the agreement they had with the Bikie group."It's no surprise they don't trust us or anyone for that matter."

He continued. "Now don't forget Thailand is a way off at this stage. We have to prove ourselves as able to deliver and able to not attract the law."

"I get that, but how come we have to deliver the first batch to Wellington" Stuttering. I-I-I-I-I mean Duke down South. Why the hell there?"

Paul responded first, lowering his voice. "Because for reasons I can't fathom Duke NSW is the paedo capital of Australia. The cops just about have a checkpoint going in and out of that fair town."

"Great so we grab five chickens and take them to a place where the cops are already on alert." Damo as usual offered his analysis and just as usually dripping with sarcasm.

"That's the whole point Damo, the Bikies have set us a worthy test, we'll be right, we're up for it. Think about that wonderful trip to Bangkok, and keep calm, all of you." Charles looked around the group with a steely grin.

"Good work on that attempted abduct at Ferny Grove Ben."

"Boss it didn't really take Sherlock Homes the guy was a dumbass, he confessed it was a spur of the moment thing. But I'm just glad we got him before his twisted mind actually formulated a plan that might have succeeded."

"Yeah, of course you're right, but every perve we scare or put inside is one less out there for a while." Looking over at a Detective hammering away on her computer. "Molly you've got court again this arvo haven't you?"

Smiling Detective Molly Herbert looked up and nodded. "I'm up at 1400 Hrs another easy one, yet another clown, they may as well just hand themselves in. Snatches a little boy at a shopping centre while mums playing the pokies."

"Honestly, Molly the friggin mother should be charged as well." Superintendent Fisher spat. Molly continued. "No fight from me, she had the nerve to carry on yelling at me to get out there and find her son instead of asking questions. I get it. She was terrified but that horse had bolted like. Anyway, I'm still at the mall interviewing her and some shop assistants and this Super perve comes out of the fire escape. Bold as brass he is holding the little boys hand and laughing."

"You're kidding?" I said amazed.

"No joke I couldn't believe my eyes. Anyway, I played it cool just in case the guy had found the kid in the stairwell and was trying to do the right thing. But my gut told me the prick was good for it."

"What happened then?"

"Well a couple of uniforms had arrived so I got them to keep the bloke busy while mum and I talked to the boy. Anyway, the little boy obviously didn't know what had happened to him in terms of sexual abuse. But he said the man touched him and showed him his 'Willy'. So I went over and formally arrested him. We took the little boy to the hospital and between his skin and his clothes Forensics found a bucket of semen.

Obviously we matched the physical evidence with the guy's blood and DNA. There was even CCTV of him taking the boy to his car and bringing him back. The vic too young to testify so my interview plus the Forensic evidence is plenty to put this guy away for a while."

The Superintendent was clearly pleased with his team. "Between you and Ben we are catching some breaks lately mixed with solid Police work by you guys. Let's hope our good luck holds and the idiots keep stepping up."

"Thanks, that's for sure boss, we all know this evil circus has all sorts of dangers not just clowns." Molly said wisely.

Wacol Queensland
Correctional Services Restricted Area

Two hours later a slight breeze was blowing left to right. A mosquito that thought I was dinner filled my ear with a whine like a turbo. My range finder placed the back door at two hundred and fifty-seven metres. It was a wooden weather-board cottage built in the fifties and thankfully that meant it had the obligatory little landing off the back door. Mr Donald Nell had lived there by himself for the last three months. It was Correction Service's idea of transition. Get him out of a cell into a home, poor little man how he had suffered. Or so his solicitor had whined at his Parole Hearing. He was due for release by Christmas and he was enjoying his new freedom even though the razor wire and guards still surrounded this cottage he now called home. I had been watching the seen for nearly four hours and so far except for some lights going on in what I assumed to be the kitchen there was nothing.

I knew he was a smoker but clearly he was happy to smoke inside watching TV or whatever he was doing. I was surprised that I hadn't seen a glimpse of Nell but patience was something I had learnt well in another place with a lot more sand. I had chosen today because it was rubbish day. I smiled at that thought because that's exactly what I was doing. Taking out the rubbish. Nell's bin was sitting at the back door on the landing I now focused on. If this plan didn't gel I was still OK with taking a shot through a window. But this wasn't my first choice. I was counting on Mr Nell doing the most domestic of chores and giving me a clear shot at him. My weapon was Remington in 308. Winchester unregistered and unknown to the world at large, but especially the Queensland Police Service.

The sun isn't up yet but it is threatening the horizon, I've made sure I'm not going to be looking into the sun when it finally arrives. My plan, my being there was against every part of my being, except for one. I am a Christian, I fear God and believe in judgement as in Heaven and Hell. However, I can't keep working in my profession knowing the people I'm supposed to be protecting are not safe. All because the system is attempting to serve multiple masters. This means the long standing guard has stood down and can no longer guarantee their safety from these paedophiles. Parents, my parents, teachers, my teachers none of them can protect the young any more.

I'm OK. But others, I can't forget the thousands of other children that are now grown adults. Scarred and scared forever by the abuse these animals have selfishly inflicted on so innocent a victim. Speaking to the universe. "I am OK, being OK puts a debt on me I feel the weight of every minute of every day. Justice must be done."

The universe responds. The back door opens outwardly to the landing. Nell comes outside and places a small bag into the rubbish bin.

The cross-hairs settle lightly on his chest and I felt the recoil of the 308. It is done, the children of this world are safe. At least from him.

CHAPTER 3

Psalm 123"7 "Children are a gift from the Lord; they are a reward from him." "Jesus said,

Robert stirring his coffee continues. "And on top of that some crazy bitch shrink, I think she's in the States has described paedophilia as a Disorder not a crime. Treat it with preventative meds huh!

Its like all these fools that push for chemical castration, ha ha! They've got no fucking idea how this shit works. If a paedo can't get it up even with a help from uncle Viagra he still wants to touch or look, right? So even if you are paralysed from the waist down you still have a mind, an imagination, a finger, two eyes, even a frigging tongue." Everyone laughs.

"Yeah, chem castration just satisfies the good citizens who want revenge it doesn't do much else."

Robert appears very excited this morning and attempts to tell the group what had occurred over night. Charles attempting to take the group to where he wanted it to go.

"Sure, sure Robbie can we just discuss our upcoming road trip first?" Robert's facial expression moves from anger to deadset sullen, but says nothing more. Charles uses the gap to push on. "Duke seems to be progressing well, lets bring everyone up to speed, where are we with it?" Duke was their code-name for Wellington New South Wales.

Paul smiling and rubbing his hands on something under the table. "Feel like fucking James Bond with all this code shit. As you know the customers ordered five hot chickens for Duke, and four are ready. We have them cooling at Paul's place, all good. They'll be able to warm them up when they get delivered." Smirks all round except for Charles of course. "I have been thinking..."

Charles sneers and cuts across him. "That's a fucking nice change Paul, only kidding. What's your plan?"

Looking like he had been slapped across the face by Charles's sarcasm Paul continues."We pick up the last hot one on the way down, should work OK. What do we think?"

Richard who hadn't contributed until now spoke up. "Yeah, can't see why that wouldn't work, maybe grab a little bird in Warwick or whenever we see one we like. We all good with that?" Nods of agreement all round.

Charles not famous for his team motivation skills effortlessly upset another member. "Get on with your fucking story Robert, if I didn't know you better I'd think you were an old queen the way you carry on."

Robert glared at the informal group leader.

"Well let's see how you'd feel if the cops came to your address hey Charles?" That had got everyone's attention; Robert allowed himself a small smile of satisfaction and continued. They all knew if the Police were questioning one of their group it wouldn't be long before they were all pulled in for questioning. Robert's introduction worried them all.

"Anyway, as you know I live in those Housing Commission units that overlook the Mooloolabah State School."

Leering he continued. "Some like ocean views but I am more than happy with mine especially on sports days." He giggles. "Anyway, I look over the oval and see a flash like a reflection coming from a parked car. Now I spend half my life and the best part of the school term making sure my telescope and camera don't betray me by reflecting outwards. So you can only imagine what was going through my mind. Was that a cop on surveillance duty. As careful as I was had someone seen my big lens sticking out the patio door? Well,

I panicked. Where will I hide my camera, all those photo memory cards and of course my laptop is overflowing with evidence? After a while I settle down a little and figure I should make sure its a cop and if that's who it is, was he actually looking at me. He might be some perve, who knows?"

Everybody laughed at this irony, easing the suspense, the fact that Robert was sitting next to them suggested he had escaped somehow. "I grab my binos and from deep inside my unit I check him out. He was definitely looking across the oval at my block of units. But get this, I could tell from the angle of his binoculars that he must have been looking at a unit much higher than mine. I can't tell you how relieved I was. Anyway, about an hour later there was a ruckus on the stairs and I snuck a look. Two cops had a guy in cuffs, I don't know him but I've seen him around and I think he lives three floors above me."

The relief around the table was palpable. The others reckoned Mike and Charles were partners of some type. Maybe to support his arguments, or maybe a vote and possibly a spy for the ambitious informal leader. Mike seldom said anything but, but he was smiling.

"Man you sure had me worried."

Charles attempted to reverse the earlier insult. "Well it took a while but man what a story? But it just shows these Sunshine Coast Child Protection cops are everywhere." The story served to remind everyone how fragile their freedom and the operation of the group really was. The story was all too close to home for everyone sitting there.

My Boss Superintendent Barry Fisher was a good cop, leader and man, but as in most hierarchies the higher you go the more pressure on you to hand out bullshit and tell everyone it's ice-cream. I was angry and he knew it. Only last week he was saying how 'lucky we were with the paedos, just about jumping into our nets he had laughed.' Well our luck was still there the only problem, now it was all bad. A paedo I had put away had applied for parole and it looked like being approved.

"Sir, that piece of crap should never get out. Raping a one year old baby, oh come on. Now boss hopefully as she got older she was never told about it. But you know family secrets seldom last the long haul. That's only her, even if she is unaware of the original crime, the fact that her father topped himself because he felt like he had failed to protect his little one. It's destroyed that family. As you know I did the Victim Impact Report for the scum-bag's parole hearing. It all had to be without her knowing. Her mum was telling me they still don't know if she was so torn up whether she can even have kids. She and her family have been given a life sentence. You know what will happen, his release will hit the news and something will identify the victim. Some kid at school will ask and then it'll all be out there. And this guy he gets to go free. They're just empty shells Sir, you look at the family photos prior to it all this and they're all smiles a happy family with a future."

"Ben, mate take it easy, I have seen it all before and so have you. I am starting to get worried this is getting to you. You need to let off that pressure. Don't get all hard hearted like some of the detectives, but try not to personalise every case either. You're good at this. I don't know what keeps you so fired up but I know you're goin to burn out if you don't settle it down a tad."

"I know you're right Boss but I hate the idea of him back on the street. I know it's been ten years but these guys just keep dreamin about it and talking to other scum-bag paedos on the inside while they do their time."

A mix of frustration and understanding was clear in the Superintendent's voice. "Enough is enough Ben. It's done and I am sure you did all you could, even the Attorney General tried to stop it. You know today everything is about rights." Holding his huge paws up to stop me from responding. "Yeah I know, what about the baby's rights, now the little girl's rights? But we work in a crazy cesspit in a fractured world."

A uniform knocks and comes into the office.

"Sir, there's a message for you." He hands a piece of paper to Superintendent Fisher. He reads it and shakes his head.

"Ben it looks like you just got your wish. Nell's parole just got cancelled. He was shot at his prison cottage at 0535Hrs this morning."

"Well Sir I'd be lying if I said that's terrible. Is he dead? Actually, it's friggin awesome. It might be wrong from a Police point of view but at least some kids'll be safe for a while."

Holding up his hands attempting to stop me before I said something that he couldn't ignore. Now knock that shit off buddy. Go and have a couple of beers, get some rest and I'll see you tomorrow, yes?"

"OK boss, see you in the morning." I said. I was feeling slack about having just acted surprised by this news lying to a man I admired and respected. More than that I had orchestrated the debate about Nell to cover my tracks.

I drove home on autopilot. My mind was going over every word the Superintendent had said. But just as vividly, I could see the crime photos of that little baby torn apart by the horrific act. My thoughts were jumping everywhere. *The original crime could easily have resulted in the baby being murdered. Everybody was trying to keep this monster behind bars. The system had all failed. Yet again. I couldn't trust the Parole Board. How would we all feel if he had been released only to hurt another baby? Thankfully, the situation had been resolved. I couldn't, I wouldn't take that chance. No choice at all.* After a scolding hot shower failed to burn off my anger I had those few beers and hit the sack before nine.

ISAIAH 59:16 The Lord looked and was displeased that there was no justice. He saw there was no one to intervene.

My alarm clock glared 0300Hrs at my bleary eyes, my sheets soaked in sweat tried to strangle me. My lungs and heart working like I had just run up ten flights of stairs. The nightmares always varied slightly. They always had me in different situations unable to escape, unable to get help and terrified. The bad dreams started just before I turned ten. Up till then I was a happy nine year old. Or as happy as a nine year old living in my family could be. I wasn't top of the class, but I was up there, and I liked my teachers and they liked me. By my tenth birthday my world had turned one eighty degrees. I was so angry I couldn't concentrate. My exam results showed it and any enquiry from a teacher that cared as to what was wrong met an angry outburst that alienated the teachers even further. All my friends abandoned me driven away by my anger, often sarcastic comments or my more adult interests. I was fast becoming toxic at school.

At home it was the same. I was angry, rude and demanding of my mother who had her own challengers to cope with. Mum and dad never did understand. I would hear mum defending me to dad. "It's just another 'stage'.

Not knowing any better Dad would say. "He'll grow out of it." Dad's solution was simple. "Get to your room and no supper 'til you apologise." Often assisted with a clip over the head. Of course at ten years old I didn't fully comprehend the rationale behind my anger. But I knew it had a lot to do with losing all respect for adults, teachers and parents. I couldn't trust them, I couldn't depend on them to protect me. I'd been betrayed.

CHAPTER 4

Joel 3:3

They cast lots for my people and traded boys for prostitution; they sold girls for wine that they might drink.

Charles smiled and left no one doubting he was pleased himself even more than his usual arrogance.

"Don't say I never do anything for you guys. I've got a massive surprise for you."

Mike asked what they all wanted to. "OK, Charles what have you done that's put such a big smile on your face?"

"Guys, I had a really interesting call from an old chicken farmer mate who happens to live just outside Warwick." Charles paused for just a moment and was rewarded with silence.

Paul who was still enjoying the use of cryptic terms like Duke for Wellington NSW and chickens for kids looked puzzled.

"You mean you actually know someone who breeds kids, a 'chicken farmer'?

Charles looked at him the same way a teacher looks at a slow student who was silly enough to confirm their stupidity, and shook his head in disbelief.

"Oh Paul, sometimes I wonder how some people can be that dumb and still breath without assistance. No he's a real, an ordinary chicken farmer, you know big sheds and silos. He sounded like he was wasting his time trying to illuminate the older man sitting across from him.

"Well anyway he has similar interests to us and is a father of three children all under thirteen." Several of the men sitting around the table turned toward the speaker, some grabbing for the coffee mugs in front of them.

He continued knowing he had them in the palm of his hand. "Now apparently he's not making near enough growing chickens. So he's started a little hire business. It hasn't been going long and he wondered if we would like to come up some weekend and hire a few things."

Richard chimed in. "What on earth would we want to hire Charles?"

"Did you two take your dumbass pills this morning? Seriously. Oh, I don't know. Maybe one of his kids, maybe all three."

Paul moved forward on his chair. "Are you kiddin me?"

"No, that's why he phoned he's looking for some customers and he knows I'm cool. This is what I was thinking. We call in there on our Duke trip. Do we need a vote?" Charles asked with a knowing smirk.

Every one of them looked so excited Charles had his answer.

The Car Park

The Power Boat Club

I had been waiting for a guy to arrive and I was feeling a bit anxious. I hadn't done any undercover work for a while and certainly not this close to home. A crystal white BMW pulled into a space, his personalised plate SMILE 01 confirming he was the target I was looking for. He looked just as he should, starting to lose his hair, but trying to camouflage it. A sparkling smile and fit looking without being threatening like some kale munching marathon running chiropractor. Climbing out of the Beamer he walked straight over to me and shoved a hand out.

"You must be Justin, nice to meet you I'm Luke."

'Yeah, nice to meet you too, happy to go inside?'

"Sure what would you like to drink?" He asked like we were old friends catching up.

We sat at a corner table in the Power Boat Club overlooking Bribie Island and I had just put our drinks in front of us. Even though I like Toby Keith they were playing, it was way too loud. I started to wonder if I was just getting old. I didn't want to have to shout our conversation but the man sitting opposite had chosen the venue.

"So Luke how long you been a dentist?"

"Ah, close on eight years but I am starting to count it like dog years and multiply by seven. Just so sick of shoving my hands in people's mouths and being lied to about how often they brush."

"Yeah, but like the plumbers say the moneys clean right?" I said lightly.

"Sure of course you're right, and one wife plus an ex means I have to make as much as I can just to be OK."

The mention of money was a good entrée for me to get to the point. I wasn't enjoying this guy's company, dazzling smile or not.

"Well that's how we got to know each other when Jack told me about your little side business I couldn't believe my luck." He said downing half his pint of Guinness in one go.

"Speaking of Jack did he ever talk about his twins?"

I plastered on a look somewhere between annoyed and offended and frowning.

"Come on Luke we wouldn't be sitting here if you hadn't already checked me out. We both know Jack never married, doesn't have any kids and certainly not twins. For a bright guy that was a pretty clumsy trap. Mate we have to start trusting each other if I'm going to feel comfortable referring customers. And you Luke, well all you have to do is pull on your pretty blue gloves and do your fuckin job, and make another Beamer payment yeah?" Holding his hands up in surrender. "Whoa Justin, I'm sorry man, no offence. It's just I gotta be careful, those child protection cops are friggin everywhere."

I swirl the ice cubes around my glass and drain my JD with a smile. "Sorry to get agro, I've always been sensitive to people challenging my integrity. But what I said is important we do have to build trust, OK? So Luke you know I shared a cell with Jack at SDL (Sir David Longland Correctional Centre Maximum Security Unit) and let that be the end of it. What d'ya say?"

Another radiant show of a smile, he raised his glass and he finished the rest of the foamy black gold. "OK, OK when's your first referral?"

"Let me get the next round and we'll talk about it."

When I got back to my office Superintendent Fisher was sitting on my desk, looking over-tired as usual. "Ben I wasn't real happy about you going undercover on this Dentist, but I must admit it's panning out perfectly."

"Yeah, he's super careful but definitely not dangerous, the good thing is he's also greedy so he's hot to trot." I said confidently.

Shaking his head Fisher continued. "Now the Police Prosecutor needs him to actually have his fingers in a kid's mouth. That plus the tapes and your evidence will be enough to shut him down."

"You know boss I thought I'd seen it all, and feel like using acid to wash myself when I get home sometimes. But this, this just stuns me. How can a parent take their son or daughter to this maniac to have all their teeth removed. How can people be so fuckin horrible to the little ones they are s'posed to love and protect."

Shaking his head the huge tough cop responded. "I agree mate, just when I think I've seen how bad things can get something comes along like this. At five grand a pop a dentist that takes out teeth so some deviate can get a head job without getting bitten. How fuckin sick is that?"

Three days later my first referral to my new Dentist knocked on the sign-written glass sliding door. Detective Molly Herbert had volunteered to pose as the 'bitch mother'. A lengthy discussion about where we could get a child to act as a potential patient had seen Molly agree to take her own five year old daughter along. Of course the little girl was totally oblivious to it all and was simply going to the dentist. Molly was wearing a body camera and listening device. The moment she, or the Dentist uttered a phrase including 'starting now' or something similar she would remove her daughter from the surgery. Then we would arrive with a couple of uniforms and make the arrest. We all hated involving a child but to be sure of a conviction it had to be water-tight.

Dressed in his snow white dentist gown and all smiles he opened the door. "Ah, you must be Mrs Smith, I'm Doctor Jim, please come through."

Holding mummy's hand the little five year old bravely walked into the strange smelling surgery room.

"Now because this is a special treatment today I gave my nurse the afternoon off. But if you're OK there Mrs.... Ah, Smith it might be a good idea for you to stay in the room."

Smiling like a crocodile the undercover Detective agreed. "No prob Doctor, wouldn't want my baby to get scared or anything." The dentist bit his tongue thinking. *This bitch is sounding like a wonderful mother and then getting me to do this.*

"Sweety we will just get you up in this special Princess' throne, how's that sound?" As children do, the little girl believed everything the adult had to say and with mum's help climbed into the treatment chair. It didn't bode well that the dentist placed a full apron on the child instead of the usual napkin type.

Molly was repulsed, and angry to the point of thinking. *If I had my Glock I'd nail this prick where he stands.* Yet for the operation's sake and ensure that her daughter didn't pick up on her mother's anxiety and anger she pushed all these emotions back into the recesses of her trained mind.

"OK, I think we are set to start." That was all it took. Molly sprung like the matriarch lion she was, ready to kill to protect her young. Tearing off the apron from her daughter and threw it on the surgery floor. Taking care not to frighten her daughter Molly grabbed the little girl and took her out of the surgery and back into the sunny day outside.

Squeezing her daughter's tiny hand Molly shuddered. "Mommy's decided you don't need the dentist today, let's see what's in those shops over there. What do you say?"

The little girl a little confused but looking forward to the shops didn't notice the two Police Officers and another man she actually knew walk into the Dentist's rooms they had just left.

The sting had gone ahead as planned. The sicko dentist was caught both on camera and in person. Molly was pleased to hear that Luke the dentist had melted into a puddle of tears on his surgery floor when the three Police Officers kicked his door in. Especially when he saw me and the realisation that Justin was in fact Detective Ben McQueen.

"Well mate you were right when you said. 'Those child protection cops are friggin everywhere.' I quoted him from our meeting. After finishing the paper work I went home after it was all done felt better than I had for a long time. A few JDs to make sure I at least got to sleep and I hit the sack.

My voice breaking in youth and fear. "But Mr Johnson, it's just a note." He is a huge man with a huge scarred nose. He also has huge hands and one of them flies from nowhere across my face, I'm nine years old. The force of the blow knocks me across the classroom. My classmates are divided between sounds of shock and a ripple of nervous giggling. But I refuse to fall down. I won't let him make me cry. In unison I hear my fellow classmates suck in a terrified breath. Somehow quickly he is towering over me again.

"You little liar, who was this note to?"

"I don't know Sir, I...." He hits me again before I finish. I know who I wrote the naive love note to, but I am not going to get her into trouble. Again he is beside me, how does such a big old man move so quickly? Whack and my legs surrender, betraying my will to stand up to him. I'm falling. I'm falling.

I wake shaking and crying. I think about the dream, but it's not really a dream because it happened when I was in Grade five I remember the girl, her name was Margaret. I remember that mean bully of a teacher. These days he'd be up on charges, maybe lose his job. Those days if I'd told my parents dad would give me a flogging because I must have deserved what Mr Johnson had done to me.

Next morning I felt wrung out worse than I had for a long time. But mostly I had anger, not just normal cut off in the traffic on the way to the office type anger. I'm talking fury. I'm talkin if you say the wrong thing I'll pull my Glock. This anger had robbed me of my education, promotion in the Army, my social life and my joy. I had to master it so it wouldn't rob me of this job which I loved so much. Superintendent Barry Fisher is standing out the front of the meeting room, behind him are display boards with the pictures of five children in the centre.

"OK, take your seats ladies and gentlemen please, there is coffee and sandwiches down the back. Before we start I want to acknowledge and thank Molly. That was one top class arrest of our friendly dentist. Well done everyone and especially Molly and her little one."

Everyone clapped softly and smiles all round. In crap work ya gotta get your joy when you can. Celebrate the wins.

"Now as you all know kids go missing every day. Especially now the Department of Child Safety have to inform us every time a foster care kid disappears for a couple of hours. That being said these five are the real deal. As far as we can tell, 'normal' parents, no big issues, totally out of character. Frankly guys these five worry the shit out of me. My gut tells me something is goin on that we can't see at present. Now I fully realise they are outside our region. But the Assistant Commissioner has requested all Regions to be on the look out both locally and if anyone has any Intel or ideas about this."

He continued for another half an hour or so and then finished off.

"OK guys, you all have your assignments. Keep in touch so we can maintain a helicopter view of this. We have no idea whether it's a paedo ring or an individual. I just hope and pray we are not too late to find these kids alive."

I had stayed quiet knowing that the molten anger in me was close to the thin crust it lived beneath. It would have been easy to transfer my rage to the scum grabbing these kids. However, I didn't trust myself to do this and not erupt in front of my colleagues. I was just as sure it wasn't any of the guys in the meeting I was angry with. I joined Molly at the boards looking at the innocent faces smiling back at us. We both memorised each child's face, even though we had hard copy photos given to us in the briefing kit. We still took notes from the description under each photo because this to some degree at least helped the memory. That's what they taught us at Charm School, the nick name for Detectives College, we had learnt through experience that it works. The board had a set pattern of description and as we worked our way along it questions immediately sprung to mind.

Missing 13 year-old-girl, North Ipswich[1]

myPolice on Aug 3, 2019 @ 15.30 Hrs

---

1. https://qld.us2.list-manage.com/track/ click?u=bc40de864c611dd173a42d2ea&id=11fc2fd9 10&e=9a8e09e60f

Police are seeking public assistance to help locate a 13-year-old girl reported missing from a shopping centre in North Ipswich since yesterday.

Family hold concerns for the girl's safety as he has not been seen since leaving Northside Shopping Centre on her own around 1100 Hrs yesterday.

The (pictured) is about 160cm tall with a solid build, long blonde curly hair, blue eyes.

She was wearing a Bronco's Tee shirt, black shorts and a red cap (pictured).

Anyone with information regarding his whereabouts is urged to contact police.

Missing 9-year-old-boy, Ipswich [2]

myPolice on Aug 5, 2019 @ 1745 Hrs

Police are appealing for public assistance to help locate a 9-year-old boy reported missing from Ipswich.

The boy (pictured) was last seen on August 4 on Platform 4 Ipswich Railway Station, however has not made contact since.

Police hold concerns for his welfare due to his young age.

The boy is described as Aboriginal, 145cm tall, slim build, dark brown hair and brown eyes.

He was last seen wearing a white shirt, long black pants and black joggers and was carrying a dark blue school back pack.

Any members of the public who have seen the boy or who have information in relation to his whereabouts are asked to contact police.

---

2. https://qld.us2.list-manage.com/track/
   click?u=bc40de864c611dd173a42d2ea&id=3ed01d9
   8a4&e=9a8e09e60f

Police and family hold concerns for her safety and well-being due to her young age and are urging the girl, or anyone who may know her current whereabouts, to contact police (details below).

Missing 11 year-old- boy, Goodna [3]

myPolice on Aug 9 Aug 2019 @ 1600 Hrs

Police are appealing for public assistance to help locate a boy reported missing from Goodna today.

The 11-year-old boy (pictured) were last seen yesterday at 0800 Hrs at a Bunya Street address.

Police hold concerns for their welfare due to his young age.

The boy is described as Caucasian, 155cm tall, slim build, blonde hair and brown eyes.

Any members of the public who have seen these two children or have information in relation to their whereabouts are asked to contact police.

Missing 5 year-old- boy, [4]Raceview

myPolice on Aug 13 Aug 2019 @ 1500 Hrs

Police are appealing for public assistance to help locate a boy reported missing from Goodna today.

The 5-year-old boy (pictured) were last seen yesterday at 1500 Hrs at a Happy Days Childcare Raceview.

Police hold concerns for their welfare due to his young age.

---

3. https://qld.us2.list-manage.com/track/ click?u=bc40de864c611dd173a42d2ea&id=198efa63 da&e=9a8e09e60f

4. https://qld.us2.list-manage.com/track/

click?u=bc40de864c611dd173a42d2ea&id=198efa63da&e=9a8e09e60f

The boy is described as Caucasian, 120cm tall, slim build, blonde hair and brown eyes.

Any members of the public who have seen this child or have information in relation to their whereabouts are asked to contact police.

My eyes were magnetically drawn to the nine year old boy and I began thinking about how he must be felt; *How scared that nine-year-old boy must be. How some mongrel had probably stolen his childhood by now either by abuse or by murdering the poor little bloke.*

My thoughts were broken into by Molly. "Ben are you still with us? You looked like you were somewhere else just then."

"Sorry Molly, just thinking about those kids. I tell ya what Molly, little wonder the boss' gut is on alert. What do you see in all this?"

Molly smiled. "Nothings changed since Charm School you were always asking me for answers and then looking good in front of the instructors and the other cops. But yeah, I'm sure you see the same thing. Four kids in one month, must be all time paedo record. Even though the media make out otherwise, normally we don't have that many abducts in the whole year."

Nodding Molly responded. "I agree, it looks like we have a serial paedo on the go. And highly likely a serial murderer as well. We both know these scum don't usually leave a witness. The chances of four independent paedos abducting kids in the same month and although they are spread out in sort of the same area too, is way off the coincidence scale."

We left the briefing room and went straight to Superintendent Fisher's office. I knocked but neither of waited for an invitation.

"I don't have to have psychic powers to know what you two want." He said as he looked up from a file he was reading.

Grateful that my job was redirecting that molten anger I had woken up with. Molly and I laugh as we sit down. Ladies first. "Boss

Ben and I are sure that you think the same thing, but have we got a serial paedophile on our hands."

Picking up his coffee mug he looked disappointed when he found it empty. "Yeah, you're the only two bright enough to see it." Shaking his head. "The rest of those guys, they're workers for sure, but dumb as a bag full of hammers in some ways. The others only do what their assigned no more no less. But yeah I'm fuckin terrified that there'll be another any time soon." He continued. "In any case that's what my gut is tellin me. How about yours?"

My turn. "It's way out there but what if it's an individual or maybe even a group assembling a collection. I don't know maybe a stable that they use or make money on. Face to face maybe, but these days there's more dollars in digital."

Molly looked aghast. "Ben that's sure is out there but I s'pose it could explain the four kids going missing in the same month."

Superintendent Fisher looked even more worried if that was possible. "Seeing you two are so smart, what's your plan? Where do we go from here guys?"

I didn't have a clue but I knew honesty wasn't what was needed here. "Well boss I think at present all we can do is chase down every interview, every lead, maybe the uniforms have missed something."

Molly understood that as well. "Boss, Ipswich City and surrounds has more friggin cameras than Hollywood. We will get a crew to check every CCTV control surrounding the abduct sites."

Molly had succeeded. The Superintendent's face lit up, at least for a moment. "Great idea Molly, you're right about Ipswich, maybe we'll catch a break."

CHAPTER 5

"Strike the shepherd, and the sheep will be scattered, and I will turn my hand against the little ones. NIV **Zechariah 13:7**

"See they finally got that Bishop fella." Mike said while chewing on his buttered fruit toast.

"Not a moment too soon. The church are like the doctors they bury thier mistakes. Maybe not always in the ground but they move them from a wealthy Sydney parish to a dusty country town a hundred miles west of no where. Trouble is nothin's changed but the map reference. After a little while the offending priest starts up again. Only difference is that farmers don't just turn the other cheek, they all have guns and plenty of dirt to hide a body. The cost of sin is death out there in the great outback." Laughed Richard.

"Yeah, the lucky ones get promoted and sent to Rome or somewhere, but they're still guily as sin." Mike stated.

Richard felt duty bound to comment. "I am constantly amazed at the cover ups that go on, whether it's a church or some big disability or age care orgainsation. It's all about reputation and reputation is all about money. If it comes out that some facility manager abuses the people with disabilities or the oldies in care then all the families and widows won't buy their raffle tickets,donate to them. No chance of them bequething something in their wills. So it goes on but seldom hits the press. The church is the same, people leave a church if the priest is caught doing something wrong. Churches lose people they lose money and even the ones who care about their wellbeing can't help them if they leave the flock." Richard is aware that was a long speech, especially for him, it was nearly a sermon and determines that he will now shut up.

Charles noticing the group members who seem to talk a lot about this particular topic without his wisdom and especially his guidance decides to end the discussion. "Not that I give a shit but it always amazes me that poor old God or the church gets the blame. It's not really fair, it's just one man, that is unless the heirarchy have covered it up then they deserve anything they get."

Symbolic of the personality traits that drove him, with a mix between sadness and anger Damien closes the discussion down. "Oh come on guys you know I hate talking about church, that fat prick touchin me up. I know it's all a bit of a cliché but, you guys don't understand. It was the stereotypical priest abuse. It doesn't make it any better talkin about it. I've had a shitload of civvy and Army shrinks try that."

Charles as usual leads the group when he senses Damo needs rescuing. " OK old mate, change of subject then. Operation Duke. Are we all set for next weekend?"

Paul responds first seeing he has the 'stock' stored at his place. "I'll be glad to get rid of them, always crying makin a mess. Honestly, it's like havin a fuckin litter of puppies or something."

"Only a few more days mate, do you need a hand?" Charles asked.

"No thanks I've got 'em into a routine and it's better they don't get used to anyone else."

Without ceasing to gaze at something fascinating in his coffee mug Paul Paul answered.

All the others confirmed they were good to go, the excitement in their voices betraying the anticipation that had been building over the last few weeks.

Charles continued. "OK, now the bus is ready. By the way, Robert's done great work on that." Charles gestured that he expected a response from the quiet man who always hid behind his sun glasses. Robert cleared his throat.

"Sure, the windows are all one way only so no one will be able to see in. There is a rear section that is totally sound proofed and can be locked up. Mechanically the bus is fine for the distance."

Charles loved this sort of meeting, he had always wanted to be President of a club but could never have made it in the Lions or Rotary. Under the guise of 'getting to know you' there's all the usual questions. "You married? You got kids?", and on and on. He would have to lie from the get go, so it had never happened.

"Once again guys I'm sure we all agree Robert's done a terrific job. Now let's work out the details for Thursday."

Just then their usual waiter Stan a young blond surfie type with a dark tan and a quick smile arrived with the coffey orders. Once again Stan noticed the instant silence and thought; *If these guys were talking about the football or work or nearly anything they wouldn't stop talking like they do. Especially the way they all stop as one as soon as I get near enough to hear them.* As he walked away he noted; t*here you go I knew they would start up again when I get to the shop door.*

Taking a mouthful of his long black Charles continued. "Now, I've been thinking about our bonus excursion and I believe it's vital to keep our cargo out of sight from my chicken screwing friend. Not a mention of the real purpose of the trip, OK? He can assume that we came to see him and then we will head home. Everyone on board with that?"

Richard responded spraying scone crumbs as he spoke. "Sure, the last thing we want is our chickens not to be whole when we deliver them. If he finds out about them he might want to swap his chickens for ours and that's not happening."

Charles nodding vigourously. "Exactly, guys please be careful. Have a great time up there." Laughing now. " But how can you trust a man who can't be trusted by his own kids, right?" The bent irony of this statement wasn't lost on anyone.

Golden Beach

Walter Maxstead had been a welder for near on forty years until a young bloke pushed the wrong button on a gantry crane and dropped a steel beam on him. That was eight years ago now and all the physio and rehab and technology meant SFA. His thoughts drifted back to when he sat day after day near his front gate waiting for the plump little girl to walk by. Weeks went by before she said hello the first time. He had purposefully dropped some letters on the path creating a scene no little girl could resist. An old man in a wheel chair who needed her help to pick up the spilt mail. A simple yet perfect trap. That seemed a long time ago but thinking about those first contacts still made him smile. Her innocence, her vulnerability her ripe little body. His daydreams became reality as he guided his wheelchair around the internal wall near the lounge room he jumped as he heard someone knocking. "You there Mr Max?" A high pitched voice enquired. Maxstead could barely disguise his excitement at his young visitors arrival.

"Sure Jenny the door's unlocked, come around to the TV room."

Jenny was a little bit overweight and the boys at school gave her a hard time, the girls were even worse. She didn't seem to eat any more than the others and was trying to walk more these days. At first she enjoyed visiting Mr Max because he didn't seem to notice she was a bit fat. And he didn't nag her like her parents had been ever since thy saw her at the school sports day. Mr Max was nice and sometimes he would buy her treats or even maybe a present. He always asked her to keep these their little secret. She wondered why she wasn't allowed to take her presents home. But he was a grown up, there must be a good reason.

"How was school today Jen?" Mr Max always asked her that when she first sat down.

"Yeah, it was OK I guess, the boys are still calling me names. I laugh when they do it. But it hurts me here." She touched her chest over her heart.

Smiling his Grandpa smile. "Oh, my poor darlin, all of a sudden you'll shoot up and be tall and skinny like one of those movie stars.

And you know what Jen all them boys will be chasing you wanting to go out with you."

Colour invaded Jenny's cheeks. "Yeah, sure Mr Max, I can't see that happening."

"Come over here darlin I think you need a cuddle. I know when I'm sad that makes me feel better."

And that was how it had started, a little touch here and another there. A "can you massage my back Jenny it's a bit sore?" Next time it was his leg. The abuse had been going on for over a year. Jenny had no real friends, and parents that were more worried about her weight than her well-being. But how could they ever know, she was always home by the time they both got in from work. She was nearly thirteen and could see no way out of the set up. Mr Max had said he would hurt her parents and her if she ever told anyone about their special friendship. And who would believe a poor old man in a wheel chair was interested in a tubby little girl like her.

Caloundra RSL

"Ben you know I'm careful not to be coming to you all the time with concerns about one of my students."

That was true. In all the years of teaching it was true, he had resisted the temptation to see abuse in every underachieving or agro student. I was very grateful for it. He continued.

"But there's just something wringing an alarm with this little girl. Her name's Jenny. A bit over weight, and as much as teachers and coaches and counsellors and all the rest try to include her she has ended a bit of an outcast, a loner."

I had known Jack Wright since High School and he was my best mate. Except for a few guys I had served with overseas he was my only mate. But he didn't know me at all.

Throwing back the last of his beer he continued. "Now I know it's a bit like some movie but between her social behaviour and now her drawings.... Well I think there there may well be something going on." He seemed to peter out at the end like a balloon finally empty.

"Jack I trust your instincts and mate often behaviours and manifestations such as weird drawings are all we have at the beginning. What would you like me to do? You know I can't speak to her 'unofficially' if there is abuse going on that may blow the case. It's either official or sadly we might have to wait for another signpost."

I had made this speech because Detective Ben McQueen really didn't want to officially blaze ahead on the little I had. However, I had instantly decided to look into it privately and see whether Jack's alarm bells were justified.

Not realising why I wanted the information I asked my friend. "OK Jack I'll keep a small note of this conversation just in case. What's the girl's name and contacts?"

"Thanks Ben, it may not be anything at all. I'll keep my eye on her at school and let you know if anything develops. I had her details here in case you wanted them. OK mate, I better head home." Smiling he stood, we shook hands and he left. Not for the first time I wondered at our friendship. After my abuse by that teacher, I could pick one at fifty metres. How could my best friend be a teacher? One of life's ironies I guess. I had half a beer left so I took my time and thought about what I should do next. I knew one thing that I couldn't put this off because every day might be another day this young girl suffered.

The info page Jack had given me included a picture of Jenny. Armed with this I parked self-consciously outside the main school gate awaiting the end bell. I was hoping no alert teacher or lollipop lady would start wondering about a lone man waiting outside the school. So far so good. At the sound of an electronic bell, like a flash flood of noise and movement hundreds of children of all different ages, shapes and colours poured out through the front gates.

I hadn't seen the girl I was waiting for. No Jenny, maybe in the crush I had missed her, school uniforms act like zebra stripes and individuals seem to disappear. It had gone deadly quiet after such a racket. I had decided to throw it in when she appeared. Every atom of her body language screamed that she was avoiding the other children for some reason. Like a timid kitten coming out after the dogs have been locked up. Cautiously this slightly chubby girl came down the steps and through the gate. Feeling strange because if anyone saw me they would think the same as I would, that I was following her home. Because I was. I knew her address, and so far she was heading that way. One street away from home she turned into a low set brick home that I would guess was a state housing residence. The home was painted in a neutral sort of brown, the yard of brown hard grass and dirt was dissected by a rough concrete path leading to a ramp with green railings.

Jenny checked the letter box as though she lived there. I saw her knock, and although I couldn't hear any response by her action she must have been welcomed inside. I was tossing up whether I should try and take a look through a window. But like following little girls home from school, being caught doing a peeping Tom could be a disaster in so many ways. I took another option. Noting the address and the car registration of the Toyota Camry parked outside I decided to check out whoever lived there. The ID and MV checks didn't turn up anything suspicious so with a few days off I decided to keep an eye on Mr Maxstead. I did notice that Maxstead had disability registration, and wondered why. The ramp may have been for a previous tenant but it was starting to look like the target may be in a wheelchair. My car was parked two doors down outside a little public park so I settled in for the wait. A little over an hour later Jenny the girl my friend was so worried about came back outside and headed in the direction I knew was home. She seemed to be adjusting her school uniform, but maybe I was imagining it. I hung around once Jenny had gone but by 1900 Hrs I'd had enough and headed home.

Driving home my mind drifted as I drove the familiar streets. I started thinking about my childhood; *My Mum was always working in our barely surviving shop. Dad was either working or drinking at the bowls club, or the RSL (Returned Services Club) or the pub. Once I'd done all my chores around our corner shop then I was alone most of the time. There was a nice old Scottish couple next door who would talk to me through the fence. Just like Maxstead may have done with Jenny.*

As I passed a KFC on my left and a warehouse size booze shop over the road I started to think about that old couple who had so long ago called to me over the back fence. In a soft Scottish brogue.

"Hello wee Benny boy, what're ye up to todae?" Enquired the plump greyed haired lady dressed in tartan with a blue woollen shawl sounding like my granny would have, if I'd ever met her. A lonely kid couldn't believe it; *Imagine that, adults who have time to spend with me, who **want** to spend time with me.*

After a while they invited me into their flat. They were nice, I never knew my own grandparents but I imagined they would have been like this couple. They would sip on sherry and give me little fingers of home made short bread. After a few visits they asked if I would like 'a wee banana cocktail' they mixed it with sweet lemonade. My face grew hot as I felt so grown up. But most of all I felt like they liked me they wanted to spend time with me. No one else wanted to. But this lovely old couple did. I can't say they sexually abused me but I can't say they didn't either. I remember warmth down there, I remember the old lady kneeling in front of me. I remember flashes like lightning that was only in their lounge room when the heavy curtains were drawn.

I had to be sure about Maxstead, it needed to happen and fast. This guy was like so many 'friendly old neighbours' just like my old Scottish couple that had introduced me to alcohol, and maybe much much more. A little child a bit plump, not one of the 'in' crowd, looking for anyone to show some interest, any interest. She was searching without even knowing she was. So was I. All of a sudden my anger is at boiling point again. I guess something I don't consciously identify, a sound, a smell but it's powerful. It happens every single time I think of my childhood that was stolen from me by those neighbours. I'm not sure what they did, but the depth of my anger makes me think a deep hidden part of me must know the truth. I s'pose shrinks would say I've repressed the memories of whatever happened. Was this guy stealing Jenny's childhood? My gut told me it was so. However, I carried a ton of guilt about being judge, jury and executioner. I needed to be one-hundred-percent certain. However, once sure I would have no choice but to proceed on down the slippery path of administering justice.

The next day was pension day so I was hoping that meant my target would leave his house to do some shopping or whatever. By the time I got to Maxstead's house his car was already missing from the car-port, I was in luck. For the benefit of any his neighbours, without any hesitation or looking around I walked confidently into his yard and headed to his back door. An old credit card flicked back his door lock and slipping on some rubber gloves I was in. By the spacing of the furniture and the height of used shelves and some damage on the walls I knew straight away what the guys disability was. Or at least that he was wheelchair bound. After a look around nothing was jumping out so that only left his laptop. It always amazed me how some people just don't lock their phones or computers. I was grateful that Maxstead was one of these trusting souls.

A search of his files didn't show anything so I went into his emails, nothing there either, but I took a copy of his contacts in case I needed them later. I figured if he was dirty he would be accessing the Deepweb or the Darkweb. At the very least he would use incognito window, and disable cookies to eliminate any search history. Now if this investigation was all official our resident geeks could open all these hidden files and searches. But as a part time freelance burglar I could only look and hope that Maxstead was sloppy enough to leave a trail. And luck definitely favoured the innocent this time. His history was virtually empty. However I looked through his favourites. There were row after row of ordinary hetero' adult porn sites. But, I figured I had time on my side for once. I opened the favourites and scrolled and scrolled and there it was. All the links went to Schools Out, Class Action, Teacher's Pet. I opened the first site and the others cascaded out like vomit.

OK, now I had something more than my mate's observations of a sad school girl and my gut feelings. But as wrong and filthy as these were did it have anything to do with twelve- or thirteen-year-old Jenny. What to do? I decided to go back to the start and check the folder names. Once again nothing. Then an icon on the Desktop caught my eye, not a file, nor a folder. An icon for an extended hard-drive Seagate Backup. I had seen some electronic leads and miscellaneous junk in the bottom desk draw. I dived into it now and there it was a thin little black hard-drive with a cable plugged into. I inserted the cable end into a vacant port. The laptop immediately read it and opened the contents file menu. There were several that I would eventually look at but one leapt from the monitor screen. JENNY.

CHAPTER 6

ISAIAH 53:5

You burn with lust among the oaks and under every spreading tree; you sacrifice your children in the ravines and under the overhanging crags.

Mike asked anyone in general at the table. "Did any of you guys know him?"

"Who?" Richard replied.

Mike couldn't believe his luck knowing something the others hadn't heard. "Old mate who got done yesterday. Child Exploitation Charges here on the Sunny Coast. Detectives from the Maroochydore Child Protection have charged a man with 42 offences, found a heap of stuff at a Kawana address on Saturday. Apparently they took a year investigating him. The bloke thirty-nine, he was asking kids for explicit videos and photos on social media. Usual story get to know them and then offer money for photos. They were onto him back in November 2018 the coppers reckon he's been paying the children by using the 'cardless cash' facility. He's in Maroochydore Magistrates Court in January."

Charles was acutely aware that any mention of the local Child Protection Unit charging a local paedo was of concern. Not just to him but all the members of his little club. They were always careful, and experienced in the game, but jail was still a terrifying thought. Especially for three of them who had done time. He wanted to change directions.

"OK, guys it just reminds us how much smarter the opposition has become. And so we need to bring our A game every time we play, right?"

Nods and murmurs all around the table. "Now, on a brighter note. Let's talk about Duke. Are we all good for this weekend?" He waited two beats and continued. "I'm sure you are so let's finalise the details."

Damo giggling like an excited kid. "I still love that Duke stuff instead of Wellington."

"Well Einstein if you always say Wellington every time you say Duke they're won't be any point in having a fuckin code, will there?" Richard said harshly, and then continued to make his report. "OK. Transport is finished it looks like a converted bus, a motorhome you know the sort; you see 'em everywhere. As you know it's sound proofed and now the windows are all blacked out as well. There are six little cages in the back with some padding so the meat doesn't get bruised. Four of us will ride with them and the others in the Landcruiser. I've set up UHF radios in both and they are on an unused frequency."

"Great work Robert. To make sure none of our chickens escape I want all of us at Paul's to help loading. Robert you have the bus or whatever at his place by 0600 Hrs Friday. Same for all of us guys. Paul and Robert wearing masks, they bag the chicks and then we help with the loading and locking of cages. I think the bags stay on the whole trip. Agree?" Everyone grunted and nodded in unanimous agreement.

The rattle of coffee cups alerted the group as the waiter came out of the coffee shop and onto the alfresco area. Once again the table went silent, the different orders were distributed. Yet again the waiter thought this was strange as he returned to the kitchen.

"What about number six?" Asked Damo.

Charles maintaining his tenuous grip on leading the group responded. "Good question. What are our thoughts, do we wait until we get to Warwick? I think that makes sense we've sought of given the Ipswich area a bit of a hiding."

Richard putting his coffee mug down in emphasis. "I agree snatching so many in one region always worried me. And I don't know if I'm imagining it but there seems to be a bit of a surge on here on the coast from the coppers."

"Yeah, but taking them so far from home took most of that risk away." Robert threw in.

"OK, let's plan to keep our collective eyes open from Warwick inwards. There are plenty of places between Warwick and Duke, I'm sure we'll find what we are looking for."

"We couldn't Recce the route guys so toilet stops are going to be adhoc, truckies stops when no ones around. And they must be quick. It'll smell like a cattle truck if we don't make the effort, but we have to be careful."

Thankfully Maxstead was staying out of the way. I copied the extended hard-drive and put the original back where I had found it. I hadn't opened the JENNY Folder but was pretty sure they weren't going to be school projects. I headed out the back door and just in case I took the long way home. I made a good JD and Coke if there's such a thing as a bad one and opened the JENNY folder. As I had assumed it was full of photos and videos of the school girl I had followed to Maxstead's house the afternoon before. I checked the dates and noted that the abuse had been going on nearly eighteen months. You could see that Jenny was a little girl when it had begun, but now projected a coldness that hadn't been there at first. The audio was classic grooming, followed by graduating steps of touching and being touched. Eventually, the usual threats came and now while Jenny never appeared to enjoy any part of it, she did what was expected of her like some sad robot. I made another JD and sat on my back deck and made a plan. The one surety was that this animal would never touch Jenny ever again, or anyone else for that matter.

I wasn't concerned about being seen or someone interrupting me as I dealt with Maxstead. From searching his house I knew he lived alone and there didn't appear to be any family or friends, no mail, photos on walls or on the fridge. I couldn't tell from the copied hard drive but I needed to make sure that Jenny was the only victim. I was going to question him so I could be certain. This time I parked two blocks away at a small but busy shopping centre and walked back to Maxstead's house. I knew how interrogations worked and wanted him to be on the back foot from the get go. His car was in the driveway as I walked up to the front door. Bang, Bang, Bang loud and intimidating as I had been trained. He wheeled to the door and went a ghostly pale when I showed him my Police Warrant Card. Reversing to allow the door to open fully he had recovered his composure by the time I stepped of his front porch.

He must have still been terrified but was trying to put on a good act. "What can I do for you ah, ah." He stuttered struggling to know what to call me.

"Detective Dan Olbas" I helped him with a lie.

"OK, Detective what's this about?"

"Well Maxstead, in a minute you might wish the Police were here but for now let's go into the kitchen away from the footpath, hey?"

"What.... D'ya mean, are you really a copper? You don't sound like one."

"Yeah I am but that won't help you. Now I want you to grab your car keys we're going for a little drive."

"No this is bullshit. I'm not driving you anywhere. I think you should leave before I phone the real cops. I'm not sure what your game is but I'm not playin. Now fuck off."

"That's a bit unfriendly, so here's what we'll do. I'll pull my gun and you will shut your mouth and do what I told you to do. And don't think for a moment I won't use this." I said threateningly pointing my privately owned Glock in Maxstead's direction. He stared at the black gun. He was catching on. I grabbed the extended hard drive from his draw so no one would ever know of Jenny's abuse.

"Now you drive and if you do anything to attract attention it will hurt, either you'll get hit or maybe even shot. So take it easy and head for ramp near the Outrigger Canoe Club down on Golden Beach."

I was ready to end this. I had him rattled, he was scared and confused not knowing what this all about and what was going to happen next. We arrived in the parking lot filled with vehicles and empty fishing boat trailers. "OK get out jump in your chair and don't say a word"

"What the fuck what are ya goin to do, what's goin on? I haven't got any money, I'll....."

"Shut up I just told you not a word."

We got out and after I pointed he wheeled beside me down towards the double width boat ramp.

"Now Maxstead I'm going to ask you some questions. I don't want a conversation I just want answers. Am I clear?"

"Yes, but.." I hit across the side of the head with my gun. He screamed, but being in the wheelchair didn't collapse or stagger. "How long have you been a paedophile? And don't bullshit. You know you are and I know you are. So that part's a given."

"Ah, sort of ever since my accident. I can't ah, ah, you know. But I can still think about it, my eyes and hands and tongue still work." As he said this a filthy leer crossed his face like I would understand and be OK with it.

"You animal what about the children?"

"I tried hookers but I'm a pensioner and they don't like old blokes with disabilities. Kids are easier you can train em."

It took all my control not to strangle him right there and then. I had a couple more questions.

He was starting to panic. "You know I was just ah... lonely and she was keen, she seemed lonely. I mean she came straight over when I called out to her over the fence."

I immediately felt a flash point angry, and then selfish because I was thinking of myself not Jenny being called over to the fence. Like her, my childhood had been snatched from me in exactly the same way. My thoughts whirled in my head; *I was here for Jenny, no one was there for me.*

"So Maxstead, are there any other little boys or girls or just Jenny?" He was clearly shocked at my knowing about Jenny by name. Then a sort of righteous anger flew across his face.

"I'm no poofter, I wouldn't go near a little boy."

"But poor little girls are fine. You sick fuck. What about it, have you ever abused any other little girls?" I asked through gritted teeth.

"Nah, you probably won't believe me but Jenny was my first and only. I started talking to her at the front fence one afternoon about eighteen months ago. It' all gone from there. She's a sweet little thing, my Jenny." There was that leer again.

I was convinced that he was telling the truth, it lined up with the time of his accident and the first photos and videos I had seen. Except for a single light bulb over the boat ramp in was pretty dark where we were standing. I had chosen the place and the time knowing the guys had long taken their boats out and wouldn't be back until the tide changed again. I didn't want to hear his voice any-more or see his filthy selfish leer whenever he spoke of little girls like Jenny.

I pushed him and his chair to the top of the boat ramp and stopped. I waited for him to fully realise what was going to happen next. I wanted him to feel the fear Jenny must have felt every time she walked into his street. I hoped in a way he would understand why I was doing this, but deep down, I doubted that and I didn't really care if he didn't. I gave his chair a big push and it flew down the wet mossy slope and tipped as it hit the water and rolled on top of Maxstead. Being a boat ramp the water was deep immediately and he struggled and flapped and screamed until he disappeared for the last time under the tiny waves. After wiping around anywhere I may have touched I left his car there. If people thought he had killed himself who cares, if they thought it was a terrible accident same thing.

CHAPTER 7

Ephesians 6:4 "Fathers, do not provoke your children to anger by the way you treat them."

Looking up from his Courier Mail, Richard quietly stated. "Seems like only yesterday when a certain tall friend of mine went the same way."

"What's that mate, what the latest?" Asked Damo.

"Oh, an eight-year-old girl was grabbed and dragged into the bushes and assaulted. Apparently, Detectives from the Gateway Child Protection and Investigation Unit have released a comfit image of a man who may be able to assist police with their investigations. Copper lingo for he fuckin did it." Richard continued. "Anyway the comfit gear these days is digital and therefore it actually looks like a person as in a photo. The old days they had stick on noses and moustaches and all looked like they were out a cartoon book. The reason it reminded me of my mate was this guy was like as tall as a basketball player. Got an OK facial plus two metres plus tall. Won't take long for him to be spotted by some Police patrol or Joe public. Same as my mate tall, curly hair and a moustache, took three days."

"OK, that is why it's always better to be completely forgettable in our line of work, like the members of this little group. I think they call it vanilla."

"Molly any action from those CCTVs?" I had just returned from my days off and needed to catch up on the multiple abductions case.

"Yeah Ben, we have found one abduct' but these guys are Pros. No face, stolen vehicle. And the fact that there's only the one caught on camera means they're avoiding those zones. Slick."

"You know what Molly, that all makes me think we are dealing with an organised group. Not some random perve nah, this is like you say a Pro job."

"What's the boss think?"

"He was a bit sceptical the other day, but he's comin to the same conclusion." She arched her back to release some tension. "I hate just sitting here sort of waiting for another kid to disappear."

"And, hope they make a mistake this time." "Want a coffee, I sure need one?"

"Thanks Ben, I'd love one."

Charles had dosed off a couple of times between the Sunshine Coast and Warwick. As the little convoy entered the large rural town he straightened up and said. "OK, guys now remember we don't let on that we are on our way to Wellington. And more importantly, that we have a bus load of kids. He's a mate, but he would definitely want a piece of that pie. While we are enjoying his sons and daughters he would expect us to share as well."

Robert was the bus driver, so he felt like this concern was his to solve. "I don't know the layout but I'll park the bus away from your mate's house. Being a chicken farm there should be plenty of room."

"Sounds like a plan Rob, we'll adjust as we need hey?" Charles replied. Now we have to make sure the boys in the car are on the same page. Make sure we remind them before we get there. At the servo when we are filling up will best."

Richard asked. "What about that kid we are short of? There's a stack of little country towns between here and New South Wales all the way to Wellington."

Mike cautious as ever. "We will have to be super careful using our current vehicles hey."

"Yes, good point Mike, the boys travelling in the Cruiser can do it. That'll be quicker and not as noticeable than our little motorhome." Charles had quickly assessed that this delegation ensured he wouldn't still be in town when they grabbed the last one wherever it happened. I think that's everything re the operation covered. Let's relax a bit and enjoy ourselves for a while?"

Robert interrupted their day dreams of the entertainment that would fill in the rest of the day.

"Servo up ahead is cheap, right to pull in Charles?" Smiling at this physical demonstration of his leadership Charles nodded. "Sounds good."

"Ben, I have no idea why but that girl I was worried about Jenny, well she seems like she's happier somehow." Jack Wright my school teacher friend said with a smile.

I picked up my beer to make sure my face didn't betray my thoughts. "Oh, that's great, what do you mean she looks happier?"

"Well it's like some weight has been lifted off her shoulders. She doesn't look scared or tired, looks like a twelve-year-old should look. I don't know why but I'm happy to see it. Her teachers have made the comment that she is contributing better in class as well. Early days but something has changed for the better."

"That's great news. Your shout mate, seein you're so happy." I said hoping a little time alone would clear the anger cloud that had just blown over the horizon. Off he went to buy the next round, not knowing that he had been right all along about Jenny. Or why Jenny seemed free for the first time in ages. I was glad to be able to help. I just hoped Jenny would be OK from now on. Her childhood like mine had been stolen, hopefully she could start being the girl she was before. I had seen lots of little girls confused and hurt who knew more about sex than a lot of adults go on to engage in loveless sexual relationships searching but never finding.

Waiting for Jack to come back with the drinks I thought; *What they did to me I can't remember but, I know that was the year my whole life changed and not for the better. How it had effected me every day from that point on.* It's not just being an angry kid, it's not being allowed to be the age you actually are. Somehow you're older. Not an innocent kid any longer. Of course you weren't aware of it until you grew up and saw children just being children. Normal to me was thinking about adult things when you should be dreaming of being a cowboy, or Robin Hood or someone. Instead at nine-years-old I became interested in sex, drawn to characters like James Bond and the cold physical approach he had to women and relationships. As a child with a covert agenda I was able to infiltrate groups of girls like my older sister's friends. As a nine-year-old kid I was no threat so I heard them talk of things, I saw them getting undressed or dressed without the usual care to shut a door. Just glimpses but enough to satisfy my immature appetites. I didn't even know what sex really meant it was more just a feeling a thirst I didn't understand. I had noticed that in the books I read and movies I saw it was always a grown up man and woman doing things. As a kid confusion filled me because deep down I somehow knew men did things to little boys.

As always my joy at stopping another abuser was short lived knowing that there were always replacements for each one I removed.

Just like every time I do this I wondered whether God would ever be able to forgive me, i remembered a scripture that on the surface justified my actions. However, I knew deep down the Old Testament approach had changed with the teachings of the New Testament.

ISAIAH 59:17

He put on righteousness as his breastplate and the helmet of salvation on his head; he put on the garments of vengeance.

CHAPTER 8

"Oh man, visiting your mate and his children was worth every penny and more." Mike stated to the bus in general.

Grunts and giggles circulated from all the passengers. "Yeah, it'd be great if we can do that every so often." Robert added.

Charles ever the wise sage. "I agree it was fun. But in my experience in these matters, they don't last long. He'll get greedy, too many visitors and someone will brag about it. And the boys in blue will pounce. I've seen it happen more than once. And they will somehow find out who has been playing with the kids. If pushed my mate will give them a list to get a shorter stay in the clink. No I'm sorry boys but at least for me that was the first and last. But I can't say I didn't enjoy his little family."

Richard looked up from his Ipad and laughed. "We wouldn't need to worry about all that if we move to the States, listen to this. There is a real push to legalise under-age sex. There's a lobby group called NAMBLA, North American Man/Boy Love Association. I'll read it out. The North American Man/Boy Love Association (NAMBLA) is a paedophile organisation that advocates adult sexual behaviour with male children. Given the considerable consensus in this society that such sexual behaviour with children is exploitative and victimising in nature, the techniques that NAMBLA uses to justify, rationalise and normalise its philosophy and its members' practices in order to avoid or neutralise censure and stigma, are of particular sociological interest. This paper uses Scott and Lyman's (1968) concept of "accounts" as a theoretical framework for the analysis of these techniques that are found in the publicly disseminated literature of the NAMBLA organisation.

Imagine that everything we are into legal, can the lefties be that fuckin stupid? And just like every such change it'll open up the door to including little girls, I'm all for equality." Richard shaking his head. "I can't even decide whether it'd be a good thing for us but I am one hundred percent positive it would be open season on anyone under thirteen or so." Charles made a mental note to look into this American group, knowing that their strategy had worked successfully gaining support for other alternative previously illegal practices. Richard turned the page and started again. "It just keeps getting better, the Labour Party have blocked a bill trying to get Mandatory Sentencing for Paedophile crimes. Thanks guys that's very nice of you."

Charles was becoming tired of Richard being the source of news and shut him down. "That's interesting but until we get the all clear from our boys in the Land Cruiser I can't think about other interests."

Charles was rightfully on edge. The sign said the sleepy little Tidy Town of 2004 the convoy had just entered boasted a population of four-hundred and twenty-two. Some smart ass local had changed this by crossing off the two probably as they escaped to bigger things down the road. The occupants of the bus had all noticed a flock of children playing on the swings near the empty school ground and no one was surprised when the radio crackled to life with a pre-arranged code that here might be a good place to pick something up. Having never served in the Military, Charles always felt uncomfortable using the radio. "Thanks for that sounds like a good idea." Contact ceased.

Damo on the other hand had done two tour in Afghanistan and anyone could tell from his correct radio technique. "Roger that, we will complete that order and RV as arranged. Out." Contact ceased.

Charles asked the others in the bus what's he mean by RV? "Robert who loved war movies replied. "Means Rendezvous, so they'll grab the kid and meet us at Coonabarabran as arranged."

Frustrated and annoyed at not being on top of things Charles lashed out at the hapless driver. "Of course I knew that, I didn't need the whole fuckin message translated into English just the RV part."

Everyone in the bus noted that Charles didn't know everything and the fact that he never swore that he was upset about this weakness. Inwardly, everyone smiled at the great man's loss of 'cool'.

Charles attempted to will himself to re-group, annoyed with himself for displaying weakness, he must be tired or stressed. Probably both. He started thinking about the money they would get for their young cargo. *Just a few more hours and all going well the kids would be safely unloaded in Wellington. And the Hunters Bikies would have their proof that his little band could be trusted to deliver when required. It was a lot of money especially when immediately converted into Thai Bahts. And even more especially when every pleasure a man could wish for was so cheap over there. He was smart enough to know that the it was no coincidence that the Ex-President of the Hunters Bikies now lived in Bangkok. He also knew that the majority of the Paedophile Tours from Australia to Thailand were organised by him and his group. It was sweet deal, they made money from on-selling the kids to the Russians all over the East Coast and then in most cases taking their money back via the Thai operation.*

"Bravo this is Lima Tango. Over." Came over the radio. Bravo standing for Bus, with Lima Tango being chosen for the Landcruiser, thus avoiding the use of Lima Charlie, and the mention of Charlie or Charles.

Robert grabbed up the microphone. "Lima Tango this is Bravo go ahead." "Ahh. Over." Robert was better than the rest but had still forgotten to say Over.

"Bravo we picked up what we needed without any bother and have left town. See you at the RV. Out." Damo confirmed.

The team members in the bus breathed out a collective sigh each one glad it had all gone so well. Charles was back grasping the helm again.

"Now that's great news guys, we can all just enjoy the rest of the trip now and dream about Thailand at the end of the year."

Everyone nodded and grunted their agreement, and the bus was quiet as all but the driver closed their eyes in fatigue driven peace.

"Ben have you and Molly come up with anything on those abducts?" Fisher asked.

"Not really Boss, just more sure they are Pros. You know what will make it even harder, if they aren't paedos but just in it for the money. What do you think of that?"

"Not much, I sure hope you're wrong. But sadly you might have something there, our entire system is geared to know of and catch paedos. The idea of mercs could make it a lot harder."

"Anything State wide?" Molly asked.

"Nothing at this stage, a few interstate but nothing to link them together and it's been two weeks since the last one in Ipswich region." Fisher replied.

The idea of little ones being taken off the street and either abused and killed or sold to some Paedophile brothel was an outrage. Especially on my watch. I could feel the anger starting to smoulder within me. But I knew at least for now I couldn't do anything as the culprits were still unknown.

"We can't just sit here and wait for another kid to get snatched. Maybe we need to look at the possibility I'm right about it being an organised list rather than a serial individual. The gap between the kids being grabbed is too small for an individual sicko. It's gotta be a group."

"Ben I think that's a good idea. I'd be surprised if they weren't already on to it but I'll give my counter-part on the Gold Coast a call."

"Boss in the mean time Molly and I'll shake the palm trees around here and see what falls out."

Molly grunted in agreement. "Give me five and we'll hit the road Ben."

At the rest stop on the outskirts of Coonabarabran the Landcruiser with its new passenger quietly sobbing but securely tied to a back seat pulled up behind the anonymous converted bus. As one all the doors opened, and the team assembled behind the bus sitting and standing on the low log fence that surrounded the rest stop. Charles was standing feet apart like the little General he aspired to be.

"Well, so far so good guys. By the time they even realise the kid's gone and throw up an Amber Alert we'll be miles away. I think we can all be happy with every stage of this operation from prep to right here, right now. Rob, how's our latest acquisition in the back there. Is he giving you any trouble?"

As usual, annoying Charles with his casualness, Rob was leaning against the bus reading a magazine. Looking up from its pages, Rob answered as coldly as someone would comment on the weather. "No he's so terrified, except for a fear sobs you wouldn't know he was there."

Charles continued. "That's good, not too much further, 'bout one hundred-and forty-five Ks. Two hour max." Shifting his feet in the fine dust to gain his maximum height. "Now is not the time to relax. OK."

Charles voice droned on. "A common failing is people start taking it easy when they get near home or the end of a race. Then the losers after having done all the heavy lifting have an accident and fail to finish. So same plan OK. Speed limit, and alert for coppers. And not just the driver every set of eyes. By all means think about Thailand but realise if we fuck up now it'll only be a picture of Bangkok blue-tacked on the wall of your cell. And you might be on the receiving end instead of the giving end." The entire crew Charles only swore to make himself seem tough. The entire crew agreed it would take a lot more than that for him to achieve that.

Molly and I had been assigned a new job out at Kings Beach, a pretty stretch of beach, blocks of units and weatherboard houses from the seventies on large pieces of land. An observant neighbour a Mrs Randolph had seen someone lurking around the garden next door. The first night she had figured it was a gardener or perhaps a tradie quoting on a project. A bit strange in the near dark, but people are busy doing stuff when they can. However, he was back again the next night and this was weird. Mrs Randolph not wanting to make a big thing of some innocent event, but she knew that her neighbour was a single woman like herself and was worried for her. Accordingly, she had spoken to her neighbour the next day. Mrs Miller was alarmed by the query because as far as she knew no one had been in the yard either night. The single mother of three children under ten-years-old noted that the time the incidents had coincided with the kid's bath times. Just to be sure she had phoned the local Police Station who in turn flick passed the matter to Child Protection. So it was now ours.

After a quick call with Mrs Miller we drove out to her home. On the way Molly must have been worrying about me.

"Ben, have you got a girlfriend or boyfriend?" She asked innocently.

"First of all we've worked together for over a year and you ask me that? What happens now you ask me out in pity or something? It's taken a long time, but here we are. You know it's the kiss of death for work partners to get involved. Oh, hang on you've got some recently divorced friend or relative you think I need or she needs me, is that it?" I spoke gently, I was angry but Molly and I had gone through a lot together and I knew she was worried about my moodiness and sometimes anger. Little did she realise my anger never really abated and it had nothing to do with loneliness.

Molly interrupted. "No, no I wasn't volunteering to make you feel better. You know me better than that. No desperate friend or relly either. Nah, I was just wondering if you had a steady you might be better off than alone, that's all. You seem sad, it's probably the work. I shouldn't have said anything."

Sounding a bit less gentle. "Well I appreciate your concern but mind your own business. I'm not gay, I just haven't got around to anyone serious, OK?" I said closing it down before I said more than our relationship deserved. We arrived at the address, thankfully.

Molly knocked in her polite Police knock rather than the warrant execution banging that drove fear into even the most innocent of hearts. Mrs Lisa Miller opened the door and tried to smile a welcome. She was mid thirties, attractive even if a little over-weight, tanned and blond with a worried look that had probably replaced a happy personality in more usual circumstances. After displaying our Ids and introductions over we sat around a large coffee table in the front room of a tidy beach theme decorated home.

"Mrs Miller, this may be nothing but we want to make sure. Just to get a context can I ask about your family?" I asked.

Looking a little confused but wanting to cooperate Mrs. Miller nodded, uncrossed and then re-crossed her shapely tanned legs. "Please whatever helps, I don't really understand what's going on. But after Joy, I mean Mrs Randolph next door, what she told me. Well, I started to get scared."

Molly nodded, and with experience waited three beats, and the answers came without questions being needed.

"See, I am here alone, just with the three kids. Two girls, eight and seven, and a boy who's only five."

OK, so no male living in the home who may have been outside doing whatever?" I asked gently.

Molly did the hard yards and enquire. "Mrs Miller, I know this may seem intrusive, but is there a man in your life who maybe visits?"

"Detective Herbert, not really, Dad, ah, my father, comes over maybe to fix something but not in the dark. He's getting on now. Then sometimes Mum and Dad come over for the odd meal or birthday you know the usual." Her voice had taken on a honey tone as she shared her intimate details.

Not really understanding Molly's goals in this line of questioning Mrs Miller looked a little more confused.

Molly went on. "OK, that's fine. We are just trying eliminate a misunderstanding like some one out there in the garden with a legitimate reason. Someone you know perhaps. Nothing comes to mind, no tradie, or a neighbour getting a plant cutting or something?"

Molly was trying to help the lady, but I could see we weren't going to get anywhere here.

"No Detective, thankfully Mrs Rudolph came over the morning after the second time so I am sure about it not being a mix up of any sort. There is no reason a man should be outside our bathroom window in the dark." Blushing slightly she continued. "Well I s'pose there is but not known to us. That's why you're here right?"

I'd made a little gesture to Molly, it was time to move on. "Look at this point, Mrs Miller, it's too early to know for sure what's going on. Now Detective Herbert and I are going next door to speak with your neighbour. We may want to have a look in your garden, if that's OK?" I asked.

"Of course, will you need me to be with you when you come back?" The single woman asked me turning her back on Molly and making it clear she wouldn't mind it at all if I needed to visit her again.

"No, I don't think so. But we will let you know how it all goes." Molly answered quite strongly.

Mrs Miller still ignoring Molly, spoke to me looking into my eyes like her words had more meaning than than was spoken. "Thank you so much. I am probably being stupid but thanks again for coming so quickly."

At that we walked back onto the footpath turned left and went into the neighbour's two storey home. "Your shout Ben, use that charm to get to the bottom of all this hey?"

"Sure Molly but I can't change it, she's only human. Were you jealous of her?" I joked.

"Don't go there OK. We don't want to talk about your love life but a merry widow might do you more harm than good that's all." She said clearly sorry she had made the charm joke.

Molly had no idea that I had just done what I had been doing since I was a kid, charming women with looks and words. Initially I was like an untrained person waving around a gun, but slowly I learnt to harness this power for what it was worth. There was a coldness inside that armed me with some weird attraction best described by mimicking James Bond. Sad in so many ways, one of my few childish traits imitating a screen creation. Something else that the past continue to rob me of. Molly had been right to ask even though I hid behind some false indignation. I hadn't ever had a real relationship. I was that cold fish that used those around him, never showing my true emotions to anyone. I knew all the terms, I had trust and intimacy issues.

Little wonder I couldn't maintain a mature mutually beneficial relationship. On a much deeper level I also knew I could never love anyone. I had tried. The people that should have loved me, protected me had let things happen that could never be undone. Love let you down, got you hurt. It was no surprise that this failure manifested in the old faithful anger. I would drive any potential partner away from me as soon as I thought she was getting too close. Of course this was to avoid the hurt of being betrayed.

Molly growled. "Seriously you men."

We had arrived so our banter stopped and we put on our serious concerned faces. The world truly is a stage, and we are but players. Thanks William Shakespeare for that wisdom.

Once again a gentle knock, and by the speed the door opened I figured the good neighbour was watching through her windows, waiting for us to come over, already knowing we had been next door. Same deal as always, Ids and intros out of the way. On the way over in the car Molly and I had discussed and decided that we weren't suspect of Mrs Randolph. However, we did need to understand how she was so alert as to observe the person or persons two nights running. Was she vigilant or was she just a nosy neighbour. Furniture that bit older, lots of family photos and a wall of DVDs. I could smell a dog, but it must have been locked outside in preparation of our arrival. "Can I get you two some tea, or maybe a cold drink?" She asked with a warm friendliness.

"Oh, no thank you Mrs Randolph. I can't help noticing you seem to have a lovely family." I said looking at the wall of smiling faces of the same people at a progression of ages.

"Yes, I'm blessed with five children, all grown up now of course. Just Jack and me now, he out trying to catch dinner. I love him but he's a terrible fisherman. I've got sausages defrosting as we speak." We all laughed.

"Is there anyone else around, maybe one of your sons comes over and visits."

"No not really, as I said they are all grown up with their own families now. Two live overseas, and the only time we get together is celebrations you know Christmas and birthdays."

"Mrs Randolph. Can you please tell us what you saw earlier this week?" I had my pen ready to take notes, this motivated witnesses because you were valuing their words and obviously it helps me with the detail when I wrote up the case notes later.

Older than her neighbour by twenty years or so, and a little worn. Probably, once her pride and joy the wavy auburn hair had lost the battle to an army of grey. Her voice was raspy like a long term smoker, but confident and friendly, Mrs Randolph started. "Detective...."

"McQueen, Ben McQueen ma'am."

"Sorry, yes well every night we watch the news, eat dinner and I clean up. So every night I am standing at the kitchen window overlooking Lisa's side garden at roughly the same time give or take." Molly and my concerns had been clarified statement sentence one. She was concerned enough to act, but not involved enough to be scared.

The old neighbour continued. "Anyway, Monday, just gone, night next door I see a shadow move from bush to bush. I wonder if I've been watching too much Netflix, or maybe shouldn't have had that extra glass of wine." We all giggled. "But no, I was sure, there he was again. Silhouetted on what I guess is the kid's bathroom window because the light was on."

Would you know when that was, if not an exact time, maybe even between this and that?"

She understood. "Yes, I can work that out, it was just after 6.30 because the sport came on and I headed out of the lounge."

Molly encouraged her. "That's a big help Mrs Randolph."

I started again. "Now, you said that it was a man, are you certain, I mean it was pretty dark?" I asked gently.

"About ninety-five percent sure, just by height, shape and he, or whoever had broad shoulders and short hair."

Nodding to further further encourage her. "Now, what can you tell us about the second night?"

"Sure that was Tuesday of course." And she went on to replay the events of the second incident. The details of which were nearly identical to Monday night's.

Standing to make it clear that we were going to proceed I asked. "OK, well that all makes sense. Could we see the view from your kitchen window please?"

Age and probably arthritis made getting out of her lounge chair a task, but once standing she quickly led molly and I into the kitchen. Even though it was day time it was easy to visualise what Mrs Randolph had described.

Thank you so much Mrs Randolph, if all our witnesses were as precise as you our work would be a lot easier. We have Mrs Miller's permission, would you be OK to show us where the person went and stood the other night?" Molly asked.

Yeah, sure I'll just put my gardening shoes on and I'll meet you at the front door."

The three of us walked down the wooden stairs and stepped onto a concrete path. I noticed that a smaller path lead off to a bright green door under the main house. Being curious by nature I asked. "Where's that lead to Mrs Randolph it looks well used.?"

"Yes, it is well used. That's where Vic, he's our boarder lives. I forgot about him when we were talking. He's been with us close on eleven years but he's never home. That's why he slipped my mind. Vic's hobby is lapidary." Molly turned to me with a quizzical look.

The observant neighbour went on, satisfying Molly's unspoken question.

"He is always away collecting rocks, and then at his Gem Club I think they call it. He even does some cutting and polishing in the little workshop under the house."

Being extremely careful not to seem excited to any level, not wanting Mrs Randolph to think my question was worth mentioning to either Mr Randolph or Vic the border, I asked. "Just for my notes please Mrs Randolph, could I have Vic's last name?"

"Madden, Victor Madden." she replied.

Walking over to the scene of the incidents we noticed Mrs Randolph appeared a bit excited with all this attention and importance. We always encouraged this in a managed way to ensure full cooperation because even volunteers sometimes cooled when confronted with Detectives and questioning. Molly and I knew that the potential crime scene had probably already been contaminated or at least walked over by the two ladies. However, we still wanted to have a close look around by ourselves.

"Mrs Randolph, please just pull up there." I asked firmly.

She wasn't going to miss all the action that easily. "But the man was in further, I can show you exactly." She started to walk deeper into the garden.

"No thank you that won't be necessary, we will take a good slow look by ourselves." placing my gentle arm around Mrs Randolph I guided her away from the garden. "Now we can't thank you enough for your alertness to spot him but also all your help. Mrs Miller is sure lucky to have a neighbour like you. Now please you head home and Detective Herbert and I will see what we can find."

Molly joined in. "Yes thank you Mrs Randolph we don't often get as much help as you have given us." With that she was gone. But we were sure she would need something near that kitchen sink and immediately. We were rewarded by her silhouette appearing a short time later. Good luck to her she had been very helpful.

"Now Molly we both know there has been two women, probably three kids and dogs as well through here, but you just never know. OK, like an American meat smoker low and slow, let's have a look."

It was difficult to truly evaluate a scene that any number of well meaning owners and neighbours may have tramped through. However, Molly and I could see where someone had stood for longer than just a walk through. There was no pile of DNA rich cigarette butts like in the movies, but there was something.

"Hey Ben."

"What Sherlock, what have you found?"

"Well it's probably snail or ant killer or something, but look at this white powder."

"I stand corrected, Sherlock." I laughed.

CHAPTER 9

The strange group of men had returned to their favourite coffee shop and were celebrating a successful delivery to Wellington New South Wales. The bonus was the fun on the way at Warwick, and a totally uneventful trip down. The cherry on top was the delivery of the completed order in perfect condition to those waiting in the shadows of the leafy little New South Wales town.

"I'd rather be toasting with Moet or Dom Perignon, but here's to a great team effort. What a few days, hey boys?" Charles said triumphantly

Everybody raised their mugs and cups and smiled, remembering the fun they had with Charles's friend's children at the chicken farm. And thinking about even greater enjoyment the trip had credited into their Thailand sex tour account.

The waiter noticed the toast but as usual couldn't make out what they were saying. And another week began.

As Molly and I drove back to the office from the Miller's place she finally asked about my Sherlock comment. "OK, smart arse, what did that Sherlock stuff mean."

"No, no Molly totally sincere. No sarcasm involved. You discovering that white powder identified our mystery Peeping Tom."

Not convinced at all she asked. "What do you mean identified?"

"Well, I'm pretty sure but, we have two things to do before we reach the one-hundred percent surety. First we need to get this sample we took to the lab. I believe that they will confirm that it is Tin Oxide."

Molly had that questioning look again. "And Tin Oxide is?" She let the **is** keep running to make it a question.

"Tin Oxide is used in the final polishing stage by lapidaries, as in those who have cut and polished said rocks."

Molly's face lit up. "And which person have we recently heard of who does lapidary?" Answering her question. "One Victor Madden. What's the second thing we need to do?"

"Run Mr Madden through the system, I'll be absolutely amazed if he hasn't got form for something kiddie related.

Within forty-eight hours Victor Madden, AKA Vince Maddox was in the Remand Centre. We were right in both cases.

Victor Madden had no criminal record, however we discovered through Centrelink that he was drawing unemployment benefits under the name of Vince Maddox who had done two stretches for paedophile related crimes. That encouraged the Magistrate to sign a search warrant for his unit and the entire ground floor of Mrs Randolph's house.

"That's terrific, I'll be over shortly to pick up the paper work. Thanks again." I looked up from the phone to see Molly walk into the office. By the smile on her face something had made her day. "Ben, does it get boring being right all the time?" She said with a laugh.

Laughing as well I relied. "I'll let you know, what's made you so chirpy?"

The lab results are back, they confirmed that the sample taken from the garden was indeed Tin Oxide."

"Awesome, we've just got our search warrant so rally the guys and let's head over to Kings Beach and Mr Madden's place. Two hours later, the search had turned up a huge collection of child porn, some photos of the children next door obviously from the garden and through their open bathroom window. We also found a container of a white powder on his lapidary bench. I was sure this perve was right for it, but we just needed to firm up the forensics to be guaranteed of a great result.

As we drove back to HQ a thought flew through my mind; *Is this guy worth me taking off the board? I figured probably not, he was a deadset paedo, and deserved punishment. At least he had not abused his victims in a physical way, and was at least for now off my radar.* The other principle that I always worked on was if the case was official, it was far too risky for me to act on in that way. Murdering a suspect might be a bit close to home for suspicions not to be raised.

By Ten the next morning the lab had tested the second sample of white powder and found that it matched the brand and batch characteristics of sample one found in Mrs Miller's garden. The evidence was nearly better than a signed confession, it was so solid. He was guaranteed to be starting another tax payer funded 'holiday' real soon.

Superintendent Fisher entered our office with a beaming smile. "Great work you two, quick, effective and rock solid. Couldn't ask for more."

"Thanks Boss, if Molly hadn't found that white powder in the garden the rest of the ducks might never have lined up."

Molly looking chuffed and a little embarrassed changed the subject. "Any further on those abductions?"

Shaking his head, his smile falling from his face Superintendent Fisher responded."No not a thing. In fact, and of course we have no reason to think this is linked to the previous but there was another on Saturday morning. A whistle stop just this side of the Queensland border."

"Have we got the details on the kid?" Asked Molly."

"Yeah, hang on a minute." Fisher went into his office and immediately returned holding a piece of paper, and started reading from it, he skipped the unnecessary parts. "Yeah, OK, taken September four at around 0900Hrs. Thirteen-year-old boy, last time he was sighted was at an Battersby Street Park 0800 Hrs and he has not contacted family since. This is out of character, who usually returns home at sunset and stays in contact via social media. He has not accessed his account since earlier Saturday morning and has not answered his phone since disappearing. He is described as Middle Eastern in appearance, with a light brown complexion, around 165cm in height, weighs around 60kgs, with a slim build, light brown hair and brown eyes.

The teenager may be wearing a dark blue polo shirt and black with white hi-top shoes. End of alert."

"So that's even harder. Still a long way from us, but on that road they could have gone any direction." I said despondently.

"Or they grabbed him and have taken on a camp for their sick fun. If they hold up there long enough any roadblocks of POLAIR will be called back. Free to go, they can kill him at their camp, or keep him and take him home if they want."

I drained my cold coffee and said. "You know it's just my gut, but I still think this is one person, or one group doing all these. I realise an abduction hundreds of kilometres from the first makes that improbable. But I just keep coming back to it."

"Yeah, I have seen your instincts give results Ben, but it's a bit of stretch like you said yourself. Listen it's been a big day, a great day of top class work. How about we call it quits and head home."

"You don't have to force me chief, I'm outa here." Said Molly grabbing her gear and standing.

"Sure why not, Molly can you give me a lift to O'Shannessy's with this early mark I'll catch up with an old friend who phoned me earlier." I said as I closed down my computer." Molly looked at me smiling. "Don't even start Mol, he, as in a man an old school friend, honestly it's like having a mum trying to marry me off." Molly laughed and we both headed for the lifts.

Pastor Rick Bell and I had been friends since our Army days and although we had gone our very separate ways remained close. As close I could be to another man, another human being. My inability to relate to people, my peers and authority all grew from the abuse I had suffered. When still a little boy of nine I had a naive interest

in sex that my school that friends my own age didn't possess. One
by one they seemed to just drift away. I had also become sarcastic
and that combined with my unharnessed anger made me toxic.
Sullenness thrived as I bucked against authority and trusted no one.
But I had learned in the Army that I couldn't survive that way so I let
in a few people that somehow had displayed qualities that allowed
me to trust them at least a little. Rick was one of them, and he had
never let me down. He was looking a mix of equal parts guilty and
embarrassed and one part scared. I knew this couldn't come from
what he drinking as he was currently nursing a double sarsaparilla.
In fact even when we served together, before he had found God he
hadn't been much of a drinker. He was however, one of the toughest,
bravest soldiers I had ever stood shoulder to shoulder with.

He had saved my life on two different occasions, both of which
he brushed off as minor incidents and definitely not involving his
being brave. He hadn't aged much, his hair was longer and the blond
moustache was now connected to a well managed goatee. He looked
like he was keeping fit and was dressed in worn jeans and a surf
themed tee-shirt.

Between my often drunk, physically abusive father and being
assaulted both physically and emotionally by my school teacher I
hadn't grown up with role models. I grew up with people I didn't
want to be like, in situations I never wanted to be in. Not all of us are
dealt great cards, but that doesn't mean you can't reshuffle your deck.
Get a better outcome. I was sitting with one of the few men I knew
was real. He was a man of faith and his life demonstrated it, unlike
so many who confessed a faith but denied it with their lives. Sitting
with this man of God, I felt ashamed at my hypocrisy. He constantly
proved he had a brotherly love and respect for me. However, I knew
I wasn't worthy of either. How he would hate me, and be so very
disappointed in me if he knew I was a murderer. He would never
condone it because everything about him screamed forgiveness and

giving people a second chance or the benefit of the doubt. Could he forgive me? Could God forgive me, as I walked towards his table I asked myself for the millionth time.

"Ben it's great to finally catch up face to face. Emails and messenger are OK, but gee it's good to shake your hand." He said with a huge smile.

"It sure is Dinger, you're right we should do this more often. I mean we are both busy, but you're only in Brisbane an hour or so."

"Mate, it's been a long time since anyone called me Dinger. Remember in our Company, hardly anyone Officers included, actually knew my name was Bell?" My Pastor friend replied.

Putting my glass down I added. "Sure and that Training Captain, oh what was his name? Yeah, Captain Pigeon who used to make fun of you misusing your nickname."

"Yeah who could forget. 'Corporal Dinner Bell' do this 'Corporal Dinner Bell' do that. He was so annoying. He just seemed to target me, I was never sure why. It took God's help and several attempts for me to forgive him for the hard time he gave me."

Laughing I shook my head. "Seriously, you shouldn't have wasted a minute of your life forgiving him, he was just an ass....."

My friend interrupted my cursing. "Mate, forgiveness is for both parties by God helping me forgive him, I was healed. Maybe Captain Pigeon was somehow blessed or released by it as well."

I laughed again. "And you don't drink. Maybe you should" This earned me a punch on the arm.

"Hey, talking about friends, some sad news you may have missed. Tim Condon took his own life just two weeks ago. Pastor Rick said in a sombre tone.

"No. Surely not he was one squared away guy I always thought he was heading for great things. Do you know what happened."

"I had the honour of doing his service, family only, absolutely no visitors. Even us because I asked. But his widow was adamant that it would be quick and no fuss." He paused and took a gulp of Sarsaparilla. I let him continue.

"Anyway, spending a little time with his widow, she showed me his suicide letter. It turns out poor old Tim was sexually abused by the local Priest. I hate to say it because unfairly it always seems to tarnish the Church or even God's reputation. It was his Priest, Bishop Len Fitzgerald. Now obviously your lot got a guilty verdict for his multiple victims you know the story there. And I assume there always more victims who never come forward. People like our Tim. Everyone, or I suppose nearly everyone was happy to see him put away. Then as you know that Solicitor David Mason got him off somehow and he's out and re-instated in the church of course."

I had to hide my fists from my friend as they were clenched so tight that they had turned white and the nails were cutting in to the flesh in places. I could hear Rick speaking but I couldn't discern his words as my emotions filled to overload. I knew if I spoke it would sound like I was about to explode to kill someone. It would have been very true. Even though I wasn't personally involved in the Bishop Fitzgerald case, I knew he was right for it, his Solicitor getting him off was the usual inadmissible evidence etc. The freed priest, a smiling solicitor claiming innocence and justice being served. In reality everyone knew the accused was guilty but the evidence or the witnesses were just not strong enough to proceed, not innocent just not put in front of a court. Appreciating the need for just laws and procedures, it still angered me seeing someone who was guilty get out on a technicality. It also sent all the wrong messages to all the victims in seeing how the system let them down.

Sensing my silence and probably misinterpreting it, Rick added. "Anyway, I know you work in that field but it can't make this stuff any easier. Normally, I would accept that he's been released so give him the benefit of the doubt but not this time. Tim's wife reckons when he saw the news of Fitzgerald being released he went into a shell. He hung himself the next day. Such a great bloke his life, family and career destroyed by the selfish evil of this one man. And it's worries me that he preaches every Sunday, feeding his flock on poison food. And who knows how many little boys he has so horribly abused?"

Finally, I was able to speak without betraying the fury that had coursed through my body.

"Rick, I'm glad you told me it was probably unhealthy for you to carry that burden by yourself. I tend to agree with you, but how can you be so sure the abuse occurred?"

After draining the last of his drink he responded. "Tim left a detailed note, basically he had battled it all his life. He said he was guilty, it was all his fault this had happened. I'm not sure what he meant. This might explain the way he was when we were all together. Remember he was always the first to volunteer for that extra patrol, or be the first through a doorway in some sandbox village. We just admired his courage but maybe..." He let the 'maybe' hang there.

We talked about many other things and at the end of the evening Rick drove me home.

"Great to catch up mate, do it again soon. I am sorry I brought the bad news but that's life I guess." He said offering his hand to shake. Taking it we hugged shoulder to shoulder, held each other for a little longer than usual just grieving quietly together.

"Yeah, keep in touch, talk soon, yeah?"

As I walked to my front door I thought about Tim. The initial rage I had felt was now replaced by a cold calm. By the time my key turned the lock I had decided that this Priest was my next person of interest. I knew the details in Tim's suicide note wouldn't result in any further charges. However, I knew Tim well enough to be sure that he wouldn't have put those things in the letter if they weren't true. Who would especially his last words. With the benefit of hindsight, I was just as sure he had lived his life in fear, dis-empowered by the man that he had given his trust. I knew exactly how that felt. Feeling guilty, ashamed and angry every minute of every day. I thought about Tim's reckless attitude, his quite nature, and inability to really be one of the boys. It all made sense now.

And, like everyone with an abusive past I could relate to his battles. I had struggled with those same social hurdles all my life like so many others. It didn't matter whether I was a Detective wearing a Glock on my hip and arresting paedos. I always had that second guessing lack of confidence. That inability to feel accepted by those around me. Never actually feeling like I was a fellow adult when among a group of men. Relationships were hard, with acceptance issues and an inability to trust anyone friendship and love were nearly impossible. We got by in varying degrees using what ever strategies they had developed. Some drank, did drugs, were over promiscuous or had other self-destructive life styles. And others like me found careers that allowed their anger to be legitimately vented against a surrogate enemy. Putting the evil doers away was rewarding, but when they escaped justice something else was require to tip the balance back toward the victims.

CHAPTER 10

"Stan, I know they worry you mate, but they are probably just some group of retired Postmen or something. You've been watching too much NETFLIX mate." The coffee shop owner liked his young employee, he worked hard and was great with the customers continued. "I've told you before mate, they put money in both of our pockets nearly every day. They're OK I'm sure of it."

Shaking his head Stan the waiter loaded the men's orders on his tray. "OK Boss, I hear ya, but I'm not convinced."

Picking up the tray in silence he left the serving area and headed outside. He couldn't help himself, he had to know one way or another who these men were. He found that he was walking much faster than usual in an attempt to catch the men before they went silent as he approached their table.

"Here's your orders gentlemen." The young waiter said happily.

Once again like a switch the group had shut down as soon as they noticed the young man coming toward their table. Knowing each man's order he placed their plates, cups and mugs before them. Glancing over his shoulder he saw that the conversations around the table had started again, and said to himself. "I know I'm right but how can I prove it?"

Superintendent Barry Fisher approached our bank of desks. "Ben and Molly a HIT just came in you guys want it?".

A HIT, was a Historical Indecent Treatment, usually the victim had gotten to an age where they felt they could finally make a complaint of some past abuse. They were notoriously difficult to investigate and harder to prosecute. That being said every victim had the right to make these claims and attempt to free themselves of the horror of their past. If it was a one time only event it became even harder, but if the abuse had gone on over an extended period, the cases had a good chance to proceed quite successfully.

It was alleged that a man Joseph Anderson who was now in his seventies had inappropriately touched, in that he repeatedly digitally raped his twelve-year-old grand-daughter. The victim Julie Anderson was now twenty two and had made the initial complaint at Kawana Police Station. The guys there had done a great job with the initial and as per SOPs (Standard Operating Procedures) had flick passed to us at Child Protection.

How these sort of cases played out was one of two ways. The perpetrator when confronted with the accusation would often confess. Often the abuser was an opportunist, baby sitting a neighbour or a relative and they kept the abuse going for an extended period. They had never done anything like this before or since they had stopped. Some would be guilt ridden stating that it was good not to have the weight on their backs any more. Others would be fear driven.

Glad in a way that they no longer have to wonder if the victim would tell somebody and their past catch up with them. There was of course the serial paedophile. What normally happened was once the case became public other victims would come forward. This abuser had multiple victims and had usually kept abusing kids until for some reason they stopped or like now they were finally caught. Sometimes the abuse stops purely because the little girl or boy grow up and are no longer attractive to the abuser.

Julie Anderson sat uncomfortably in the interview room, clearly stressed, she hadn't stopped wiping her eyes since her arrival at our office. To minimise the victim's embarrassment Molly was conducting the interview, which was being videoed. The alleged abuse had gone on throughout 2007 and 2008 at her Kawana Island home. Julie claimed she was further abused during a family holiday to Cairns in early 2009. The interview continued and although teary the victim Julie answered Molly's questions accurately and in sickening detail. Two hours later we had a sequence of abuse that contained enough solid points to support further investigation. Julie's parents were still living on Kawana Island and would need to be interviewed. Julie stated that they were aware of her claims and had reacted by withdrawing and refusing to discuss the topic with Julie. Julie's grandfather Joseph Anderson had moved to South West Rocks in New South Wales around Easter 2009 for reasons unknown.

Historical Indecent Treatment cases relied heavily on times, dates and locations and this one was no different. Once Ms Anderson had left our offices Molly and I divided up the leg work that her interview had generated.

"Molly, what's your take on Julie?"

"One-hundred-percent solid Ben. It's always a bit safer when the vic is of an age they are a little savvy, they remember details that a four-year-old wouldn't notice, or be able to verbalise. I think we proceed. We have locations, we have a set patterns of when he would baby sit her, maybe not dates as such but every Thursday night her parents went ten pin bowling."

I had watched the interview and agreed with Molly's evaluation. "Obviously, we will need to confirm that the family stayed in Cairns in early 2009, that could be hard."

"No, I've asked Molly to check the family photos for a date to help us pin it down."

"Good thinking Molly, see how it goes hey?" I responded thinking it was a bright move on my partners part.

I had seen a few of these Historical Indecent Treatment cases go no where when the investigators discover the alleged abuser is dead. Sometimes the victim wants more but where can law enforcement go when the perpetrator can't be brought to justice.

"Molly give me all you have on Grandpa Anderson and I'll make sure the old sicko is still on the top side of the lawn." I asked hoping he was still with us.

Molly laughed at my joke and understanding where I was coming from tapped out an email with the information I had requested. Within twenty-minutes I had found him.

"Molly, I found Grandpa, he's in NSW so an extradition will be needed if the case proceeds that way." The excitement beginning to build in my voice. I had hated the idea of him escaping justice.

Molly replied. "That's a relief. Ben, what do you reckon, line up the incidents and then talk to Mum and Dad. My gut feeling is they knew something. Hopefully, not everything but enough to either exile Grandpa or for him to flee the family and the State".

"Yeah, that makes a lot of sense. Where to from here?"

Julie Anderson phoned as Molly and I were planning out our next steps.

"Julie, how are you going?"

I couldn't hear the reply, but I'd heard it from hundreds of other victims. It took courage to do what they did coming forward after all those years.

Molly encouraged her and then put the call on speaker. "It can be tough dredging up those old memories but it was necessary. I assure you it'll be good for you in the long run."

"Oh. Detective Herbert, yeah I know I feel so stupid crying all the time. They haven't said so but I'm sure my parents would have liked me to just forget about it and not rake it all up. But I had to, he did those things, and he's supposed to be protecting me, loving me in a proper Grandpa way. It doesn't feel right at the moment but I think, well I'm hoping doing this will help me feel better about myself, about everything." The young lady said trying to be more convincing than she sounded.

"Julie you are one impressive young lady, and for what it's worth I believe you are right. By sorting this out as painful as it is to your family. Well, I think you will find you do feel a weight shift off your shoulders. How did you go with those photo-dates?"

"Yeah, you were right I got the dates off the photos and even better the name of the motel we stayed in is in one of the shots."

Molly wrote down the info and after letting Julie talk some more finished the call.

"OK, Ben we all good, as you heard, I got the name of Motel and a date that must be two or three days either side of checking in."

After talking to the Motel Manager we had confirmation of the booking. Of course after all this time the Motel staff wouldn't know who stayed in what room. However, the Andersons had occupied Rooms Ten and Eleven. Yes, those rooms had an interconnecting door which supported Julie's claims about her Grandfather's accessing her room and abusing her on several occasions when her parents went out.

After a phone call to Julie's Mother, Molly and I headed out to Kawana Island, a beautiful mini-suburb built on a man-made island North of Caloundra. The house was two storey, modern rendered in a sort of sand yellow, no yard but on the canal.

"Please come in Detectives, can I get you a cold drink perhaps?" Asked Julie's mother who was identical to her daughter plus the extra years. There was an aura of weariness or despair that had robbed the spark from her startlingly blue eyes.

"Frank, this is Detective-Sergeant McQueen and Detective Herbert."

After the introductions we sat in a bright lounge area looking out over a small pool and then the wide canal, a retirement village could be seen on the other side.

I kicked off. "Now I know this is a very difficult situation for any family to confront. However, we have investigated Julie's claims and we are proceeding further. Has Julie spoken to you about what she alleges her Grandfather did?"

Julie's father Frank projected a confidence born of being used to running his own company with people following his orders.

However, as much as he attempted to lean on his usual position you could see he was out of his depth. Way out of the world he normally had control over. Torn between hope that his own father hadn't hurt his daughter and knowing deep down that he probably had. Parents were often reluctant to confront the issue because it suggested a sickness or some deviate trait within their genes and also that they had failed to protect their child.

"Yes, Julie has spoken to us and told us things. She's our daughter and we love her dearly but we are not sure doing this after all thee years is beneficial to anyone."

Molly understood how this stuff tore families apart. However, after the law our first priority is always the victim. "I get that it's terrible. Now thinking about 2000, or 2008, at any time did either of you think something was going on, did you see anything. Did you notice Julie change in any way?"

Often when speaking to a couple you got conflicting answers. Mrs Anderson started to reply. "I saw a change in Julie."

Mr Anderson cut her off. "Yeah, but you know girls becoming teenagers they all change right?"

Molly and I looked at each other and she was about to say something but Mr Anderson spoke loudly to make sure he was heard

"Look we love her, but he's my Father, her Grandfather. If we were sure at the time we would have gone to the Police for sure. You're always hoping that what you saw, or felt in your gut was rubbish, it couldn't be. Marcy talked to Julie at some stage but Julie said everything was fine with Grandpa. What could we do?"

Marcy, Julie's mother nodded. "You can't believe it, no it can't be happening in our family. Until one night we came home from bowling a bit early I think I had a headache or something."

The father chimed in. "Yeah, and same thing, there was just something that seemed off. Dad was acting strange, Julie stayed in her room. I can't remember it was so long ago. But it was enough. I fronted Dad, I didn't accuse him but I asked him if he and Julie were OK. That was about it. He said they were but I could see something in his eyes. I let it drop and he went home."

"That's right Frank, and the very next morning we found a short note in the letter box. I wouldn't know where it ended up. It said something like he had decided to move on, that we would be better if he didn't have anything to do with us. And that was the last contact we ever had with him. Nether of us have any idea where he moved to or where he is today. He could be dead for all we know."

We discussed the case all the way back to the office, as we walked into our building Molly stated. "Let's take all this to the Boss and see what he thinks." Molly said confidently.

Superintendent Fisher looked up from the file he had been reading while Molly and I had sat in silence awaiting his assessment. "Well, I think we have enough to drag the old guy back to the Sunshine Coast. Once the extradition is authorised you two liaise with the NSW boys. Have them pick him up, and then you fly down and bring him home. Early days I know, but that looks like great work guys."

"Thanks Sir, yeah these can be tricky. It'll all depend on how Grandpa reacts under questioning. Let's hope he does the right thing and comes clean."

Two days later an old man who looked just like someone's grandfather should look like was sitting opposite Molly and me. That's the problem, these monsters never look menacing like Hannibal Lecter. That's how they operate so freely, under the families radar, or the soccer mum's antennae. Thankfully, it took very little for this old man to brake down and confess to sexually abusing his the twelve-year-old granddaughter. That was a big relief because it meant that Julie didn't have to give evidence in court. Anderson senior would confirm his confession before the Magistrate and be sentenced. Smooth as glass. With a no-contest case to prepare the hearing was held just three weeks after our investigation had begun. Joseph Anderson a seventy-five year old man residing at South West Rocks New South Wales was sentenced to four years with a parole possible no earlier than two years. At seventy-five there was a good chance that he would die behind bars and good luck to him. Molly and I were very happy with the result as was our Boss. Molly advised Julie Anderson of her grandfather's sentence and her reaction was one of stunned acceptance that it was all over. There wasn't celebratory gestures or words, just an understanding that the cloud that had hung over each one of them including her Grandfather was now gone. She wondered how her parents would take the news.

On another matter, unbeknown to anyone in my office I had run some checks on the Anglican Bishop, Fitzgerald who had been charged with abusing three altar boys in his local church when still serving as a Priest in his parish. Two had given evidence in the case, one had withdrawn his statement due to mental health issues. Studying the court transcript and victim's statements, I was not surprised that the original Magistrate had returned a guilty finding. Fitzgerald had been sentenced to fourteen years, and to me it appeared that this was a good outcome. His Barrister David Mason had a reputation for getting high profile scum-bags off on technicalities rather than through alibis or defence evidence. He had taken the case to the Supreme Court and had the finding overturned on a technicality. This meant that Father Len Fitzgerald had been released amongst a media frenzy and reinstated to the post of Bishop. This meant in reality I had two persons of interest, a paedophile Priest and a Barrister who seemed to profit by defending paedophiles. I understood the concept that everyone deserves the best legal counsel they can get. However, Mason seemed to be specialising and was worth a look.

I had been thinking about the way I needed to handle this. I had faith that my Army friend Tim wouldn't name a specific Priest and make allegations of sexual abuse without reason. Especially, in his last communication before he died. All the other paedophiles I had put out of action were confirmed sickos deserving more justice than the system was providing. However, if I was to execute Father Fitzgerald I needed to be completely sure he had abused Tim or was indeed a pedo. With this in mind I decided that I would wear a mask and interrogate the good father. That way if I believed he was innocent I could just disappear, leaving him to decide if he wanted to report the incident to the Police. I doubted that he would want to draw such attention to himself, but who knows?

I also researched David Mason the high profile Barrister who had gotten him off. He regularly appeared in the newspapers and on TV. I was biased whichever way you looked at it, as a cop, and also hating paedophiles. However, he seemed to specialise in cases that appeared to be watertight prosecutions and yet faltered at court. The defendant would get off on a technicality of law rather than say, evidence. In other words he was not pronounced innocent, just not guilty due to such and such. Or in several examples, the Crown Prosecutor chose not to proceed stating a lack of evidence. Everyone understood this translated to the accused is guilty as charged, because we can't prove it. This was why several such cases had been re-opened and resulted in a conviction with the advent of DNA analysis. Thankfully, samples taken from the crime scene years ago had been preserved. Now with the benefit of DNA technology the samples were tested and matched to the accused. In the past police may not have been able to prove a suspect had been present at a rape or murder. Now, by matching a suspect's DNA with the sample collected at the scene police could prove the accused had been there.

As you could imagine security around the Bishop's residence was extremely low. The Diocese had employed guards after his release to discourage any journalists or camera crews. However they had been dismissed a week after he got out, the hierarchy hoping that everything would settle down now. As I silently came through the unlocked back door I pulled down my ski mask. Sitting at the head of a huge mahogany dinning table he had his back to me reading the racing form. Momentum and fear were my strongest allies. I slapped him hard across the side of the head causing him to tumble off the chair. Maximising the shock he was now feeling I jumped straight in.

"Now we are going to have a talk. I will ask a question you will answer, nothing more nothing less. Got it?"

"Oh, young man I don't have a lot for you to steal, but you don't have to hurt me. Take whatever you want."

I slapped him again, but this time on the other cheek. It crossed my mind to make the connection about turning the other cheek, but I fear God too much to joke about such things.

"Wrong answer. I asked you if you understood how this talk was going to go. I'll explain it again. Now I ask, you answer. Not hard at all. Do you understand this time?"

Wiping a tiny stream of blood from the side of his mouth he stuttered a scared reply. "Ye...Yes."

"Great, now we are getting somewhere. Is there anyone else in the house?" I asked

"No, I'm alone." He answered softly.

"OK. Are you expecting any visitors?"

"No."

"See this is lovely now, it's not hard once we all understand. Now I'm here about your court case. I know all about your appeal and subsequent release. And the last thing I want to hear are claims of your innocence. I'm here to decide that." I hesitated to give him some time to switch on to the topic and stop guessing why I was in his dinning room.

I continued. "OK, now I am unsure whether you're are guilty or innocent. However, to seek the truth I'm willing to hurt you more than you can imagine. I know, I know, that's so unfair if you're innocent. But, look at at it this way, if you aren't guilty of molesting those altar boys you will get out of this OK. A little damaged but alive." Once again I paused to let the fear smoulder within him.

"I didn't touch those bo..." I slapped him, hard this time with a cupped hand over his left ear. He screamed and grabbed his ear, attempting to soothe his probably shattered ear drum. He went to apologise for his infringement of the rules, but thought better of it.

"OK, now I am going to walk you through the victim's statements. Answer me truthfully and you will avoid being totally deaf by the time I leave."

I read from the reports, and asked him questions and details. He too had studied them and had answers probably developed and coached by his Barrister David Mason. I was looking for eye movement and body language more than the words. I was sure that he had delivered the same responses in court word perfect and with practised facial expressions. However this time he was alone, terrified, in pain and deep down knowing that he was in truth guilty as sin his acting ability was paper thin. This man sat proudly, if not arrogantly before me. His perfectly groomed grey hair, and his expensive black suit with his big gold cross hanging under his dog collar spoke of righteous authority and superiority. I was probably eighty percent certain he was guilty. Guilty as sin. Now the first two victim's statement were clearly named, and birth dates and addresses supplied. I got to the third statement and noticed something I had missed when I'd read them at my place. Due to withdrawing his statement and accusation the third victim's name, birth date and address had all been redacted. It had been left in the file for administrative reasons but was no longer active.

"Now, this third victim, tell me about him?"

"Well, Tim was always a troubled boy. I'm not surprised he lied about all this when the police contacted him." He kept talking on and on. However, I didn't hear a word he was said after 'troubled boy'. Fitzgerald wasn't aware that I hadn't known the identity of the third victim and off course that Tim was known to me and that was why I was interrogating him. The revelation hit me like a freight train. I'd had no way of knowing that Tim, my Army buddy was the third victim. The person, who due to mental health issues had withdrawn his statement of accusations against this Priest sitting before me. Tim had killed himself straight after he saw Bishop Fitzgerald released on the six o'clock news. It all came flooding back to me. I remembered my mate Pastor Rick talking about Tim's suicide note; 'He said he was guilty, it was all his fault this had happened.' At the time neither of us understood the meaning of his guilt comment. The guilt he expressed in his suicide note was related to him being unable to continue with the court case. He felt responsible for the paedophile Priest being set free because he had withdrawn his statement. He blamed himself for letting this animal get free and maybe abuse other kids.

I was sure. He was good for it as we say in the police when we are sure someone is guilty. "Now Father." Sarcasm dripping from my words. "The problem with you guys is you dirty the good work of all the other Priests and Pastors who a real. You talk God with your lips and deny him with your actions. Well I'm sure you've preached these words many times, now you can understand them. 'The wages of sin is death.'" He whimpered softly as I stood up from the dinning table and walked behind his chair. Silently drawing my custom made Filicietti hunting knife I grabbed a handful of that manicured grey hair. Dragging his head back, he screamed and then fell silent. I whispered in his good ear. "Tim was a war hero, a great bloke and a good friend of mine you piece of self-righteous shit." I gave it time to register, and when he began to squirm I knew it had.

I drew the razor sharp Damascus steel blade across his stretched throat and stood back. The room filled with the smell of copper and faeces as the paedophile's bowels failed him at death. I had worn gloves and crime scene overalls since I had left my vehicle so I had no concerns about fingerprints or DNA being left at the scene. I looked around and saw his laptop and nearly as an afterthought took it as I left the room.

Same thoughts and doubts about forgiveness, same lame justification from the Old Testament. Just like those ancient times parents sacrificing their children to gain a selfish outcome.

Leviticus 20:2

"Say to the people of Israel, Any one of the people of Israel or of the strangers who sojourn in Israel who gives any of his children to Molech shall surely be put to death. The people of the land shall stone him with stones.

CHAPTER 11

Charles looked around the group and deep within made the decision that he had really made after they got back from the Wellington trip. It was time to leave, to move on. He had learnt long ago that one way or another you get trapped by staying some place too long.

"Anyway, Robert tells me the Bikies have placed another order." Smiling like a shark, Charles continued. "This is wonderful because it means the Wellington delivery has proven to our hairy partners that we are trustworthy."

Robert looking at Charles for approval, and receiving a nod added and several murmurs. "Now the order isn't as big, but it is very specific. They must have orders of their own. I s'pose customers have certain preferences and the Hunters Bikie Group are in the business of satisfying those needs. And so are we."

The others looked around the table and noted that everyone was nodding in agreement. Charles enquired.

"What are the details Rob, can we fill the order from here on the coast. It would be good to hit this fast and hard." Individually, the rest of the group stifled a laugh at Charles' attempt at some Jason Statham imitation, or some unidentifiable tough guy at least.

Without missing a beat, Robert replied. "Four in total. One, Middle Eastern boy no older than twelve, two Asian girls under ten, and one Asian boy no older than five."

Richard commented. "I know it's a little riskier collecting near home. But, it is sure a lot easier, and I'm always worried operating somewhere unfamiliar to us."

Surprising the group due to his usual cautiousness, Charles agreed."I think this time Richard is right. What do you guys think, can we get that variety locally?

The discussion continued like the men were planning a shopping trip.

Stan the young waiter was looking down at the array of coffee mugs, tea cups and milk jugs and didn't see them at all. He was deep in thought; *I know the Boss is probably right, but I'm just as sure these guys are up to no good.* Then he had an idea. Picking up the first part of their order he exited out the back door instead of the usual front entry/exit. Quietly he headed around to the side of the coffee shop. This meant that he had just a few steps to put him at the group's table, he thought. *I might just be able to catch some of their conversations and finally know either way.*

"So as far as the Asian kids there are so many on holidays here they will be easy. As for the Arab well he mi...." Mike had been talking but when he saw the waiter coming from around the corner of the building stopped mid-word. The group caught on immediately, and as usual silence fell like the proverbial 'cone of silence' until the waiter left their drinks and returned to the get the rest of their order.

Charles looked anxious and asked. "Do you think he heard anything?"

Robert responded. "I can't see how he couldn't have heard at least something."

"Yeah, but maybe one isolated sentence what would he make of it?" Richard added looking hopeful.

Shaking his head Charles continued. "I don't like it, not one little bit. We can't just hope he didn't hear, or didn't understand. I think we have to assume he's an immediate threat. The question is what do we do about it?"

Charles didn't want the entire group as witnesses to planning the waiter's demise so he took control of the discussion. "OK, it's unlikely, but it means the cops might turn up here and ask questions." Charles saw a hardness enter Damo's eyes and immediately knew what he was thinking, and that his deadly seed had taken root. Looking around the table Charles stated. "OK, we won't come here for a week or so. If we disappear completely, like forever, the owner might get suspicious. Damo, how about you and I catch up later?"

Then the front door of the coffee shop banged open as Stan the waiter pushed the door open with a tray carrying the rest of the group's order and asked. "OK, gentlemen is there anything else I can get you?"

"Ah, I think that's all mate." Said Charles making the pretence of seeking a response from the others when he knew they didn't want the waiter near them.

"Fine thanks again." And with that the young waiter walked back into the coffee shop.

"So did anyone notice anything strange?" Asked Rob.

"Yeah, well the most obvious is that in all the time we have been coming here he's never come from behind us. Now all of a sudden he does. And then straight after that he's back to normal using the front door." Richard replied sounding uncertain and like he was already regretting speaking.

"No, I think you're are right Richard, it is strange. I wonder if he was trying to catch us talking. I s'pose it might seem strange the way we always clam up when he brings out our order." Damo who had made up his mind about what had to be done said supporting the theory. As the group split up going their separate ways Charles took Damo aside. Charles was torn between caution and deep down knowing that Damo was right on all counts. He wanted to unleash his attack dog without it being obvious. In that way he could if necessary, plead that Damo must have misunderstood his intentions.

"But Damo we're not even certain that the young fella heard anything. It's a big step, that may not be necessary."

"Firstly, Charles you are fine as a leader when it comes to the day to day, or the operational stuff. But, I'm the only one in the group that's had hot metal shot at me, and returned it as well. Like I said

I not going to gamble with my freedom. I know we aren't sure if he heard anything, but are you really willing to go all in on it?"

Charles wanted to distance himself from what he knew was inevitable. "OK Damo it's your call." As he said it he turned sharply and left Damo standing alone, he smiled knowing the button had been pressed but he hadn't left any prints. Damo, already in attack mode hadn't noticed the older man's departure and talking quietly to himself said. "It always was you silly old prick."

After leaving the late Bishop Fitzgerald's home, I turned on to the Gateway heading for the Sunshine Coast. I started thinking; *Executing the Bishop was only stage one of gaining the justice my mate Tim deserved. Sure his abuser had been removed but that Barrister was just as guilty by allowing paedophiles the freedom to re-offend, as they always did.* I got home and grabbed the bottle of JD. Hitting the series of keys one of the computer boys at work had shown me I bypassed the password protection on the laptop I had taken from the fallen Priest. He hadn't even bothered to hide anything it was riddled with kiddie porn. I was sure before, but now I was absolutely certain. He had deserved to die.

Looking at his emails I went into Sent and searched for Barrister David Mason. There were hundreds of them. I systematically worked my way backwards noting the more recent referred to the Bishop's Supreme Court appeal. As you would expect there were multiple emails back and forth discussing tactics and what the Bishop was to say when questioned. Going further back I noticed that most of the emails had attachments. I opened the first one and was confronted with a video of a little girl, maybe five years old kneeling in front of a man. I opened several other attachments and found they were all kiddie porn with emails flowing to and from the Barrister. So, he wasn't just a Lawyer who wasn't choosy about whom he defended he was a paedophile as evil as they were. I noticed some of the emails that the two perverts had exchanged were forwarded from other people. I studied the addresses and took a photo of them so I could research the list later. I knew our Lawyer friend was deserving the same reward Bishop Fitzgerald had received. For now though, he could wait.

"Boss I'll hit the road, every thing's done. I've done all the lunch prep, and filled the fridges." The young coffee shop waiter said, looking forward to going for a surf.

"Thanks Stan, I'll see bright eyed and bushy tailed tomorrow hey?"

"Yeah, whatever that means I'll be here. Thanks Boss. See ya."

Laughing at the young guy not understanding the old saying his Boss replied. "See ya then."

By the time the waiter's shift had finished the group of men had gone their own ways. But Damo hadn't gone far. He had seen the waiter around, his transport was a push bike with the surfboard rack on its side leaning near the coffee shop's gas cylinders. Resting in his Jeep Wrangler, Damo had slouched down so as not to present an obvious silhouette. He was in the shade ensuring a good view of the coffee shops rear parking area. Eventually, Stan came out of the coffee shop and was talking on his mobile phone. "Listen Wax, Dicky Beach is all Ankle Busters, but Kings will be Bitchin, there's a great Northerly blowing. Should be there in ten, OK?" He disconnected.

Damo followed Stan and had already decided how this would go. He too had checked the surf and was pretty certain where the young waiter was heading. Stan could hear the throaty engine of some 4WD just behind him. He thought; *Why doesn't this dickhead pass me? It doesn't really matter I'm getting off the road just here anyway.*

He swung his bike into the entrance to the lookout and was surprised that the vehicle he was concerned about had followed him into the smaller road. Stan wheeled toward the track that lead down to the water. Damo made his move.

The Wrangler's bull-bar struck the surfboard but that was OK. The bike, surfboard and its rider were knocked sideways towards the verge. The bike caught on a bush and the rider flew over the handlebar falling over the three-hundred-and-twenty foot cliff landing on a rock ledge below washed by the pounding surf. Damo was no amateur, he wasn't about to stop and look. He had chosen the site quickly, but with local knowledge and was certain no body could fall that far and survive. He slowly drove around the U of the road and rejoined the main thoroughfare. Careful to maintain the 40 speed limit he headed for home. At the base of the cliff momentarily revived by the cold salt water Stan's eyes opened. He smiled because he loved the waves. His shattered organs began to close down one by one. And then as his lifeless body was rolled by another wave his sightless eyes closed for the very last time.

From the Hebrew Bible Adrammelech, Anammelech, Moloch (also **Molech**, Milcom, or Malcam) is the biblical name of a Canaanite god associated with child sacrifice. Where parents would burn their children to gain some reward or protection from the god Molech.

CHAPTER 12

Molly and I were reading from our computer monitors, Molly looked up, frustrated as usual because I was a slower reader. "Ben, can you believe this shit?"

A grunt was all I could manage, stunned and angry at such a horrible betrayal.

There had been a major break on an Australian wide case. A Melbourne woman originally from the Netherlands, one Lotte De Vries had been charged with sixty-four cases of Child Exploitation. The woman, because you couldn't call her a mother, had sold her own son on the dark web on at least sixty-four occasions. She had been sentenced to just twelve years for this heinous crime. The woman's partner and stepfather to the victim, Bramm Bakker, was also sentenced to 12 years in prison in connection to the crime. After the pair complete their jail time, they will be required to comply with numerous restrictions to ensure they do not re-offend.

The couple was charged with multiple crimes, which included rape, aggravated sexual assault of children, forced prostitution, and distribution of child pornography. The couple themselves had also sexually abused the young boy for at least two years and made custom-tailored videos of the abuse for sale on the dark web. They had advertised their son for sale and allowed multiple abusers to engage in sex acts with the boy, charging the abusers as much as $12,000 at a time in order to do so. As I read further into the case notes I found this. The woman who thought it would put her in a better light stated the following. "There was one customer, a Chinese man who I let have my son for a day. But this man offered to pay more for the right to kill him." The horrible bitch thought that rejecting that offer made her look caring in some twisted way. However, every cop who read it, including me would have thought she had decided a dead son brought no more income. Yet again, the sentence was grossly inadequate but I had enough on my plate. I did however create a private file with photos and all the details of the offenders. I hoped they would move to Queensland when they got out of jail.

"You guys finished reading about that Melbourne case?" Superintendent Fisher asked.

Smiling Molly looked up."I've read it twice, Ben's still on his first. Grade four was the longest three years of his life."

Looking up I replied. "Very funny, not. I think as I read and it slows me down, OK?" All of us laughed at this incriminating statement.

Fisher pulled us back to centre. "Guys, I didn't give you that file just for interest. The Victorian computer nerds have somehow followed the money and identified a number of the customers this pair sold their son to. And guess what we have two players right here on the Sunny Coast."

I stopped reading and looked up to see that Molly was clearly excited by this news. "Boss, you're kidding."

"No we've got two local celebrities, known to us but no recent form. Richard Cook and a..." He looked at the printed email he was holding. A Paul Simpson. When Simpson had his psych eval he fitted the Macdonald Triad as a child. Turns out he was a frequent bed-wetter as a child, which caused him much humiliation. Simpson also reported that he sexually abused animals. As usual both bed wetting and animal cruelty are components of the Macdonald Triad, a classic set of childhood behaviours that can point to violent pedo tendencies later in life. I want you to come up with a plan, I know we can grab these sickos for the Melbourne offences straight away. However, you know what these grubs are like. They're always up to no good in other ways where ever they live, and in this case here on our patch."

I agreed with him. "I think that's a great idea Boss, we know where these guys are. They'll get what they deserve for hiring that boy but lets put them away for as long as we can."

Molly and I read up on each of the men mentioned in the list of buyers and ran them through all our registers. For the next hour or so we hashed over different ideas and possible ways to see what they were currently doing. We had decided that we would be covert at first, holding back on search warrants that, when served would immediately alert them. All of them had stayed off the radar for some years which suggested they were being clever covering their tracks, rather than suggesting that they had reformed. So, for us to charge them with as much as possible we had to know what they were really up to. Molly and I were about to head out our to start watching our first Target, one Richard Cook. He'd done time eight years ago for Sexual Assault of a Child under 16 years old, the twelve year old daughter of his long term next door neighbour. Neither of us believed the leopard had changed his spots. Sadly, it meant that we hadn't caught him, rather than he hadn't re-offended in some way. Just as we were thinking of going for a drive-by to check out Cook's known address there was a knock on the main office door.

Two Detectives were waiting when I opened the door. They didn't have to show their badges for me to know.

"Hey, I'm Jack Nolan and this is Dennis Conner, I'm hoping our Boss talked to your Super about us visiting?" We shook hands. "Ben McQueen and that's Molly Herbert over there."

Shaking my head and hoping they weren't here for what I was guessing I smiled. "Not that I know of, but things are a bit hectic here at present. Maybe it was forgotten." I gave them the benefit of the doubt. They had said where they were from. That's the sort of bullshit Internal Affairs would pull, just showing up trying to rattle you. But these guys weren't IA, that I could tell. I still wondered where they were from. "Grab a coffee and a chair, I'll be right back.

Where you blokes from anyway?" I asked as I stood to head towards the Boss' office.

"Homicide" Nolan replied.

"Sir, there's two Detectives outside, they say their Boss phoned ahead. I just thought I'd check with you?"

"Oh! Ben I totally forgot with that Melbourne stuff getting us all excited. Yeah, they're investigating a death, they think it might have been murder over at Golden Beach last week." It took all my self-control not to stagger at the shock.

Recovering and hoping he hadn't seen my reaction I asked. "OK, Boss do you know why they want to talk to us?"

"Not, really something about the vic being one of our sickos. They didn't give me any details." He said casually.

Walking back to our office and the waiting Homicide Detectives I felt my gut tighten so hard it hurt.

I entered my office to find Molly and the two visitors chatting and laughing like old friends. In the most casual tone I could muster I asked. "So, what's this all about?"

Detective Nolan responded, he seemed the senior of the pair. "Well we are still waiting on the Coroner's findings but the Caloundra Coastguard pulled a floater out last week heading out to sea from Pumistone Passage. Now, he was very helpful, because he had his wallet in his pocket. When we ID'ed him it turns out he was a paraplegic, wheelchair bound. Then something interesting happened, a guy heading out from the boat ramp at Golden Beach hit something metal. And guess what, it was a wheelchair."

Looking like I still didn't get the connection I asked. "Sorry Jack, I'm confused. Are you investigating an accident, a murder, or maybe even a suicide? And without seeming rude. What's this all got to do with us?"

"Of course you're right Ben. It could be any one of those three. And my money is that we may never be sure. That's the answer to your first question. The answer to why are we here is easier. When we searched the dead guy's place we found he had a heap of kiddie-porn." Detective Nolan stated.

His partner Conner chipped in. "Well obviously we checked for any criminal record and he came up clean. We know sometimes we can be onto someone but just can't slam that cell door. So we figured that your mob might have known of him even though he looks clean on first glance."

Molly responded and then turned to her key board. "Give us his name and DOB and I'll see if we have anything on him."

Jack Nolan opened his Police notebook and read from it. "Walter Maxstead DOB, 6/2/54."

In less than a minute Molly turned back to the three Detectives. "Sorry guys, nearly nothing. His rego was noted by an alert school crossing lollipop lady who thought he was parked and looking rather than picking up a son or daughter. Anyway, we ran it got nothing, and of course told her if she saw him again to let us know. We've never heard of him from our section ever again. Whether it was nothing or he got spooked we'll never know, especially now."

"That's a bummer. We were hoping for a list of victims who would immediately be persons of interest. You know seeking revenge of their abuser. All too easy I guess."

I felt like I had held my breath for the last twenty minutes and hoped my anxiety wasn't as visible to them as I felt. I hadn't thought about the possibility of Maxstead's possessions leading an enquiry in my direction. However, scared I was I had to remind myself they were here for information about the paedophile. Not, because of anything even vaguely related to me.

"That's good work following that digital breadcrumb trail to here. I'm sorry it didn't really help." I said sounding to me insincere hoping again it wasn't that obvious to them.

They both stood up. "Molly, Ben, thanks for your help in any case. You know how it works shutting doors is most of any investigation. Then all of a sudden there is one or two open for us to step through. Please thank your Boss for your hospitality, even though that coffee is worse than the mud at our office." We all laughed. "We'll get out of your hair now. Good hunting, most of the people we put away are just ordinary mum and dads who lose it and go too far. Your mob though they don't deserve to live for what they do to the innocent little ones." With that the two Homicide Detectives were gone. I sat down after letting them out of the office smiling for the first time since I had opened the door to them. The irony of Jack Nolan's parting words echoing in my mind. They didn't deserve to live.

"What did you make of that Molly?" I asked, more to break the silence than to gain a reply. Molly stretched the tension from her neck and replied. "Good work, like he said, victim revenge could have steered them toward the killer, if there is one. When you put it together, what have they really got. A sixty something fella in a wheelchair, easy an accident, or maybe he'd had enough. I sorta feel like murder is the least most likely scenario."

I wasn't about to disagree with her on that.

CHAPTER 13

Peter Hook had just put out the last of the chairs into the alfresco area of his coffee shop. Sadness hit him as it did every time something like this task reminded him of young Stan's death. He had a new kid starting the next day but a staff member wasn't the issue, Stan was great young man and Hook had always treated him like a son and friend in spite of their age differences. It had been two days since Stan's accident and the coffee shop owner could still hear the raw grief when Stan's mum had called with the terrible news. He looked over at the table that the group of men always occupied at this time of day. Interestingly, the men hadn't been in for the last couple of days. Hook started to think; *That's a coincidence they disappear the day after Stan's accident.* He had never put much stock in his waiter's concerns about the group. However, he found the men's absence caused him to remember Stan's comments regarding his belief that they were up to no good. He resolved that he owed the young man a chance to find out either way. Hook looking around and finding the shop empty phoned triple zero, and asked for the Police. The Operator was used to handling vague calls from well-meaning citizens but was also trained and experienced enough to know sometimes even the smallest tip from Joe public could lead to a breakthrough in some case.

She put the call through to the Caloundra Station where a Senior Constable Brett Ashney took down Hook's details and concerns. He was about to respectfully brush it off with. "If you see something else" sort of comment when the coffee shop owner said. "I have CCTV videos of the men."

SC Ashney trusted his gut, and that little jump when this Mr Hook mentioned CCTVs changed the direction he had planned to head by dismissing the call as imagination.

"Sir, I will have someone down there later today. Thank you for calling us." The call ended, Hook looked up and saw he had customers waiting at the counter. He felt good that he had remembered Stan by his actions.

Three hours later two Constables from Caloundra Station were standing in front of counter of the coffee shop. The owner Peter Hook had been so busy he looked surprised they had shown up, but recovered quickly. After introductions were completed he asked. "Would you like a coffee while you're here?"

"That would be great Sir, if it's not too much trouble" The younger of the two cops replied.

"What would you like?" Asked Hook.

The Junior Officer replied. "A flat white double shot for me and a cappuccino for Constable Worthington, please." The female Officer nodded to confirm his ordering on her behalf, they'd had plenty of coffee breaks on patrol.

Hook set the two coffee mugs in front of the police officers. The coffee shop owner had transferred several instances of the CCTV video capturing the group of men to a USB in preparation of their arrival. He handed the memory stick to Constable

Tilly who had only been out of the Academy five months, but was a thinker, he asked. "Sir, is there audio?"

"Sorry mate, just pictures, I know it's probably all a waste of time. I wish I could tell you they did any thing wrong even. It's just, they just seem strange."

Senior Constable Margaret Worthington was experienced enough to know that the Senior Sergeant who ran the station would ask questions on the constables return. And she had learnt the hard way it was always best to have the answers.

"Mr Hook, what seems strange?"

"Well, a staff member who has served the group of men for months now always thought they were sus'. Every time he would bring their orders to the table it was like a cone of silence descended and didn't lift until he was well away from them." Peter Hook explained.

"Yes Sir, but what caused you to call us now after all that time?"

"Well, you'll probably think I'm crazy. Now, that waiter Stan, he died in an accident on Monday just gone. Those men haven't been back since." Hook said shaking his head sadly.

Worthington was not about to discourage the coffee shop owner, but was thinking maybe he'd watched one too many crime shows. "You're probably right, it sounds a bit of a coincidence, but one thing at a time. We'll take the CCTV videos back to the station and have a look-see. Who knows what we might come up with? Was there anything else you can think of while we are here?"

There wasn't anything else, so the two Constables finished their coffees and headed back to Caloundra Police Station.

Molly and I had decided to have a casual look at the first name from the Intel the Sunshine Coast man who had hired the boy in Melbourne. Richard Cook was a resident of Moffat Beach and drove a Ford Ranger registration number; PPE 762. We headed down to his address, a rendered brick low set with neglected gardens with the Ford Ranger parked in the driveway. Now we were pretty certain he was home, we returned to HQ. Molly and I had decided that we didn't have the resources to run surveillance on Cook 24/7. Both of us couldn't be away from the office and other cases at the same time for long, and we didn't know how long this surveillance would last. We settled for two ten hour shifts, helped by two uniforms from downstairs. Molly had drawn first shift, so after signing out an old Toyota Camry that no Police Department would use she drove to Moffat Beach. Parking three doors down from Cook's home she settled in with her M&Ms, and Red Bulls to keep her on the ball. Unlike the movies, police work was ninty-percent staring at a monitor or sitting in a smelly car waiting for something to happen.

Molly settled in Cannon with White long distance lens sitting along side the snacks.

"So was that a total waste of time Margy?" Asked Senior Sergeant Spud Murphy who ran the day to day at Caloundra Police Station.

SC Margaret Worthington replied. "Probably Serge, the coffee guy gave us a USB of the men he was worried about. I thought I might run it through Facial Recognition, who knows?"

"Sure, worth a try, but don't take all friggin day. Did you think of me when you were drinking your free coffees?" The old cop asked with a smile.

"Of course, I wouldn't forget you need to eat." Laughing the Senior Constable handed over a paper bag containing two vanilla slices. Compliments of Mr Hook's coffee shop.

"Margy me girl, your next evaluation just sky-rocketed." they both laughed as the Senior Sergeant returned to his office bag in hand.

Molly answered on the second ring. "Hey Ben what's up?"

"Just thought I'd wake you up, figured by now you've run out of Gatorade and M&Ms"

Laughing she replied. "Well, it's impressive how well you know me. But it's Red Bull, Gatorade makes you pee, and the next guy mightn't like a damp seat."

"Far too much info thanks." I said laughing as well.

"No, I wasn't asleep, but I may as well be. He hasn't moved in over four hours."

"Surveillance, is synonymous with boredom remember they taught us that at the Academy. Anyway that uniform will be there in an hour or so. Have fun I'll see you tomorrow Molly."

"Cheers mate, see you then." She disconnected.

I was due to do my shift watching Cook in five hours so I headed home early, looking forward to some time to myself. I had some things to think about. I had a dead paedophile's laptop hidden under my couch. At this stage I hadn't checked the addresses, but tonight would fix that. With a heated frozen pizza, a JD and Pepsi Max and the dead Bishop's laptop my dinning table was complete. Opening the computer I quickly headed into the addresses. After searching alphabetically I'd found no one I recognised, then I noticed a Group address. Opening the Group I couldn't believe my eyes. I am just a Sunny Coast Detective, but here were the names of four Members of Parliament, several Judges, Barristers and lawyers. That's the ones I recognised, who knew who else was there. Now I had an even bigger problem. I knew from experience that the Argos boys at Child Protection Investigation Unit Queensland HQ in Brisbane would harvest a ton of Intel from this. They would be able to manage the investigations and resulting prosecutions on this grand scale better than I ever could. And more obviously, how could I give them this laptop? I may as well give them a signed confession for taking the Bishop off the board at the same time.

Everything in me shouted that this was too important to powerful in bringing paedophiles to the courts. I couldn't ignore it, I sure as hell couldn't execute them all. There were too many people, in high positions and it would be a full time job for the next few years. In any case, due to their seniority, their killer's motivation would be distorted every which way. The other factor was these pillars of society should be publicly outed. I had no desire to harm the institutions or governments these high profile people represented, but they had to pay for their sins. And then I knew what I had to do. After cleaning the computer for my prints and vacuuming any DNA from it's nooks and crannies.

My plan was to leave the laptop somewhere that would guarantee it would be found and find its way to the Argos Section of Child Protection Investigation Unit Queensland. Once their experts took a look they would know whose laptop it was and open it up file by file. I was sure they would find what I had discovered quicker than I did. It meant a trip to Brisbane, and identifying a safe place while still avoiding any CCTVs. This was an incredible risk to take. However, my safety came second to the importance of revealing this evil group. I knew what I had to do, I knew I couldn't sit on this, it had to break now. I decided that I would deliver the Bishop's laptop the following day. I clipped my holster on my belt, grabbed my thermos full of coffee and headed out to Dickey Beach to do my shift watching Richard Cook.

The tired Constable I relieved had a similar report to Molly. Out Target must be hold up or living a very boring life. Starting at 2000 Hrs. I sort of hoped for some action. Like cockroaches crims of every type seem to become more active when its dark. Apparently, this cockroach didn't get the memo. Not a movement, he didn't even put the rubbish out. It did give me time alone to think things through. By the end of shift I knew exactly how I was going to pass the laptop over. Driving home I was looking forward to some sleep before my quick trip to Brisbane. Next morning as I parked well away from my destination I assembled my disguise. This wasn't Mission Impossible, all I needed to do was not look like Detective Ben McQueen. Even though it was warm I put on several layers of jumpers topped by an oversized snow jacket. I had purchased a stick on moustache and beard, and although it was far too corny to pass close inspection the overall result was fine. Last thing I put on a pair of aviator's sunnies, the wig and a Brisbane Lions footy cap. I knew enough police procedure to know what I was about to do would cause a ruckus. However, I also knew once it was inside the building it would guarantee that the laptop was searched thoroughly. One look at the stored photos and the computer would quickly find its way to the Argos who specialised in kiddie porn and paedophiles chatting with children via the net.

Walking slowly, perhaps befitting my overweight appearance, and suggesting that I was older than my true age I headed towards the Queensland Police Roma Street HQ, the home of Task Force ARGOS, a highly successful anti-paedophile group, where I wanted the laptop to land. I couldn't be seen hovering in the shadows next to the brightly lit staircase leading up to the main entrance of the Police HQ. Hesitating just long enough for two Constables to get into a uniform car parked at the bottom of the stairs, I slowly walked diagonally up the stone stairs. Reaching about half-way across I placed the laptop bag on a step, and without the briefest pause kept walking. I changed direction and headed down to the footpath. There was no reason to believe I was being followed but I had to be sure.

Walking in the opposite direction from my car I took several unnecessary turns. Stopping several times to look into shop windows, I surreptitiously surveyed the footpath I had just walked. I was sure I was alone. Standing in the shadows adjacent to the car park I waited a full five minutes to ensure police weren't waiting to arrest me as I returned to my vehicle. I was being overly careful, but the risks were huge. There was no movement in the car park except for a dirty white cat that traversed the concrete cave and disappeared in the yard next door. I couldn't drive all the way to the Sunshine Coast dressed as I was. I was melting from the heat for one thing, and I wouldn't have been able to explain my dress to a cop if I was unlucky enough to be pulled over. Quickly, I took off the layers, the fake hair and beard. Starting the motor, my heart was beating faster than normal as the air-conditioning kicked in.

"What's that on the stairs Trev?" Asked Steve, a retired Police Officer, now a civilian Guard at the Roma Street Police Headquarters.

Trev, his fellow Guard peered down the stone stairs and replied. "Looks like a bag of something. Some wino probably dropped it. I'll take a look, stay on the radio mate."

He descended the stairs to within three steps of the item. "Yeah Steve, it's a bag, maybe like a computer bag. What should I do?"

Both the Guards were retired cops and they knew the SOPs Standard Operating Procedures backwards. "SOPs mate, I'll phone the bomb squad. I know you're right but imagine if that is a bomb some unhappy citizen has left. If we brought it up here and it went boom. You know what they say when the shit hits the fan it is even distributed. If we were alive we'd definitely be unemployed mate."

He had been dialling the Bomb Disposal Squad while he was speaking to his partner. "Come back up mate and leave that thing alone. I'll get some uniforms down here to cordon it off. And so he did. The Bomb Disposal Squad's van arrived and they went to work. The entire exercise went precisely as I had predicted. In fact the laptop was delivered to Task Force Argos much quicker than even I had expected. Once the techos got in and the team thought it was an early Christmas and began unwrapping their presents.

Chief Superintendent Daniel Koles was in charge of the task force and knew the Intel that had been placed on his desk was potentially the most damning indictment he had ever seen in almost thirty busy years as a Police Officer. His first action was to ensure total confidentiality from the nerds who had harvested the Intel. This was in a way unnecessary as the very nature of their work demanded the highest level of confidentiality, however this information was so hot he had to remind them. There was no reluctance on his part to act, however he was aware of the dangers involved in being the messenger of such revelations. No layer of society was missing from the toxic list, politicians, clergy, teachers and sadly police officers of every rank. There was a well known case in South Africa where a Detective, who exposed an elite paedophile ring was found dead killed after exposing a multi-level paedophilia network. It had been made to look like suicide but nothing made sense. However, the findings suited a lot of senior people and so the outcome was accepted, with the body buried for eternity. Koles was very sure he didn't want the same fate as his South African counterpart.

Having said that he knew that the Minister for Police was as straight as a die, he could trust him. The Chief Superintendent was also just as certain that it would be career suicide if he went to the Minister before informing his superiors. The last thing a Police Commissioner wants is the politician to be better informed than him or in Queensland's case her. Now it was a bit old school, but the way Koles thought meant the Commissioner being a woman all but guaranteed her integrity when it came to paedophile cases. However, the higher one got in organisations the more influenced by politics and public relations one became. The Assistant Commissioner was a close friend of the Argos Task Force Commander, he would start there. Koles picked up his phone and punched in the numbers before he changed his mind.

Fifteen minutes later he was in the Assistant Commissioner's office looking distractedly across the desk at his friends shoulders displaying his rank, one pip and crossed tipstaves with laurels. He caught himself staring at the badges of rank and returned to the conversation. "Well Bill as I was saying this Intel doesn't miss many people. Pollies, coppers senior ones too, teachers, heaps in the legal profession, a couple of magistrates. You start to understand some of those light sentences now, it's a nightmare."

Assistant Commissioner Bill Wilson felt sorry for his long term friend and colleague. "Dan, this could make you the hero of the decade, but I understand how it can also be a poison chalice."

A clever political copper he asked. "What are your thoughts on how to proceed from here?"

"Bill, firstly I am talking to you to make it official, but as a friend I'd really appreciate your guidance on my next moves. You know me talking to you doesn't in any way infer a lack of trust in the Commissioner. I figured you were the right place to start in the Chain of Command, so we could work this out to make sure the messenger doesn't get shot."

The meeting went on for nearly an hour, with both experienced Officers nutting out the best strategy to inform the Commissioner. This Intel was toxic to everyone who came into contact with it, including the most senior cop in Queensland. A meeting with the Commissioner was convened straight after lunch. Superintendent noted the presence of the Crown Solicitor sitting in the corner taking copious notes and unsuccessfully trying to keep a poker face. The small group discussed the Intel, some of the names shocking everyone in the room. It was decided that every individual involved must be brought in simultaneously so as not to tip off anyone. The paedophile ring was Australia wide, so the Commissioner suggested that the Federal Police be recruited to handle any arrests outside Queensland. The Crime and Corruption Commission (CMC) and the Ethical Standards Command in addition to the Child Protection Investigation Unit Queensland were brought into the fold, forming the most powerful task force ever assembled.

CHAPTER 14

"I don't know about you Molly, but I think we are wasting our time watching Cook. We've got him on toast for buying that Victorian boy. Let's see if the Boss will approve his arrest. Maybe we can get something out of him after some time in the lock up, or from tossing his house."

Looking tired, Molly rubbed her eyes and replied. "Ben, I agree, I thought I had no life. He goes out less than the average elderly pensioner. It's nearly like he's hold up in there keeping low. But Vic Child Protection Investigation have kept the parent's arrest quiet giving all the other states a chance to bust the buyers like Cook. So why would he be hiding under the radar when he doesn't have a clue we are on to him?"

Just then the phone chirped. "Detective-Sergeant McQueen, how can I help you?"

"Detective this is Senior Constable Margaret Worthington Kawana Station."

I thought to myself; *Some bloke hanging around that school next to the cop shop probably.*

"Well we got a concerned citizen call, you know vague, worrying about a group of males meeting at a coffee shop over your way, Kings Beach."

I was still tired from my surveillance shift and my quick trip to Brisbane to drop off the laptop, and showed it."Yeah, yeah Senior, what have you got?"

A little less confident after hearing my tone she continued. "Yeah, well the coffee shop owner gave us some videos. I ran them through Facial Recognition and got no less than three hits. Anyway they're all paedos, so that's why I phoned you guys. One of them is a Richard Cook lives over Dickey Beach way."

I was momentarily stunned, I hadn't even heard the other two names. "You still there Detective-Sergeant McQueen?" Asked the young Constable.

"I sure am, what was your name again?"

"Margaret Worthington, Kawana Station." She replied sullenly, I had been rude earlier and now insulted her by my forgetting her details so quickly.

"That Senior is great work. I'll mention it to your Boss. You don't realise how happy you've made me. Now I need those videos, and the coffee shop details ASAP. Drop whatever you're doing and get them here yesterday." Realising I'd been a bit abrupt with her. "Please Senior Constable."

Respectfully reminding me that I wasn't her boss she stated. "If its OK with my Senior Sarge I'll bring 'em straight over. Any trouble I'll let you know otherwise see you in twenty minutes or so." The connection closed.

I got off the phone feeling like I'd just had two shots of espresso, nearly shouting in my excitement I called. "Molly, where are you?"

Molly eventually arrived adjusting her clothing, having just returned from the bathroom. "Ben, you look like you just won Lotto."

I told her about my call from the switched on Senior Constable at Kawana Station.

"That's great, three scum in one place and did you say there others in the group.?"

"Yeah, some unknowns, or more likely not caught until now, hey?"

"Three hanging out, we know they wouldn't be talking about the weekend footy. This will be interesting. How do you think we should go from here?"

"Let's work that out once we've seen our happy little group. Then we talk with the owner of the coffee shop and go from there, OK?"

"Let's go tell the Boss, and guess what? No more need to sit outside Cook's place. We've got him on the Victorian charges and this confirms what we all knew once a paedo always one. You don't hang out with at least two other paedos that have done time unless your sharing happy snaps or up to no good some other way."

After what only seemed a few minutes Molly finished speaking there was a knock on the door. An attractive female copper poked her head in and asked. "Detective-Sergeant McQueen?"

"Sure, that's me." I said as I jumped to my feet. "Come in please."

I offered my hand as I introduced both of us."Margaret, that was really great work, this may well have confirmed something we were working on. We really appreciate your help. Sorry for being a bit short on the phone. Would you like to stay and walk us through the whole report from the get go?"

Feeling good about herself and excited to help a specialist group such as Child Protection Investigation Unit, Senior Constable Worthington handed over the USB with the videos on it.

"My Sarge said I should stay around in case you had any follow ups so let's take a look."

She replied as Molly plugged it into the TV mounted in the meeting room and we sat expectantly as it opened. Molly and I knew all three paedophiles on the video, but were also interested in the other members sitting around the wooden table outside the coffee shop.

"Mr Hook that's the owner, he's a good guy, he's not jumping to any conclusions but one of his staff picked up on these guys acting weird and so Hook phoned us as a general concern."

"Molly and I will go talk to him as soon as we finish here. You said the men had been coming to to the coffee shop for some months. What prompted the owner to contact the police now?"

She flipped some pages of her official note book and said. "Mr Hook stated that Apparently, Mr Hook had a waiter that had been telling him that this group of men were acting strange. Although it's pretty normal in a way, every time the waiter approached their table they would all stop talking like a switch. The young bloke kept nagging his boss that they were up to no good."

"Oh, OK. We'll need to talk with the waiter for sure."

"Well going back to your question about why the owner phoned us now. The answer is that the waiter was killed in an accident last week, and the group haven't been back since."

"Wow. I can see why, but surely he's not suggesting the waiter was murdered?"

"Well he didn't say it, but it is sort of strange that the group is lying low all of a sudden the day after the accident."

Molly and I looked at each other and didn't really need to say a word. "Molly you thinking the same thing as me. Cook is holed up, no wonder he didn't leave his house. The ducks just keep lining up."

Not understanding the young Constable looked puzzled, but she was smart enough not to ask questions.

"This is awesome Margaret, leave it with us and we'll let you know how it all goes." I said sincerely.

Smiling Senior Constable Worthington knowing that Detectives didn't keep uniforms informed, thought; *Sure I'll make Commissioner too.* As she drove back to Kawana Station the young Senior Constable had no way of realising how valuable her initiative had been to our case.

Molly and I walked into Superintendent Fisher's office after knocking but not waiting for a reply. We knew he would be happy with this interruption. After explaining everything we had so far the excitement in the office was palpable. His shaved head glowing under the downlights of his office, the Boss smiled. "Boy oh boy, Christmas really has come early this year. It might even work out that this Intel becomes the gift that keeps on giving."

I was itching to get out to the coffee shop and clear up all the questions I had rattling around in my overloaded brain. Top of the list of my thoughts that I needed answers about; *Was the waiter's accidental death tied up in all this. And of course if it was, then it was murder.* I phoned Mr Hook the coffee shop owner, who informed me that he closed in about an hour and would be available without interruptions from then on. I was being super careful, not knowing if he was being watched by the group. The last thing I wanted was another body, and to lose a new source. I arranged for him to meet me at a local shopping centre. Here, alert to anyone following him I would watch him for a while and once sure he was alone pick him up for an interview. After a few minutes I was sure that this was the case and came up beside him I spoke quietly. "Mr hook follow me to the C level car park please." Thankfully he complied without discussion or even looking at me, and when he came out of the big glass doors on Level C I walked him to the anonymous car I had signed out.

"Detective Ben McQueen Mr Hook pleasure to meet you. Please call me Ben."

"Pete's fine with me as well." The coffee shop owner said as he thrust out his moist hand. I could see he was nervous, and I would have been surprised if he hadn't been. Dealing face to to face with the police is threatening enough to a civvy. I had probably multiplied his stress with this James Bond meeting procedure, but I had to take care of him. Fifteen minutes later we were back at my office when once he had met Molly we moved into the meeting room.

"Now Pete one of the Officers who spoke to you two days ago have given us the video and a transcript of her notes. I'm sorry but Detectives always like to hear it first hand. I'll probably ask some of the same questions, but please bear with me. The other thing is we are coming from a different angle to what the Constables were."

Peter Hook looked scared and confused, but he was committed to help. "That's OK, you go for it and I'll do my best. Like I said to the girl, I mean the Constable the other day, really all this could be just a big waste of time."

Molly edged forward in her chair. "Pete, let me assure you we are way past that. Three of the group are well known to us, and that means your information may well be valuable."

The coffee shop owner visibly relaxed."OK. Well that's good news because poor old Stan always thought they were bent in some way." Still nervous he coughed. "I feel guilty now, I used to tell him he'd been watching too much Netflix." His eyes went a little misty as he spoke.

I desperately wanted to talk about the dead waiter but needed to stick to the plan Molly and I had devised in preparation for this interview. We needed to be very clear about the details and about the timing of events. I ignored his personal comments and continued.

"Firstly Pete, has the group returned to your café since you spoke to the Constables?"

"No, still no sign of them, they have disappeared for a day or two in the past. It was the timing that struck me as weird this time. Stan's accident, then I haven't seen 'em since."

We questioned Mr Hook for the next two hours. We could see after running his coffee shop since early this morning he was beginning to wilt.

"Would you like a coffee Pete, its been a long day for you?"

"No thanks. With all due respect, I figure the coffee in here would be just slightly better than hospital brew and I'm used to my special blends."

Molly and I laughed, lightening the tension that filled the room. "You're not wrong mate." Molly agreed.

We had shown him stills of each of the individuals from the video, he didn't have any names but confirmed that they were indeed the regulars he had doubts about. I knew from our time together Mr Hook was very bright. We had seen him catch on to the direction of a line of questioning, understanding why the question was being asked and not being offended by it. If only all our witnesses were this helpful. We had noticed the tremor in his voice when he mentioned Stan Croft the young waiter who had died.

"Pete, I know this might be a bit hard but let's go back to the day of Stan's accident."

All three of us had our doubts as to whether the young guy slipped of a track he had used a thousand times and had gone over the cliff. Perhaps it was a hit and run accident, or even a premeditated murder. But, at this point there was no proof that we were aware off regarding this. However, most people's answers fitted their beliefs of that topic. So to try and get to the truth I had to sound like I believed the boys death was an accident.

"Now I know it was a terrible accident that happened to Mr Croft, but we need to talk about it. Pete, take us back to that day, did anything happen with Stan that was out of the ordinary. Did he have a run in with a member of the group, or did he hear something that he told you about?"

We could see he was doing just as I had asked, digging in his memory for something he hadn't thought of before or mentioned to Senior Constable Worthington.

Hook was nice bloke and clearly grieved for young Stan."I feel bad, like I let him down now you say this group is of interest to you. A stack of times he had tried to talk to me about them. He was freaked out by how they always shut up like clams when he approached them with their orders. It had gotten to the point where I closed him down, I didn't want to hear it any more. They were regular customers that paid some of my bills and he was young guy with too much imagination."

I had let him run fuelled by guilt by the sound of it. He had answered several questions by doing so. However, he hadn't actually answered my original question. I tried to calm him a little by using the term mate.

"Mate, I need to ask you again. Take us back to that day, did anything happen with Stan that was out of the ordinary. Did he upset a member of the group, or did he hear something that he told you about?"

"No he was too good with customers, even the one's he thought were acting strange he wouldn't clash with them. Nothing comes to mind nothin strange." I could see him digging again trying hard to recollect that fateful day.

"Hang on. I was too busy to even ask Stan what was going on or why but he did something really strange that morning. Now because there are so many of them, their orders always takes two trays, you know, two deliveries to the table. I noticed that he took the first tray out through the back door and around to them. I meant to ask him why but totally forgot about it. It was especially weird for Stan to do that because he then took their second tray out the usual way through the front door."

Speculating with a witness can be dangerous but I figured that with this guy and what I was looking for it made sense. "Pete, why would a waiter take the long way, probably dodging buckets, mops and garbage bins?"

"Oh Stan, you couldn't let it be. The crazy kid, he's snuck around that way to catch them talking. That's what I figured anyway. I wonder what he heard?"

And I thought; *Yeah, and I wonder if it cost him his life?* We asked a few more questions and concluded the interview. I had one of the young Constables change into his civilian clothes and in a different car from the pool take the super helpful Peter Hook back to near his car at the shopping centre. Meanwhile back at the office Molly and I looked at each other stunned by what we had learnt.

"If we are going to flick this to Homicide we need to talk to the Boss and see what he thinks yeah?" molly asked.

Assigned to Stan Croft's death the same two Homicide cops that we had met earlier were back.

Detectives Jack Nolan and Dennis Conner were like most Detectives overworked and under-resourced, and it showed.

"You serious, a surfer falls off a cliff and now you want us to open a murder investigation on it."

"Come on Jack, we all know some accidents seem so obvious we confirm our opinions, the Coroner does the same. No one's saying it wasn't an accident but it sure seems that way. However, we've got testimony that might suggest this kid was playing detective with a group of suspects to do with one of our cases. He may well have stumbled in on something, now whether it lead to him being murdered." My words drifted off suggesting a huge maybe. "Yeah, it might be stretch, but surely you can re-open his file and just take a look." I said trying to sound casual and friendly.

"OK Ben. We will have a quick look but we 're not opening anything on all the maybe babies you've given us. Neither of us had anything to do with it. I think they even looked at it as a possible suicide because they found his bike and board at the top of the cliff. So don't hold your breath mate. We'll look at it, but no promises more that that."

Molly smiled her most charming smile and said. "That's all we're asking boys, just a look to see what happened to young Stan Croft. You guys know the drill, elimination is usually the biggest part of detective work."

So off they went, neither of us knew Nolan and Conner. All we could do is trust that they would keep their promise and have a good look at Stan's 'accident'.

CHAPTER 15

Charles had phoned around the group and no one had heard or seen anything suspicious. Maybe he had been over-cautious telling everyone to go into lock-down for a while after the waiter business. Even Damo had sounded happy and friendly on the phone. It sounded like everything was fine, the boy's death had been reported as an accident in the local TV and news Papers. They had gotten away with it. The informal leader confident it was safe to raise their collective heads above the parapet called around again arranging for everyone to meet for breakfast the next morning. Calling the group to adopt a low profile had a risk if anyone associated their absence with the boy's demise. However, to his knowledge there was no reason to believe they were under anyone's scrutiny so he had decided to order the group away from the café. Charles smiled at being proven right right about the situation.

The excitement in Peter Hook's voice was unmistakable. "Ben, those guys are back, same as always, same table everything as usual."

"OK Pete, you be careful not to show any interest or act differently OK?" I said avoiding sounding scared that he might just do that and blow everything.

"Sure, I'll stay in the kitchen out of sight anyway."

"Great, leave it with me, by mate and thanks again." I disconnected the call.

Charles felt good being back in his favourite chair commanding his little kingdom he raised his OJ. "Welcome back everyone, it's nice to catch up."

Everyone raised their juice or coffees and grunted in agreement.

Confirming what he had already asked each individual he enquired of the group. "We all good, no strange cars, or feeling you're being followed, anyone." Charles asked looking at each face at the table.

"Nothin with me." Richard replied naively. Everyone said the same so Charles continued, business as normal.

"Ok, now we still have plenty of time to fill that latest order. Has anyone seen a likely subject?"

Without missing a beat, Robert replied. "For at least part of the order I've been scouting the locals rather than the tourists. The Middle Eastern boy no older than twelve is easy. He lives with his family and is at Kings Beach every Saturday, always the same place. We need two Asian girls under ten, and one Asian boy no older than five. I've found the girl at Little Mountain. However, I noticed that new hotel California Towers on Golden Beach is real popular with the Chinks. I'm wondering whether it makes more sense than one here and one there, if we are better off doing our shopping in one place."

Richard chipped in. "California Towers, should be easy with school holidays coming up."

Charles was impressed with Robert's work and said so. "Well done Rob, there's enough of us to grab all them and do same day delivery to the Gold Coast. Nice and clean and easy."

"We could call ourselves UBER kids at this rate." Mike added, and everyone laughed.

Mike stated the obvious attempting to impress the group with intelligent comment. "Yes, it would be good not to take the risk of having them stored at Robs like last time."

His attempt failed miserably even though what he said made sense. Charles took back the reins. "OK, Rob can you show Damo the lay out for Kings Beach. It's always good to stay away from the shopping centres, movies and entertainment arcades. Great places for kids, but too many security staff and CCTVs and witnesses." Charles added.

As an after thought Charles continued. "I was just thinking our plans are good, I think we all agree they make sense and minimise the risks. However, we are too thin on the ground at the Towers. Three kids to grab, get back to our vehicle and secure, then leave and do it all again twice more. The way I see it, is there are four of us for that part with Damo and Rob over at Kings. Two groups in the hotel grabbing, transporting and then someone staying with the vehicle."

Damo whose strength was in analysing and planning agreed. "Charles is right, all we need one of the kids to scream at the wrong time or some surfer to walk past our vehicle with a Chinese kid or two trussed up on the back seat like Peking ducks and we'd be history."

"I hate to say it but we need some help, maybe one more person on the day to secure the kids and the vehicle. Does anyone know anyone we could count on to do it, and to keep their mouths shut?" Charles asked.

Richard replied. "My cousin is visiting, he been a full time burglar since he finished high school so we can trust him. He'd be keen for a fee and I'll vouch for his silence, he's no grass."

"Great Richard you make sure he stays in town until that Saturday at least. We'll make it worth his while."

My phone rang. "Ben, its Jack Nolan. Is Molly nearby? She'll want to hear this."

"Yeah mate, I'll put you on speaker." There was click. "You still there Jack?"

"Sure am. OK. Now we are not at the point where I can say its definitely a murder case. Having said that, we are very interested in a couple of things. Not just covering my arse, but without your input providing a possible motivation no Homicide Detective would spend any extra time on this."

"No worries Jack, we hear yah. Accidents happen all the time and I guess that male, teenager surfies are in that high risk taker demographic."

Encouraged by my support he continued."Anyway, we knew the victim's remains wouldn't add anything to the Medical Examiner findings. Thankfully, the boy's bike was still in our holding yard." He was driving me crazy with all this process talk. However, I held my tongue in faith that he would get where we needed to eventually.

"Well anyway, Ben and Molly the bike was a surfie style with two large hooks on one side to carry his surfboard. There was a dent in the board that the coppers had noted but they all assumed it was a 'ding' from hitting the rocks washed in on a wave."

I had to say something just so I could take a breath. "Right mate so what did you find?"

Detective Nolan continued. "The 'ding' had a small black bruise, now you wouldn't look twice based on the assumption of the normal damage a board experiences. However, when you look at the damage without the narrative you'd ask yourself a question. What in nature would leave such a mark?"

Speaking in unison with Nolan I responded. "Nothing."

The Homicide Detective was on a roll. "And, you would be correct. Normally. We gave it to the lab, early finding is automotive paint. They have promised me a make and model by close of business today."

"Jack, that is awesome. It's even better than you probably realise." We all knew that in most hit and run cases such forensic evidence would result in a wide net search. It would identify every owner in the State who drove that particular brand of vehicle and perhaps the model if you were lucky.

"Anyway Jack, because we believe someone from the group we have on our radar may be responsible this could point at one individual and become rock solid evidence for your murder."

The Homicide Detective was being careful. "You're right, but I'm not calling it a murder yet, but I see what you mean."

I understood his caution, but this was too much for me. "Yeah, yeah, I know. But, we'll know this arvo though, and I'll bet your killer is there in our little club."

"I sure hope you are right Ben. I'll get back to you as soon as forensics lets me know."

"Cheers mate, we aren't sure what we have ourselves so please talk to us before you do anything please."

"Will do, but not pushin it murder outweighs your stuff OK? Now anxious to get off the line he said in a cheery tone. "See ya Molly, catch ya Ben." He was gone.

We looked at each other in stunned silence that proceeded into laughter, Molly was even clapping. Neither of us were celebrating the death of young Stan but if he had been murdered it would be good to seek justice for him. Molly even started clapping like an excited school kid.

The Boss came through our office door looking puzzled. "I suppose I should be glad my investigators are so happy. However, what are we celebrating, did I forget a birthday or something?"

Although he too joined us in being more than happy with the progress on our case Molly and I could tell he was distracted. After we filled him on the latest news he had some of his own.

"This has come straight from the Commissioner." Putting on his most serious face he continued.

"Nothing I'm about to say leaves this office. Intel from an unknown source has identified no less than forty-seven high and middle level Politicians, Public Servants, Medical Professionals, Priest, Legal Eagles and embarrassingly Law Enforcement Officers."

Molly and I spoke in unison. "Wow."

"Wow in fucking deed girls and boys. Imagine how difficult this has been to coordinate. Who do you trust, who has the balls, pardon the sexism Molly, to arrest a serving Member of Parliament, a Judge or a State Police Chief Superintendent. That one really hurts because he was a friend of mine going back to our Academy days. He's the last person i would have expected."

"Anybody up here on the coast Boss?" Asked Molly.

"Thankfully, no. Most of them were Melbourne, Canberra and Sydney, unbelievable. Apparently all forty-seven of these scum were exchanging kiddie porn for the last nine or so years." Superintendent Fisher replied.

Angry at the thought I stated. "Yeah, and how many paedophiles were let off or sentence reduced because the Judge or prosecutor and the pervs were internet mates?"

The Superintendent continued, avoiding eye contact with me. "From experience we know some of them will trade information for a lighter sentence so who knows what will cascade out of this?"

"You're not serious Boss, that might be Ok at some low level peeping Tom but nah, not these paedos they're s'posed to be protecting the kids. No way Boss you can't let these grubs escape anything we can hit them with." I said angrily.

"Sorry Boss, you know I'm over the moon about catching them, but....." I let my apology die of it's own accord.

While my anger was sincere, both Molly and Superintendent Fisher would assume that my reaction was predictable but I was still happy because a high level paedophile ring had been destroyed, and they were right. However, they had no way of knowing that I was smiling for another reason. I was absolutely certain that the destruction of this evil network was the direct result of my leaving that laptop on Police Headquarters front steps. The plan had worked perfectly.

Within days of our Boss informing us of the pending arrests all along the East Coast high profile people were picked up. Papers and TV News reports couldn't get enough of it. A Brisbane Judge was charged with filming himself sexually abusing a twenty-two month baby. Despite the damning video evidence he continued to deny these charges. He said he had been wiping potato tomato sauce off the child. A New South Wales Minister for Agriculture, Mr Graham Martin a fifty-nine-year-old man stood trial and was convicted in the District Court on eight counts of child sexual abuse committed between 2012 and 2018, including persistently engaging in sexual conduct with a child under 16 and producing child exploitation material. Mr Martin's recordings of the abuse were discovered when police raided his Dover Heights residence, along with tens of thousands of child exploitation videos and images he had downloaded from the internet. He had also shared the majority of these with his fellow ring members.

Two of the victims were sisters aged between 6 and 10. He also produced child exploitation material of another girl when she was aged 11 or 12. Martin was a high ranking member of the serving state government at the time of his crimes. His arrest showed that these abhorrent scum can literally be found in any part of our society. No socioeconomic status, no race, no creed, no religion is immune from the scourge of child abusers. They can be found literally everywhere. Although of course I wish the abuse had never happened, I was enjoying seeing the results come through. Paedophile after paedophile taken off the streets, reputation destroyed, fortune diminished fighting ongoing legal battles. These were absolute monsters. By filming the abuse they perpetrated upon these innocent children the abuse continued forever. We know online predators and members of these evil groups insist upon members supplying videos and pictures of children being abused in order to become, and remain, a member. These heinous groups allow child predators to participate in swapping and sharing the multitude of child abuse images they make with other like minded predators usually around the world. This evil ring was a little different in that as far as the Computer Specialist Detectives could tell the paedophile ring was

Australians only. This didn't make anything better, but it was worthy of noting as the detail may be valuable at some later date.

In a world of Avatars, 2D and 3D animation, robotics and every other Hollywood trick anything was possible in movies these days. But watching this filth you had to remember that every single child featured in these abuse images is a REAL child. Their emotions are REAL, their torment is REAL, and the horror and pain on their little faces is also REAL. And, sadly their pain will usually last until they die. Thankfully, none of the children had to testify during the trial, because the case hinged on several hours of these videos. Several members of the jury looked physically ill when they were forced to view samples of the videos and photos in a closed court.

The female Judge assigned to several of the cases was quoted as saying. "There was a high degree of perversion and persistence involved with the indecent dealing offences contained in the videos and photos. All the children were very young and they could not have been more vulnerable." She said.

The media frenzy was justified due to the extent of the abuse and the obvious high profile of most of the perpetrators. The crimes were also brazen given others were nearby on some occasions, including the mother of a victim. A detective described the child exploitation material as some of the most graphic he had seen "in a long, long time." More than 2800 of the images were in the two most severe categories and some showed the children in visible distress. The magnitude of the Police action provided a wonderful opportunity to reinforce what all Police and Child Safety workers knew. No one can be trusted with your children. Not even the lollipop man at school, who we trust to guide our children across the road safely. Sadly, having a position of trust is not the same as being trustworthy. Just as being a 'nice' person, is not the same as being a 'good' person, differences we need to teach our children. All the usual anti-abuse organisations put out emotive statements regarding the seriousness of the crimes and the anticipated minimal sentencing that had become so common in Australian abuse cases. These groups spoke the truth, but were naive in the contemporary environment where the criminal's rights seemed to supersede those of the children they abused.

Reading the news paper I rationalised my own actions. This injustice is why I do what I do. I may be in constant battle with my personal values and beliefs, however the system cries out for justice. However, I have so much empathy with these vulnerable innocent children that I find myself doing things abhorrent to my normal life and certainly my role as a Detective. I have long ago surrendered justifying and rationalising my executing these low lifes. Deep in my soul I know I use the word execute but it really means murder. Is my sin as heinous as those I punish? Will God forgive me for the things I do? For many reasons I was glad there were no paedophiles identified on the laptop living in my region. All I could do was wait to see if anyone I had seen on the list slipped through the net. So far as I could tell from the media reports everything seemed to be proceeding properly.

CHAPTER 16

Not for the first time, Charles had thought about never returning to the group. He had nearly turned left instead of right on his way to their first get together since the over inquisitive waiter's 'accident'. However, he had an investment, a share accumulated in the Thailand travel account. Of course the other members didn't know he had been taking three shares and then dividing the rest between them. That was only fair, after all, he was the brains, the planner, the General of this little army. The Wellington delivery had not been paid for in cash. That was a bit tricky but he had a deal with the Bangkok end, so all was good. The ex-Hunters Motor Cycle Club President who ran the Bangkok sex tours along with a couple of night clubs was holding the value in credit. He had moved there to avoid some outstanding warrants and besides Thailand was a gold mine. He catered for every taste from straight hetro to anywhere the depraved mind of the next Aussie tourist wanted to visit. The men sitting at this large coffee table would go to Thailand in the cooler months and claim their tour. The irony didn't escape Charles, they would ravish Thai children slaves for weeks paid for by Aussie the boys and girls they delivered to Wellington.

However, the brokers who they really sold the children to were the Hunters Outlaw Motor Cycle Group based on the Gold Coast. Although they were resentful of the Anti-Bikie laws that had been introduced two years earlier their businesses had flourished. They often laughed at the laws, not being allowed to wear their colours in public and no more than two members together at a time didn't even slow them down. In reality, it meant that they went about their criminal enterprise staying well below the radar just a guy on a bike. They weren't being pulled up every five minutes for licence, drugs and weapon checks by every ambitious pig with a badge. They just operated without any fuss with minimum harassment.

Sure, there was the odd assault, domestic or drug bust. However, now it was an individual who happened to ride a bike not twenty hard looking hairy bikies making the six o'clock news. While the politicians were winning votes closing the Outlaw Club Houses down, the police weren't out there stopping trade and the clubs flourished. Especially the Hunters. There were several reasons, all of which was related to the Russian Mafia. There was a temporary vacuum created when the anti-bikie laws first bit. The clubs took a while to stop kicking against it and adapt. In this hiatus the Russians every alert to openings in criminal business moved into the Gold Coast. At first they hit the ATMs with card scanners, then other deals extortion, blackmail and the inevitable chain of nightclubs. The Gold Coast where all the Southerners and the International tourists came to defrost, plenty of money and looking for fun. Even their legitimate businesses thrived. Then as naturally as breathing the Russians moved into drugs with venues and tourists clamouring for escape. They couldn't get enough. The next enterprise was prostitution which with the correct licences and approvals was also legal. As long as the name on the documents was a person without any criminal record. This was all a bit too legitimate for the Russian Mafia bosses, it was good but it could be better. Often alongside the legal venues they established illegal brothels to cater for every sexual preference and deviance imaginable. Anything and everything was available for the right money.

Charles had decided that one more deal, one more 'free' trip to Thailand and he would retire. He was sick of these guys slurping their coffees and depending on him for their next original thought. And he was sick of looking over his shoulder all the time.

"OK, this weekend we fill that next order, then it's overseas on a well earned holiday. What do you say boys?" The leader said.

The 'boys' hated it when Charles tried to be matey, they all knew he looked down on them and saw himself as smarter than the combined intelligence of the group. The dumb ones in the group didn't notice and so didn't care, the educated, more intelligent members put up with it because he had good contacts in the seamy world they loved.

"Sounds good Charles, we are all organised for the pick ups, we know California Towers is favoured by the Chinese tourists so Mike and I are going to target that hotel to fill those spares. We have the bigger order so we might need some help." Richard stated confidently, Mike who never ventured much just nodded.

Richard added. "We were thinking that Mike and I would do the snatches and bring them to you spare guys. That would speed the process up, you secure them for the trip to the Gold Coast and we concentrate on grabbing the next one."

Charles shook his head, not impressed with Richards assessment and resulting plan. "I think it'll take too long, everyone else mans the vehicles, zippy ties the chinks."

Nodding, Robert gestured toward Damien."Damo and I have the Arab under control, we have it all planned out shouldn't be any problem at all."

"Great, so it sounds like we are on track for Saturday afternoon. We'll have to wait for the Sweet and Sour to arrive Saturday morning, when they check into the hotel. But the rest we can do first thing and be ready to go. The great thing is after Wellington now, the Bikies trust our ability and this time we only have to go to the Gold Coast. Should be home in time for the Bronco game Saturday night." Charles said far more confidently than he really felt. *Fake it 'till you make it hey.* He thought to himself.

"We got any dates for Thailand at this stage?" Asked Robert.

"Yeah, we fly out twenty-third March. Of course we are on different flights and times but it all starts then." Charles answered.

Molly and I had been discussing our next moves for over two hours. Between the possibility of one or more of the members of this group being involved in the waiter's murder and the fact that three of them were known paedophiles the Boss had no difficulties getting a warrant to carry out surveillance on this group. Phone taps had been placed on each member's phone and listening devices had been installed under their favourite coffee table. We had discussed putting Molly in as a waitress. However if they shut up as reported previously when she approached them the results wouldn't be worth the effort of her working undercover. The phone taps were already producing although at this early stage we were unable to interpret some of what we were hearing. We were set up in the back store room of the café listening to the target group. Molly and I had just heard the discussion about Chinese spares and Arab something. We would analyse the tapes sentence by sentence later, when we got back to HQ. Both of us were wondering what the Gold Coast had to do with anything. We had heard some interesting key words though, Wellington and Bikies. What did all this mean? In our down time we would search all those key words. If they didn't produce now, they might provide us with a bluff when we eventually got these scum in front of us for questioning.

My phone rang, looking at the ID it was Jack Nolan. "Ben we got some more info on that possible homicide, the paint on the surf board came off a Jeep Wrangler. I've run all the Wranglers up here on the Sunshine Coast, not that we can be sure that it was a local hit, or if it was a hit at all."

"That's awesome Jack, I might be able to save yourself some time if we are really lucky a Wrangler will show up as owned by one of the guys in the grub club. Send me the regos and owners names. I'll cross-check and let you know, my moneys on it being one of them." I said confidently, I was starting to see the ducks line up like a military parade. By the time I had finished talking to the Homicide Detective the target group had left the coffee shop and Molly looked she wanted to go too.

"I was busy listening to those grubs, who was that?" She asked.

"Very interesting, it was Jack Nolan. Turns out the vehicle involved in that possible hit on the waiter was a Jeep Wrangler. He's gonna send us a list of all the Sunny Coast owners, I'm hoping that one of out paedos here shows up on Jack's list."

"Wouldn't that be great, collect some more Intel, understand what they're up to and maybe even nail one of them for murder."

We packed up and headed back to HQ, entering our section Molly stuck her head into Fisher's office. "Boss, we need a hand if you're free, we've got an hour or so of cryptic, random discussion. They could be planning to rob the Reserve Bank, or they were talking about a BBQ this Saturday."

Superintendent Fisher smiled. "OK, seems like you guys are making a lot of progress. It's all coming together, all your hard work paying off."

"Yeah well, some work and a bit of luck, all of a sudden the dots seem to join up." Molly said.

We spent a while filling him in on the new information we had collected and then split the tasks between us. Molly and the Boss assigned themselves to listening to the conversations the listening device hidden beneath the coffee table had recorded.

"Molly, I know there is a heap of content but, could you start with trying to identifying the players? Once I have a list I can start cross checking first names, I know it's a bit slim but it's somewhere to start. Jack Nolan came through and a list of the Jeep Wrangler owners who lived on the coast. I quickly checked the list for the three Grub Club members that we knew by name and nature. I was disappointed but not surprised to see that none of them drove a Wrangler. I guess that would have been far too easy. Returning to the list this time more slowly, I worked my way down the thirty odd names. Once again nothing, my disappointment was now frustration. I was sure one of our paedos would be there. I got up to make a coffee. "Do either of you want a coffee or tea?" I asked Molly and Superintendent Fisher.

"That would be great Ben, we are both concentrating so hard I have the start of a headache." Replied my Boss, Molly nodded her request as well.

I placed the mugs of steaming coffee on the table beside each of them, and Molly looked up. "Thanks mate, you have any luck with your Jeep list?"

"Not so far, I'm going to have another look now to see if I missed someone. I was sure one of our blokes would be there." I answered.

Molly looked tired. "We're the same, there's some bits that are easier than others, we need to keep going with it, but the Bikie connection is interesting."

"It's interesting trying to put names to voices and guess what we are dealing with. It's only a gut feeling but when that guy Damo speaks the hairs on the back of my neck come to attention. That guy is ex jail or military, he's the hard man in that bunch." Superintendent Fisher said as he picked up his coffee.

I exclaimed excitedly."Boss, you've got it. I didn't put Damo to Damien. The Homicide boys will still have their work cut out for them but I have a Damien Edwards on my list. I was either tired or a dumbass but I didn't catch the idea of a nickname. Thanks Sir. If he's the tough guy in the club, it makes sense that he might be the one who hit young Stan."

The Boss laughed at my comments."Your no dummy Ben, just occasionally need a hand. Pass that info onto Jack Nolan but make sure he doesn't act on it until we know what we are up against. With all that high level activity arresting Members of Parliament, Judges and so on we probably won't get any help with our stuff. Really, we're not sure what we are up against."

"Yeah, you're right again, if they barge in and take Damien Edwards in for questioning the rest of the Grub Club will head for the hills for sure, never to be seen again. I was listening in live at the coffee shop, but I got the impression there was something happening this weekend. Did you guys get that too?" I asked.

Superintendent Fisher answered. "Yeah Molly and I were just saying the same thing before you came in. That gives us a little more than seventy-two hours to know what we are doing and do it."

"First thing first Boss." Thinking out loud. "Sir, I get on well with Jack Nolan, but he'll be like every Detective including me. His case will be more important. I suppose a murder case will take priority over a paedophile case especially one that's not even fully developed. Can you give me five minutes to give Nolan a vague heads up before you talk to his Boss?"

"That's the way to go alright Ben, you call him and let me know when I'm right to make my call."

Homicide Detective Jack Nolan reacted exactly as predicted and precisely as he should. He appreciated the call, but not the content of it. No copper likes someone going over their head, although he appreciated my empathy for the situation. He pushed me for details I wasn't willing to give. I suppose this showed to both of us I didn't fully trust him. After all we didn't have years of history together to access for more trust. Once again though, annoyed as he would have been he still understood. We ended the call on a cooler note than we had started, but he'd be OK in the future. I gave the Boss the thumbs up and he immediately picked up his phone. Looking worried Superintendent Fisher came into my office.

"Ben, of course you were right, Nolan's Boss said just about word for word what you had said about Homicide cases being more important that half baked paedophile ones. Anyway, after much discussion he's given us seventy-two hours. After that they'll pick up our mate Damo and nail him for the waiter's murder."

It wasn't great but it sure could have been a lot worse. "Great Boss. Surely with what we have we should be able to tie these scum-bags up by then. You guys need more time to analyse that tape?"

Shaking his shiny bald head from side to side he answered. "Mate, I think we could listen to it another six times and get six new theories on its meaning. Come in and Molly and I will share what we think so far."

Taking my cold coffee with me I went back into the meeting room where they had been listening to the Grub Club recordings.

"Ok, what have you got?"

Molly looked up and handed me six or seven pages. "OK. Those are the transcript of what you and I heard at the coffee shop this morning. I've highlighted what we think is important. I looked at my sheets moving the cover detail page to the rear of the set. The first sentence was highlighted.

"OK, this weekend we fill that next order, then it's overseas on a well earned holiday. What do you say boys?"

Molly explained. "Now we are pretty sure the speaker is Charles, he appears to be the group's leader, if there is a hierarchy at all, even informal. Obviously our interest is in the words 'fill that next order'. Now if we just assume, and this assumption is based on all we know, such as at least three members of the Grub Club are known paedos. Anyway, what sort of order would this particular group be filling?"

I had decided not to ask any questions or offer any comments to enable Molly and Fisher to lay out what they had found or thought.

"Sounds good Charles. We are all organised for the pick ups, we know California Towers is favoured by the Chinese tourists so Mike and I are going to target there to fill those spares."

Superintendent Fisher took over. "We were able to lip-sync the video at that point. That was said by Richard Cook, who of course we know all about. When you couple that with the first highlighted sentence, it sounds like they are going grab someone from the California Towers. Now Saturday morning that place will be full of tourists checking out and checking in for a holiday or a weekend away. My money is their target is Chinese and logically a child. What are your thoughts Ben?"

I believed that they were on the right rack. "I'm being careful not to shoot my arrow and then paint a red bullseye around where it hit. However, I think I have to agree with what you and Molly have worked out. It make sense on a few different levels. What's scary is these guys talk about this like they've done it all before and they are going shopping not planning a kidnapping."

Molly arching her back to release some pent up tension agreed. "Yeah, the Boss and I had the same discussion, it's sick for sure, they are so blasé it's not scary, it's friggin terrifying. Wait until the next one opens up."

"Damo and I have the Arab under control, we have it all planned out shouldn't be any problem at all."

Molly's turn. "Again, we cross checked the audio with the CCTV at this point. We already had Damien Edwards photo from his Drivers Licence. The other face is Robert Walsh, the Boss has got more on him later. Getting back to what he said, they seem to need something or someone Arab. This when you look at it beside the Chinese pick up at California Towers sounds like someone has placed an order, and we don't think its dinner."

"The great thing is after Wellington now, the Bikies trust our ability we only have to go to the Gold Coast."

Molly continued. "Now we wondered what Wellington meant, was it a code or a nickname for something? Then I ran it through the system. Guess what, there are more registered Sex Offenders and Paedophiles in Wellington New South Wales per capita than anywhere else in Australia. Don't know why, just are. We can't really get much more from that except it sort of adds to the Intel I suppose."

"The great thing is after Wellington now, the Bikies trust our ability we only have to go to the Gold Coast."

Superintendent Fisher took point two. "Now the other key word 'Bikie', we figured they must be doing business with one of the Outlaw Motorcycle Clubs. What business? Drugs, weapons? No, let's go back to what we know for sure about this Grub Club here on the Sunshine Coast. What's their core business likely to be. Not even likely, close on definitely. Answer, something to do with paedophile stuff, kiddie porn, importing DVDs, or more likely dark web these days. So what are they into, live kids, abuse of some sort. So what have Bikies got to do with it?" He asked seriously.

Cutting in Molly couldn't hide her excitement. "Our team on the Gold Coast helped us here. They haven't been able to get anything solid enough to proceed yet. However, they are sure the Hunters Motor Cycle Club based out of Nerang in the Gold Coast hinterland are somehow involved in the paedophile scene down there. They are on the fringes too often not to be doing something, the local cops just can't see it so far."

I was impressed with what Molly and Fisher had achieved in such a short time. "Wow, the pieces are just coming together to make a clear picture. We might be missing a few but we've got enough to be sure we are heading in the right direction at least. Could the comment about the Gold Coast be talking about taking what these sickos grab down to the Gold Coast? No even better Nerang?"

I could tell Superintendent Fisher was as excited as Molly. "It gets even better Ben. Later in the tape a Robert says something. We ran him through Facial Recognition and then Criminal records and got lucky. This guy is one Robert Clive Walsh is ex Sergeant at Arms for the..."

I interrupted. "You're fuckin kidding me. The Hunters MC on the Gold Coast."

Nodding my Boss continued."Yep, as you so poetically stated. Our Sunshine Coast coffee drinker is the missing link, we had a few but this one is strongest."

"Great, so it sounds like we are on track for Saturday afternoon."

I couldn't help but to state the obvious. "So that's our time line, hey? They're going shopping Saturday afternoon. Chinese at the California Towers, but we don't know where they're heading for the Arab?

'Yep, that's how we saw it too. We can stake out the Towers from Saturday early AM. I figured seeing we know who are doing the Arab pick up, we follow them from Friday onward." The ex Military Cop who was now our boss was ready for action.

I was fascinated by how all this was cascading into a natural order, after all the work and wondering it was all here in front of us.

"Now there's still some more Intel on this tape." Superintendent Fisher said.

"We got any dates for Thailand at this stage?"

"OK, looks like they are all going to Thailand, great for the family holiday, but also well known for it's sex tours both adult hetro and paedophile.

"Yeah, we fly out twenty-third March. Of course we are on different flights and times but it all starts then."

"That's sure helpful, we have the date, and we can check the bookings with the info we have to get more details re names and addresses of these clean skins who we haven't had any dealings with before." Molly said as she arched her shoulders trying to lessen the stiffness accumulated over hours in front of a monitor.

"I'd love to know their contacts in Thailand. It's so hard to get anything from here. We could put them out of business forever."

The next day I had briefed the surveillance teams tasked to follow the targets. We had assigned the name Alpha to the team watching Damien Edwards and Robert Walsh the two Grub Club members who had talked about the Arab pick up. Team Delta was to cover the California Towers and due to the size of the complex requiring a staff of twenty made up of Constables and Detectives all dressed in beach wear.

I looked at the motley crew before me, knowing some of them would be feeling a bit anxious I smiled.

"Now guys you have been chosen because your Senior Sergeants reckon you are the smart ones at your various stations. I sure hope he or she is right. I can't impress upon you how important the next forty-eight hours will be. Important to our operation and case, but more so to the little boys and girls you are going to save if you do your jobs properly. Senior Constable Worthington please come and see us after this briefing I have a special role for you."

I covered everything that Superintendent Fisher, Molly and I had planned and then dismissed the group. We were sitting glued to the TV located in the back storeroom of the coffee shop. Looking very pleased with herself, Senior Constable Margaret Worthington and I were monitoring that morning's meeting of the Grub Club. She was taking copious notes. Conversations we had recorded were in some cases disgusting, while others as banal as listening to two children ague over their favourite superhero. Clearly, we couldn't take the chance of missing something important. Molly and I had so much to do we were glad that the meetings seldom went longer than an hour or so. However, we came up with the plan of employing Margaret Worthington. This would free one of us on each of the remaining two mornings. Molly was coordinating the surveillance with Team Alpha.

"Margaret, you've been seconded to us indefinitely, it's your choice, have a good look and if you like what you see request a transfer to Child Protection full time. The Boss will need to approve it first."

The young Senior Constable smiled happily. "Oh, thank you Sir, that's wonderful, ever since meeting you and Molly the other day I have been thinking about the work you do."

"What you come up against can and will be sad, frustrating and discouraging at times, but you have to keep trying otherwise the evil wins, and kids suffer." I warned. She smiled but I knew she had no idea what horrible things she would see if she stuck around.

I continued. "Now let's focus on Team Delta you happy with our plans to cover the California Towers?" I asked.

"I think so, the beauty of a busy block of holiday units is there are always people coming and going, standing around waiting for one thing or another, especially on Saturdays. I just hope I do OK as the Receptionist." She added humbly.

Molly reassured her. "The real one will be right beside you, we need you to note the floor number of any book ins that look Chinese. Then we can close the net in a little."

"How's it going Boss?" I asked as Superintendent Fisher came into my office.

"I think we are all good Ben. In the Army we used to always say every plan is good until the first shot. Molly's all organised and you and the new girl are OK. The Towers operation is the tricky one three roads, seven entrances and eighteen floors to cover, plus a cast of thousands. What can go wrong?" He sarcastically joked.

Friday morning saw Molly and Worthington on coffee shop duty, the last member of the Grub Club had just arrived.

"Well, exciting times guys. Damo you and Rob all set?"

Lowering his voice Damo replied. "Yeah Charles one Arab no more than twelve-year-old boy. Shaken not stirred." Everybody around the table laughed. We know where he is and should have him before ten AM."

Turning to Richard Charles asked. "What about the rest Richard, your California Towers team ready."

"Sure, all under control. We'll be stationed near reception and the main entrance. Any Asian kids fitting the order we'll follow and snatch. Four in total; one boy under twelve, two girls under ten-years-old, and another girl under five. From what I saw at these units over the last two weekends this should be fine.

Lots of Asian families with every age group represented." On finishing his report Richard was seen on the CCTV to look around with a satisfied look on his face.

Charles too, looked just as satisfied. "Great work both teams. It sounds like we will fill the orders without too much difficulty. Now, after we've done our shopping the two teams will meet at the Wild Horse Mountain Roadhouse. Park outside on the service road that way no CCTVs will see us."

"Then we head for the Gold Coast, are we meeting them on the coast or going to the club house?" Asked Mike.

Robert being the liaison with the Hunters Motorcycle Club answered. "No way they want you or the kids at their clubhouse. That's how they've kept the cops in the dark. Everything is at arms length, they might be violent, anti-social criminals, but their not stupid. We will contact them when we get near the Gold Coast and they will tell us where to meet them."

Charles was happy with the arrangements and felt good about how things would go the following day. "I'm looking forward to tomorrow, but I'll also be glad when we are safely back here on the coast. Let's hit the road and get some rest before the big day."

Slowly, in ones and twos the Grub Club members left the café.

"I was starting to wonder if they were staying for lunch." Molly said to Senior Constable Worthington.

"I tell you what Margy, if we had any doubts about their filthy business we don't have any now. No codes, innuendos, just blunt genders and ages. Goodness, I hate paedophiles. In a group like these their will be some of all the types. Some might just be here for the money selling images and live children, others will get off on digital kiddie porn, some are just abusers simple sickos not complicated."

Margaret Worthington beach tan had paled. "Molly, I so want to make a go of it here in Child Protection but those men talking like that about somebodies son or daughter. How can they be so cruel?"

"I know it's tough, and we've got to be careful not to get too hard, but we have to keep fighting this stuff." Molly said far more gently then she was really feeling.

CHAPTER 17

Saturday morning was predicted to be a typical Sunshine Coast day, bright and warm with a nice breeze coming off the ocean. Two team members from Team Alpha had maintained a light surveillance over night to ensure we hadn't lost contact with Damien and Robert. This was vital because their target location had never been revealed while they were talking at the coffee shop. If we lost them they could carry out their plans to snatch an 'Arab' (whatever that meant) and we would be none the wiser. Seated around the large meeting table drinking coffee was the balance of Team Alpha and all of Team Delta. It was 0500 Hrs, and most of the police officers looked like they had just woken up.

"Morning everyone. Well, today's the big day so if you're not awake now's the time to drink plenty of that crap coffee we have here." A few nodded, others laughed quietly.

"OK, Team Delta first. You all know your assigned locations around California Towers. We thought long and hard about that unit block. Your locations maximise your fields of view in different directions while minimising any blind spots. Stay on point, look busy with your bags and bogey boards, look the part, but stay alert. Detective Herbert is in overall charge of the California Towers op so any command issues are for her. She will be in the underground car park. For several reasons we think this might be where they attempt the grab. It's badly lit, less people and easy exit. Senior Constable Worthington will be at Reception and will control the main entrance and ground floor. The two sub-teams we have assigned to each end of the road, you're going in early so parking shouldn't be an issue. What are your orders? Constable Jones?" He was one of the Officers assigned to the front road.

"Sir, we are to be alert to any foot traffic, targets Caucasian male adults walking with Asian looking children. We are also tasked to

153

identify the target's vehicles, they will probably have more than one. Probably, with a driver waiting in the vehicle."

"Good work Constable. Everyone. Today is all about alertness to the described targets. As with Jonesy, today's a bit different to usual, we know who the crims are and we know who they are planning to grab, as in Chinese children. Now one thing that is extremely important. I hope that none of these scum get as far as the street. If the rest of Team Delta is awake we'll grab them inside. The last thing I want is some poor kid being dragged along the street, or used as a hostage. Now I know at the Academy they teach you that paedos are only violent towards children and are therefore not brave with grown ups. But please don't take their word on that, be careful. We all got that? Alert, Execute, Safely Contain." Everyone was wide awake now.

"OK, Team Alpha. I am coordinating, bit different because as we all know we haven't got a location. Smart surveillance, sub-teams rotating so they don't know they are being followed. We follow Damien and Robert to where they have targeted an 'Arab' kid. I think we can safely assume this means a child of Middle Eastern appearance." I picked up my coffee and took a swig, making a face as it's bitterness.

I continued. "Now, flexibility and calmness is what we need here. There are so many variables that we can't predict or plan for. It's reactive but careful. Now two Alpha boys are outside Damien Edward's place now. Thankfully they bunked together last night which saved having two overnight teams in different locations. This let you guys and girls get your beauty sleep, and from where I'm standing you needed more." Everyone laughed letting the tension leak from the room. I paused to ensure my next words were heard and remembered.

"Now Team Delta your targets have been assessed as a low threat from a resisting arrest perspective. Team Alpha, because we believe Damien Edwards the threat is assessed as much higher. He may have already murdered a witness so your threat is high. I say again. Team Alpha your two targets are to be approached with extreme caution. He's ex-Military, so don't take any chances. We have no knowledge of either group being armed. However, as always be careful, don't be reluctant to draw your Glocks. Use them if you have too. Stay safe, look after your mate."

I continued. "This group are smart, experienced and organised. We'll do a radio check as soon as we get on post. Then stay off the radios, these guys see someone talking into their sleeve or pushing their ears they'll be gone. They may have Police Scanners as well, OK? Now, once we see them grab a kid radio silence is off. I want everyone to know things are on the move so everyone is looking around, even more alert. If the rats run I want them cut off quickly and safely."

One of Team Delta raised her arm like a school kid. "Sir, who calls the go, when these grubs grab a child?" Dressed in her beach gear her red hair pulled back with a band she looked young enough to be a high school student.

"Good question. Because we are so spread out as much as it worries me, I think the only way we can do this is as follows. If the grab goes down in the underground car park Detective Herbert will call it. Around the main entrance and reception, near the lifts Senior Constable Worthington will call it. All units nearby will converge. But all you other girls and boys don't get excited. Stay on your spot and wait just in case they come your way. Having said that, if you can't raise the Team Leader or you're sure they can't see what's happening call for back up and move in." I stated more confidently than I felt.

"Senior Constable Margaret Worthington and Detective Molly Herbert please stand up. Now everyone take a good look, make sure you know them, what they're wearing so you've got no doubts about who's who in zoo. OK, It's been a long briefing but the key points are simple. Be alert. Stay off the radio, move in when the targets grab any child. We can't have children traumatised while we wait for a better angle or something. Listen for the Team Leader's call. Be careful these are serious crimes and these paedos may realise they're looking at some serious time. As you know this might mean they get desperate and violent. Let's do this and take this evil club off the streets. See you out there. Remember protect the children, then yourselves."

With that everyone stood up and after dropping their coffee mugs in the kitchen bin headed out. Molly and Margaret were left sitting at the table.

"You guys all good? I think we have everything covered, but you know, plans don't always go the way we thought."

Molly responded for both women. "We're fine Ben, as long as the paedos don't spring us. I think our side of the op should be alright.

Yours is the shaky one without a location anything could happen. On top of it you have the highest risk of violence if Damien gets cornered. You take care mate." Margaret Worthington nodded as Molly expressed a solid evaluation.

Full of coffee and adrenalin I was wired.

"Will do, the risks are there but man how often do you get a shot at closing down this many paedophiles in one day?" The briefing had taken just over an hour, we still had plenty of time for everyone to get into place.

"You guys take care and happy hunting. I'd feel better about catching Damien and Robert if we didn't have to make it up as we go along. But it's the hand we've been dealt so we just have to play it the best we can. Let me know as soon as you have anything." I said as I picked up my phone and headed out to rendezvous (RV) with the two Constables form Alpha Team sitting on the targets Damien and Robert.

"Anything happening Sam?" I asked the Constable who had been on duty all night. He and his mate had been taking turns at two hour on, two off watching the target's home and driveway.

"Nothing Sir, their lights went out at around eleven, not a sign of anything since then." He replied.

"OK boys, I am sure it won't be long before they'll be on the move. As soon as they go, the rest of Team Alpha will take over following them. You guys have earned some sleep, so head home hey?"

"Matt and I have already talked about that and we can't hit the sack when you guys are out there at it. I'm sure we aren't sharp enough to slot in too close, but we could cover the end of a street or something."

I was impressed by their dedication to seeing this op through even though they were probably exhausted. "Great attitude boys, you're right though I couldn't expect you to be sharp after a broken night, but sure your help is appreciated.

You go last car in the follow, and that's where you stay. You don't take part in any following car rotations, understood? Two of our cars will cut in and loosely follow the two targets. Once the targets stop, Sam's idea is a go and you block the end of the street or road you are on. I'll have another of our cars on the other end. Any questions?"

"No Sir, thank you for including us, neither of us have been on a job like this before so we are looking forward to the experience."

"That's all well and good but don't get hurt. Damien Edwards the bigger of the pair may well be armed and violent. Take care." I said sounding like their father.

The Team Alpha follow cars were parked out of sight in a back street, I would call them up when the targets came out of the house. They were ready to proceed along that street paralleling the black BMW currently parked in the target's driveway, and then fall in behind the Beamer. All was set, everything was quiet, like we were waiting for the umpire to blow his whistle and start the game. We didn't want to have much radio chatter, however it was vital that the chase team knew when to fall in behind the target vehicle.

"All Alphas, this is Alpha Bravo. Radio Check. Over." I called over the radio. All four units answered clearly. Then we all returned to radio silence.

I responded once. "All four Alphas loud and clear. Out." The radio went silent.

Without warning the blue front door swung open and two men walked over to the black sedan. The bigger man, who we knew to be Damien Edwards held out what was a remote and the car's indicators flashed. Unlike the other man, Robert Walsh, he stood outside the driver's door.

As he had been trained to do his eyes systematically searched up and down his street looking for anything that was out of the ordinary, out of its usual place. If he saw the unmarked police car he didn't show it. The young Constables had parked four doors away from where he now stood and the car fitted in with all the others parked around it. Robert was already in the car when Damien climbed behind the wheel, backed out of the driveway and drove off in the opposite direction to where we sat a few houses away.

"Solo, Solo. Out." This was the coded message designed to minimise the use of the radio and avoid alerting the targets that the message was related to them. Let the games begin.

Damien and Robert didn't go far. The four chase cars didn't even get through one full rotation, changing the lead car only three times successfully avoiding the target realising they were being followed. When the black BMW parked at the Kings Beach car park I was in the back seat of the lead chase car.

Damien ever the cool professional was frustrated by being paired with this fool, he had never served and didn't understand operations like Damo.

"OK Rob, now just take your time, we know where this Mussie family sit...."

Rob interrupted, stuttering from nerves. "Oh, Damo, it's a lot more crowded than when we checked it out the other day." He said sounding shaky.

It was Damo's turn to interrupt, this time not attempting to hide his annoyance at the other man's fear.

"Now harden up man, it's a good plan and we stick to it. You with me on this Rob? We slowly walk over, we have a look and then grab the kid, and holding his hand tightly we walk him to the car. Easy. Damien said as they walked towards the main steps down to Kings Beach. He was wondering if he'd need to hold Rob's hand at this rate. Damo was thinking he had misjudged Robert who seemed so confident most of the time.

"Stop your fuckin whining Rob. What's wrong with you? You just about ran the Wellington job and now you sound like you're going to piss your pants. Come on mate there they are."

Up ahead there was a family set up with a shade gazebo and several chairs and beach towels. An overweight man in his sixties was under the gazebo reading the paper. The older woman probably the mother and a teenage girl wore a black Burkini, a full length ankle to neck swimsuit with a built in covering for their head. There was a small girl of about five, but no ten-years-old boy.

Slowing down the couple's pace he whispered. "Damo, he's not there, where the fuck is he?" Looking around Robert had propped in the sand.

Damien once again systematically scanned the beach.

"Settle petal, you're starting to make me nervous. There he is coming this way but he's a fair way off. Let's go mate, we'll lift him while he's away from his mummy, and then we get outa here, now move." Damien ordered.

The two men looked out of place dressed more for say a shopping centre or going to a movie rather than being on a sunny beach. However, no one appeared to notice them, but appearances can be deceiving. Except for Team Alpha Three and the night shift boys all the other Alpha Teams were calmly but rapidly closing in on the two paedophiles. No one noticed the police teams as they were all dressed in board shorts and tee-shirts. Damien and Robert who were focused on the dark skinned boy were oblivious to the Police Officers who now surrounded them. The two men intersected with the boy of Middle Eastern appearance. Each man taking the child by a hand, and turned him towards the steps. He said something that must have been more of a whispered exclamation to himself as he dropped a huge ice cream he had been carrying. Going unnoticed by all the other people enjoying the beach they dragged, half carried him away from his family. Whether the boy was in shock or they had threatened him he was silent and within ten paces stopped struggling and walked along side the two men.

"All Alphas GO, GO, GO. Over." The Alpha Teams on the beach were moving before my radio call. However, it confirmed that they were to grab the two paedophiles as planned. It also warned the Teams guarding the road to be alert in case one of the paedos slipped through the cordon of Officers. One of the Senior Constables followed procedure. "Police don't move." He shouted at the two men. Robert nearly fainted from shock. As the two Officers in Alpha Team Two went to restrain Damien he in turn grabbed Robert and flung him into the two Constables. On the unsure footing of the beach they were knocked backwards, Robert ending up on top of them. Damien made the best of this and took off towards the steps to the walkway. I took off after him. It was hard running in the soft sand but I thought I was gaining on him. He hit the steps and took them three at a time knocking a mother and pram over as he reached the walkway at the top. I hurdled the mother and baby and nearly laid hands on Damien. I dug deep and was just about to tackle him when he propped and turned in one action. I saw a glint of steel and had to throw myself sideways to avoid the knife I now saw clearly grasped in his right hand. He took off again and had gained a few metres on me by the time by the time I had recovered from the feigned attack diversion.

I was reassured that a couple of my team were following closely behind. "Alpha Bravo we are fifty metres on your six and in pursuit of Tango One, Over." The voice was puffing as the Officer ran along the walk way trying to catch up. I didn't answer. Damien cut through a path beside a block of holiday units, tipping over several rubbish bins as he went. I hurdled these, but my legs were telling me this chase had gone on too long. He broke onto the back street turning left and right trying to orientate himself. Making a decision he ran uphill to the left. There wasn't time for a lot of radio procedure. "Matt and Sam coming your way any minute." My message wasn't needed both the young Constables were already out of their car and waiting on the footpath looking in the right direction. Matt was a big lad and probably possessing the confidence born on a Rugby field. He ran onto the road blocking Damien's escape. Cleverly, Sam ran to the front of their vehicle preparing to back his partner up from behind Damien once Matt had grabbed him.

I could see it all folding out before me in slow motion, and was filled with fear for the brave young man. *Matt draw your gun, have it ready.* Three more paces and Damien fell on Matt, the big Constable opened his arms like a fullback ready to block a winger. Hardly slowing, Damien arced his arm from left to right. Matt, stood up straighter with a look of total amazement on his young face. Involuntarily he spun towards the car, his back hit it and then he slid down ending up sitting on the bitumen his life blood coursing from a badly severed carotid artery. I had kept running but now I skidded to halt.

"Don't move Damien. I'll blow your fuckin head off and I'll enjoy it." I was breathing heavily, my Glock moving up and down with each breath.

Damien turned, and smiled. I was sure he was going to run again. I was wrong. He turned and ran straight at me knife raised screaming something I couldn't understand. Bang. Bang. He wouldn't need a third, two holes had appeared on his chest and were now starting to bleed. He nose dived into the bitumen and now lay in a twisted mess. I could hear Sam on the radio. "All Alphas target down I say again target down." I pulled out my phone and called Crime Scene and the Coroner, ambulances would arrive but sadly for the young Constable there was no hurry.

An hour later the street was taped off there were white forensic suits and flashing blue and red lights everywhere. "You alright Ben?" Asked Superintendent Fisher looking very concerned.

"Terrible business losing that young bloke Matt. I feel like it was my fault having those two on an op after working all night. They were keen to see it through, good blokes, good coppers." I couldn't speak any more without emotion overwhelming me. I was a bit surprised how upset I was, guilt emphasised my grief.

"Ben, you didn't kill that young Constable. That scum-bag paedo did. It's terrible, but the kid knew the risks, he did his duty. Maybe a bit of young, from what you said overconfidence cost him dearly."

All I could do was nod, appreciating my Boss's efforts to make me feel better, I knew I would take time to heal. For now, all I could start by thinking about how good it was to end Damien's life. For once it was even officially sanctioned.

Knowing getting back to work would be a good distraction, Superintendent Fisher re-focused.

"We've got Robert Walsh sealed tight. We'll let him sweat for a while, you want to talk to him?"

"I sure do, how's Molly going, anything happening?" I asked.

"Nothing so far, but we figure that most of the new holiday makers can't check in until the cleaners finish preparing the rooms. So we think around lunch onward we'll see some action."

"Yeah, somehow we didn't really think that through, but it's still good for Team Delta to be in place early."

"I agree, and who knows, the Grub Club boys may well have the place under surveillance as well."

CHAPTER 18

Molly was starting to worry that her team was set up at the wrong hotel. They had been in place at the California Towers for close on three hours and nothing. The organised tourists or the ones without kids had packed up and checked out early. The swarm of cleaners had descended on the recently vacated rooms in preparation for this Saturday's booking to move in. The hotel was abuzz, but Team Delta was starting to wilt, an early morning briefing and standing or sitting around like this dulled even the most alert of minds. Molly had done her radio check as soon as they were all on site, and then went quiet. She decided to break radio silence to wake the troops. "All Team Delta, this is Delta Mike, radio check. Over."

"Silly bitch must have dementia, we've already done that dumbass." Spat a Senior Constable named Gilliland from Noosa whose nose was out of joint because Margaret Worthington of the same rank but with less true seniority had been put over him.

All stations answered including the Noosa cop. Molly was happy to hear they were all on line, although she had hoped that no one would be dosing it was good to rattle their chain.

Her thoughts were interrupted by the squelching static of the radio. Molly smiled thinking. *One of the clods has kept squeezing his or her mike.* Then she could hear someone whispering. "Delta Two to Delta Mike. Over"

"Delta Two, you're a bit quiet. Over." Responded Molly.

The inexperienced Officer had whispered even though the targets couldn't possibly hear him from inside their car. "Delta Mike, car load of targets has just pulled into my loc. Over."

Molly's heart rate felt like it doubled. Delta Four was just inside the entrance to the underground car park. It was about to happen. "Delta Four confirm Targets, how many? Over." Molly asked.

"Delta Two, I confirm targets identified, Papa, Mike, Romeo, Charlie. Over."

Molly checked off the first name initials on her notebook. Delta Two had confirmed that Paul, Mike, Richard and Charles had entered the car park. The whole team had heard the comms between Molly and Delta Two. However, Molly wanted them to move to the next level of readiness prepared to spring the trap. "All Delta Team Targets are on site, follow orders, don't go too early. Over."

Molly had to assume the targets had parked near Delta Two's location as the Constable was still whispering. "Delta Mike, they have split into two teams of two. One team in lifts other team staying in this loc. Over."

Molly smiled the young Constable, Delta Two was doing a great job. She hoped he could stay out of sight, Delta Three was at the car park exit. They were briefed to join each other to arrest any targets as needed.

In the lift going up to reception a nervous Charles was with Paul the oldest member of the Grub Club.

"I glad there is a lift, I'm getting too old for stairs in these high-rises." Paul said slightly puffed from the walk up the hill to the hotel. As he regained his breath he looked calm as a corpse.

Meanwhile Charles was deep in thought. *This isn't good, usually I can plan things so I'm the waiting in the car or back home. Because we a so thinly spread, I've gotta get my hands dirty. I don't like the risk, but what choice do I have? And, I'm still not sure if we can trust Richard's cousin back in the car, but it's too late for that now.* The lift doors opened with a bell tone and the two men exited into the Reception Lobby. Senior Constable Margaret Worthington looked up and successfully disguised her excitement at seeing the two faces she had only seen on the coffee shop CCTV and the stills they had printed. The Two men nonchalantly walked over to a series of racks holding brochures advertising all the Sunshine Coast tourist attractions. They stood there looking collecting one and making a point of studying it. Occasionally, they would turn to one another seemingly discussing the attraction. Worthington entered the office behind reception mindful she couldn't leave the two targets unattended for long. She forced herself to take several deep breaths and returned to the reception counter.

We were running two separate ops in different locations. Superintendent Fisher, Molly and I had decided that whoever got an arrest should proceed with the questioning and subsequent charging without waiting for the other to return. Without another Police Officer present, I'd been questioning Robert Walsh for about forty-five minutes. He had called his Solicitor, but he hadn't shown up yet. I was bending the rules, and I didn't think I'd get anything special but I was busy planting seeds of doubt in Robert's brain. This would have been a lot harder to get away with once his Solicitor arrived. Especially, when I was keeping the fact that his partner in crime Damien Edwards had left this world and I hoped he was burning somewhere. Lying to scum-bag was what he deserved.

Sitting back in my chair and lowering my shoulders I started.

"Robert, can I call you Robert?" He nodded his permission. "OK, thanks, now this is how these things work...."

He interrupted me. "You're not s'posed to talk to me with my Solicitor being present, I know my rights."

We had made sure that he didn't know Damien Edwards' was dead, but that didn't mean that he couldn't still be useful to me.

"Sure, sure mate, but Damien's Solicitor has already arrived. Now, as I was saying this is how it works. The pair of you have a wheelbarrow full of charges coming your way. You know it, and I know it. Now if Damien blames you for everything, you know you're the leader, it was all your idea. You know the stuff. This is like a runaway train and he is gaining momentum fast. Well he'll do a deal and become our witness for the Prosecution." Raising my voice just a little to infer urgency.

I continued. "Now guess who we are prosecuting? You mate, Mr. Robert Walsh. Now Damien will still do time, but you might end up doing double his because he made you look bad and grassed on you." I paused, I could see Robert was visibly shaking, he was bordering on tears.

"Now Robert, I can help you, but only if you help me."

"OK. OK, I'll tell you everything as long as I get that deal not him."

"Fine mate, now you're absolutely right, we should wait for your Solicitor, so we will."

I stood up and gathered my paperwork.

"Sir, do we have to wait, I'm happy to talk now." He said anxiously, now his decision had been made.

Resisting an urge to laugh at how easy he had turned, I headed for the door, turning at the last minute for dramatic effect.

"Robert, to even open that deal, I need you to promise me you will keep your end of it when your Solicitor is sitting beside you. Will you do that mate? It's your very best move."

Robert looked relieved, his tight frown relaxing and even a little smile appeared.

"I promise, I know stuff that will be a big surprise for you."

The white Audi's tyres squealed on the smooth cement of the car park driveway as the Chinese woman behind the wheel flew down the ramp way too fast. She had left her sunnies on and was caught by how dark it was in the underground levels. The smooth sedan flew past Delta One's hiding spot and slithered like an eel down to the parking level below. The tyres chirped as she applied the brakes on the polished driveway. Two children clearly excited by their impending holiday, were jumping around as they looked out the windows. The Constable had seen the dark haired children and noted the targets reaction having done the same. Finally they were on the move. The two paedophiles left their vehicle and walked casually towards the BMW. Clearly, they had seen what they were looking for within the white sedan and were about to grab the innocent children.

"Delta Two, you there Delta Mike? Over."

"Go ahead Two. Over."

"Confirm P and C must have gone in lift. R and M have just left their car to follow an Asian woman to Level B over."

"Roger Two, are you able to follow? Over."

"Roger that. On my way. Suggest Three heads down as well for back up. Over."

The Police Officer moved out of his shadowed hiding place, grateful to stretch his legs after standing sentry for so long.

Three had heard. "This is Three, heard request Delta Mike, OK to join Two? Over."

"Two go for it. Over."

"Delta Two and Three proceed with plan. Be careful. Over." Molly ended the comms.

Richard and Mike had walked quickly down the vehicle ramp to Level B. They could see the woman and two children getting out of the Audi which was parked near the lift. The mother was handing small bags and bogey boards to her children a girl of about eight or nine and a boy who was three or four-years-old.

Richard gently tapped Mike on the arm and whispered.

"Unbelievable first car in and two out three orders filled. Now Mike I have a plan, just go along with me." Mike grunted in agreement.

Walking towards the lift ignoring the Chinese family the two men waited looking up as the lift lights showed it's descent to their call. When the lift arrived Richard said.

"Mike you hold the doors mate?"

While Mike put one arm in the lift stopping the doors from closing Richard got into the lift and pressed the button for the fifteenth floor. Stepping out of the lift again, he whispered. "Whatever you do don't let that lift get away."

Smiling widely Richard appeared to have noticed the stressed mother and her children.

"Can I help you with some of that. My friend will hold the lift so take your time."

Relief replaced anxiety as the woman smiled at Richard and replied. "That would be wonderful. If we can get everything into the lift we can unload it on our floor in one go." She handed Richard a large suitcase and a folded stroller. Richard put everything else in the back of the lift and the mother stepped into the elevator. As she turned she said. "Thank you so muc......" She screamed as Mike released the lift doors and she realised what had happened.

Trapped in the elevator crowded by the families bags and bogey boards she hurtled towards the fifteenth floor without any ability to reverse the per-ordered lift. As she travelled further away from her children she hoped it was just an accident, but dread filled her as she willed the lift to end it's journey upwards. Eventually she reached the fifteenth floor and immediately pressed the B Level Car Park button. With a lurch the elevator began its descent.

The lift doors flew open flooding a yellow light onto grubby concrete and the mother peered out into the dark empty car park. Her cries became a heartbreaking whimper as she sank to her knees beginning to realise what had occurred.

Holding the arm of one child each Richard and Mike dragged their terrified captives up the ramp back to Level A and headed for their car. Standing in the shadows the two Police Officers had seen enough to engage and make the arrest.

"Delta Mike this Two Targets have abducted children. About to detain now. Over."

They walked towards the targets without a warning in the hope
that no harm would come to the children and that the targets would
have no chance to escape. Richard was about to brag to Mike about
how easy this had been when he saw the approaching men. He nearly
stopped walking but controlled the instinct and continued. He
quickly assessed their clothing and demeanour and assumed that
they were just holiday makers staying at the hotel and relaxed. The
pair of undercover Police continued as if they would proceed past
the two men. However, just as they got past them the Constables
turned and grabbed each man. The two would be abductors in turn
let go of their frightened young captives. The children were so scared
they immediately hugged each other sobbing on each others
shoulders. The mother had heard their cries had recovered and had
staggered up the ramp. Seeing her children she ran to them and
lifted them off the ground smothering them in hugs and kisses, her
tears of terror becoming tears of joy instead. Grateful that they could
focus on their prisoners now that the children were once again safe
the Constables cuffed their prisoners. Then unceremoniously they
marched them back to the undercover Police car parked near the car
park entrance.

Molly wasn't sure if she had taken a breath since the last comms
with her Car Park team.

"Delta Mike, this is Two and Three, you there? Over."

"Two, SITREP. Over."

All coppers knew SITREP was demanding a Situation Report so
Delta Two gave Molly the details. "Targets R and M in custody, all
safe. Over."

Molly was ecstatic, two in the net and no casualties civilian or
Police. She would get all the details later but for now there were two
more targets Charles and Paul to catch.

Calling Margaret Worthington. "Delta One, this Delta Mike,
you there? Over"

"Delta One. Over."

"SITREP. Over" Molly requested.

"Delta One, Targets are hanging around Reception, no change. Over"

"One, You heard the chatter? Over."

"Roger that, my Targets couldn't have heard no reaction here. Over."

Molly had hoped that the paedophiles didn't have their own comms, and was grateful to be proven correct. She also noted although she wasn't surprised how sharp Worthington was.

Robert Walsh's Solicitor had driven up from Brisbane and was dressed accordingly, hopefully he would melt if he spent any time on the Sunshine Coast. A man in his late forties, a mop of salt and pepper coloured hair, the expensive suit coat straining just a little around the girth. We had commenced the 'official' questioning, this time I had Sergeant Douglas in with me. At this stage I had just set the scene and made the possible charges clear to all concerned. Formally I started the questions.

"Mr Walsh, you know we have you every which way, we have about two hundred witnesses who saw you and Mr Edwards attempt to kidnap that boy on Kings Beach. The Solicitor chimed in.

"My client was just unlucky to be walking down the beach when that terrible man tried to grab that child. Mr Walsh doesn't even know the other man. I think you are desperate Detective, you have your kidnapper and my client is an innocent bystander. His part of all this is no different to the other two hundred witnesses you speak of."

Smiling viciously I calmly stated. "Your client was unlucky, He was unlucky that we were there to stop him and his accomplice kidnapping that little boy. Now it would appear that he may have mislead you regarding him not knowing Mr Damien Edwards the other man at the scene. Supported by a separate warrant we have video and audio record of the two men sitting with each other and talking on several occasions."

The Solicitor looked askance at this and glared at Robert. "Can I have a private word with my client please?" He asked.

After informing the recording device that were suspending the interview I stood up, my chair made a scraping noise. Sergeant Douglas and I then left the room. This was going absolutely to plan.

The Lawyer client conference took about two minutes flat, then the legal eagle opened the interview room door and beckoned us in.

"My client, a concerned citizen wishes to assist your enquiry. He believes he has information that you may not currently have in your possession." The pompous Lawyer had recovered and was now ready to deal.

We sat down and started the recording again. As an encouragement, I gently kicked Robert's foot under the table as I began to speak. "Robert, I'm glad to hear that. Now, as a concerned citizen what were you doing on that particular beach grabbing that specific Middle Eastern looking child?" I asked sarcastically.

His Solicitor knew he and his client deserved that and much more.

"Now Detective there is no denying my client's presence at...." He referred to his notes. "Kings Beach, and he may have been allegedly involved in a very minor way in the alleged misunderstanding regarding this young person." He was earning his money, that was for sure. He continued.

"Hypothetically speaking. If you were to charge my client and he was to furnish you with information. Information regarding that other despicable man who apparently had the ability to manipulate or may I say even dominate my client. And possibly even provide details that you are not privy to at this time regarding other matters. My client was wondering that if in exchange for this assistance whether you may be open to assisting him in return. Possibly lesser charges, or a statement to the court requesting a lesser sentence."

Nodding like all this was a surprise to me and a wonderful strategy by the Solicitor I went for it. I needed to avoid being too eager so I replied cautiously.

"Depending on the severity of Mr Walsh's role in all this and the value of this promised information we may well be able to support such an arrangement."

Molly knew she had people watching the road, but she hadn't been able to alert the team members to a specific vehicle or vehicles to look for. She decided on a strategy to attempt to identify the getaway car.

"Delta Five and Delta Six you there? Over."

"Five here. Over"

"Six here,. Over."

"OK, Five and Six I want you to take opposite sides of the road and walk towards each other until you swap ends. Search for any suspicious vehicle or persons, maybe a guy sitting alone. Acknowledge understanding of instructions. Over."

"Five. Roger that. Over."

"Six. Roger that, Over."

"Delta Mike, inform as needed. Be careful. Out."

Molly was thinking; *This is a waste sitting on this floor when two are in the holding cells and the other two are obviously keeping an eye on Reception.*

"Delta Mike to One. Over."

Senior constable Worthington answered immediately.

"Delta One, go ahead. Over."

"One, I'm coming down, are targets away from the fire stairs? Over."

"One, affirmative, that will be your best way to the office. Over."

"All Call Signs my loc is now Reception. Out."

Molly ran down the steps three at a time exiting the stairwell door into the Lobby.

Smiling at her protégée to cover her worry she asked.

"Margaret, what are these guys up to?"

Shaking her head from side to side was answer enough, even so she replied.

"Don't know Molly, but I hope they do something soon, them hanging around the Reception Lobby is wearing a bit thin."

Charles and Paul were now sitting near the front entrance to Reception, the older man pretending to read a local business magazine.

Charles felt very exposed and was thinking that they had been hanging around Reception too long. "Paul, I don't like this. The other crew was supposed to come to us when they had grabbed some kid and tell us the age and gender. The order needed two girls under ten-years so logically that's what we need more of. We can't wait for them. The next Chinese girl under ten we grab, OK?"

Paul knew this was risky. He too was worried that hanging around the Lobby had to get noticed soon. He bowed to Charles' leadership, the logic sounded OK to him in any case. So they waited. It was nearly two in the afternoon when they were startled by the automatic doors opening beside them. An Asian man and girl of about eight or nine walked through the main entrance. There was red Jeep Cherokee with a Chinese looking woman sitting in it parked under the hotel's portico. The little girl was a few paces behind her father, her mother had her head down reading her phone. The Chinese man was half way across the Lobby, the little girl just stepping though the big glass doors. In one movement so smooth it was nearly invisible Charles grabbed the Chinese girl's wrist and was gone. Paul walking behind the struggling girl blocked the view from the Reception desk. Margaret Worthington hadn't really seen it but sensed something had changed. The two men were gone. Calling over her shoulder for the real receptionist to get Molly, Worthington sprinted out the door.

"All Alphas targets have a captive heading for Queens Road. Go, Go."

Senior Constable Worthington could see the back of the plump man who had been hanging around the Lobby all day. He stumbled and although he caught himself fell to the right a little, allowing Margaret just a glimpse of Charles and a little dark haired girl. Drawing her Glock she pushed herself to run faster.

"All Alphas two targets, Asian girl approx eight year-old, blue beach dress. I am in pursuit North along Queens St."

The two Police Officers who were guarding the road had not finished their search of the vehicles parked along that section of Queens Road. As instructed they had walked on opposite sides of the road towards each other. They were about to meet in the middle, outside the California Towers Hotel as two men, one dragging/carrying a small girl child burst onto the footpath, and then ran into the street.

Both the men looked towards the front of the hotel and started frantically gesturing for someone to come to them. Each Constable drew his gun as they ran onto the road blocking the men's escape. They heard a car engine start and with a squeal of spinning tyres a dark blue Subaru WRX fish-tailed out of a parking spot. Seeing the two men with Glocks at the ready running in their direction abandoned the child who ran towards the footpath sliding between two parked cars. Clearly, this was their get away car. However, the driver didn't slow at all. Paul the oldest member of the Grub Club, in his sixties and overweight was slow to get out of the WRX's way. The speeding car hit him with a sickening thump sending him into the air, his lifeless body falling onto the shiny blue bonnet. The driver flicked the steering wheel just enough for the vehicle to shed itself of Paul's battered body. The corpse was slung into the side of a parked

Ford leaving a red smear on it's white duco. The Constables having witnessed this action turned simultaneously towards the speeding sedan and aimed for the driver. There was no time for warnings or demands, the speeding rocket was now choosing which of the Police Officers stood in its path to freedom.

Bang. Bang. Bang. Each Officer fired their Service handguns, two shots from one. There was no time for a second shot from the other as the two young Constables jumped left and right out of the way of the WRX. The rally bred Subaru flew towards where only moments before the two young men had been standing. Unexpectedly, the squealing tyres silenced as the car slowed, it rolled about three car lengths and then swerved into a parked Hilux 4WD. Recovering quickly, the two Constables cautiously approached the WRX guns aimed at the driver's window. The engine was still running as the front door was wrenched open. The driver was slumped over the steering wheel, Constable Dodds grabbed his shoulder and pulled him back into the seat. The driver's sightless eyes were already glazing over, his lap was covered in his own blood cascading from wounds in his forehead and chest.

Charles was still standing on the road, staring at Paul's lifeless body. Senior Constable Worthington stood between two parked cars her gun trained on Charles. He moved suddenly, Worthington thinking he was going for a gun or try to escape nearly squeezed the trigger. However, he bent forward and vomited onto the hot black tar road. Glock shaking fractionally, Detective Molly Herbert stood a little behind Worthington after having arrived on the scene just in time to witness the whole calamity. Everyone, except the Police Officers who had shot the get away driver had frozen like garden statues hypnotised by what had just occurred, staring at the twisted bloody corpse of the late Paul. Charles looked to capitalise on this hiatus and walked calmly up the road ducking between some parked cars and disappeared from sight. Now, the reality of the situation returned. Worthington snapped out of it, and rushed over to Paul, while she phoned for all emergency services. Kneeling beside Paul's supine body, as she attempted to find a pulse she could tell that his neck had been broken. She would leave him for the Ambos, he was beyond even their help.

Molly, still on the footpath saw Charles make his escape off the road. Looking up the hill she immediately saw him walking as quickly as he could without actually running. Molly sprinted after him and was surprised that as she crested the rise he was nowhere to be seen. She swore to herself. There was a lane down to the beach that he must have run down once he was out of sight. Molly still had her gun out so she walked with it pressed against her leg so as not to scare the public. She could now see the ocean and then the golden sand as she continued down the path. Standing on top of the wooden steps that took you down to the beach she had a terrific vantage point. Systematically Molly searched every inch of the beach. A man dressed the way Charles would surely would stick out a mile. Nothing. Where could he be? A family of four was coming up the steps after enjoying their morning on the beautiful beach. Molly stood aside to allow sandy bodies, beach umbrellas and bogey boards past. A pretty little girl of about six or seven looked at Molly and whispered. "If you are playing hide and seek your friend is hiding right under these steps." Giggling at her innocently betraying the man's secret she skipped after her family.

Molly smiled, happy to know where her quarry was hiding but also because of the irony of what had just happened. A paedophile attempting to kidnap a child was now about to be arrested because a child thought he was playing a game. Well Charlie boy you might have been but for you the game is over. Molly casually walked down the steps to the beach looking everywhere but behind her so as not to spook him. As soon as she reached the sand she pivoted towards the steps. Simultaneously, the Glock came away from her leg and she looked along its black barrel. Charles's head rested nicely between the Glock's sights. For the smallest of instants Molly thought how much this scum-bag deserved to die. All the suffering he had inflicted on the innocent and vulnerable children he had abused or sold.

"Please don't shoot, I'll come quietly. Please, please." Charles pleaded.

Molly laughed out loud when she noticed the paedo had wet his pants. He would get what he deserved. "You're done Charlie boy. Guess what, we see you as the leader of that little Grub Club. You know what that means mate? It means that you'll go for what you did, plus and it's a big fucking plus. You get a share of everything else because you ordered it or knew about it. By the time we are finish with you Charlie boy you will start wishing that Michael Schumacher in your getaway car you had run you over and not poor old Paul."

Molly shut up then, she had vented enough and scared Charles enough to set him up for the inevitable questioning that would come once she got him back to HQ. But the dirty wet bastard wasn't getting in her car.

CHAPTER 19

Robert had needed a toilet brake and had just returned to Interview Room Two accompanied of course by his trusty Solicitor. The recording machine was back on and everyone was exhausted.

"OK, Robert you've done pretty well telling us about what's been going on with your little club. I get it, you were just there, didn't really do the things you've told us about. It was all those other horrible men. Have I got it right?"

The Solicitor slid his arse forward on the hard iron chair. "Now come on Detective, my client has been more than cooperative. I think it is clear that he was what you'd call a fringe dweller in that group. Your sarcasm seems uncalled for."

I was way beyond exhausted but this stuff couldn't wait until tomorrow.

"OK Robert, we'll leave that for now. Let's move on. Now once the others had grabbed these kids where were they going then? We know they were an order of some sort, these kids weren't for the use of your club members, were they?"

I asked, hoping the question would give Robert the chance to tell me what he had offered as a bargaining chip.

"Well we were s'posed to take 'em down to the Gold Coast." Robert offered.

"OK. So what's the Bikies got to do with it?"

Surprise covered his face, he obviously didn't realise I knew about them. I was hoping that wasn't his best bit of Intel. Not being any revelation to us it was no good to me or him.

Robert sensed that he had lost ground, he was slipping away and needed a rope to cling to. "Yeah, the Bikies are the Hunters Motorcycle Club, you heard of them?"

"Yeah, of course I have. Is that all you've got? We didn't need Sherlock Holmes to work that out. You are an ex-Hunters member so the relationship was there right? Not a mystery."

The Solicitor realising Robert's established relationship with the Bikies incriminated him as more than a labourer in the group stepped in.

"Ah, that's not a strong link Detective, my client's past affiliations don't confirm any current or future relationships. He strongly asserts that he just did what he was told and that wasn't very much."

I shook my head in frustration at the legal mumbo jumbo he was trying to spin.

Ignoring the Solicitor I looked into Robert's sad eyes. "Look we are way past that bullshit. Robert I need something from you. Something I haven't got, Intel I don't already know. I'm friggin tired out and getting close to calling it a day."

After a small pause to let him worry a bit. I continued.

"Robert if I leave here now, that heavy steel door is going slam on any possibility of me helping you. Mate, you gotta help me first. My Superintendent won't back my supporting you if I don't give him some Intel that makes it all worthwhile. So far, it's all been yesterday's news."

After a short pause where Robert must have been weighing up his scant options. My speech was rewarded as I observed Robert's last resistance drop along with his shoulders right before my eyes.

"OK, I'll tell ya. So you know I was in the Hunters, I wasn't just a soldier, I was Sergeant at Arms. That meant I was in on deals and arrangements you know. Anyway when that bitch Premier brought in the anti-bikie laws none of us knew what to do, or how it would impact us. In the mean time the Russian Mafia took the initiative and moved in on nearly everything going on in the coast."

"Yeah mate I'm too tired for some fuckin history lesson, OK."

Ignoring my anger Robert continued.

"Sure, I was just trying to give the background. Anyway, the Russians are running a few brothels even some legal ones. But, they have a different angle on things to most. They provide for all the sicko weirdos you know, whatever they're into the Ruskies provide it."

Normally, when I wasn't exhausted I would have let him run, But today wasn't normal.

"Robert get to the point for fuck's sake."

Discouraged by my attitude, but desperate he continued. "Yeah well anyway, I don't know how they've kept under the radar but they've opened a special brothel. One that caters for special tastes, babies upwards and no meat older than about thirteen or so." He smiled and licked his lips at the thought of it. It took every ounce of my weary self control not to launch across the table and throat punch him. I took in three very deep breaths.

Even though I was starting to see the food chain here, I needed him to confirm what he was saying.

"What are you telling me Rob, what's the link between your Grub Club, the Bikies and the Russians? I don't see it mate."

He must have had a burst of confidence because he went smart mouthed again.

"You **must** be tired, it's pretty obvious. We get the kids, we sell 'em to the Hunters. Then the Hunters on-sell them to the Russians. Then the Russians hire them out at their brothel. The Ruskies work on the old saying; you always sell the milk and not the cow principle. That's why we had to get pacific kids for this order."

Shaking my head again. "Specific not pacific. If they were Pacific kids they might come from NZ or Fiji.'

"Seriously Detective my client is attempting to cooperate with you best he can. Your sarcasm adds nothing to the equation. Robert looked confused, not realising his use of the wrong word, my joke, or his Solicitor's statement.

I moved on, yeah, I was tired. "Anyway, what do you mean 'this order'?"

Happy to understand what we were talking about he returned to his explanation. "Whatever, anyway we had to get what they wanted; one Arab looking boy no older than twelve, two Asian girls no older than ten and another Asian younger than five years-old. That's why we split up. Damo and I were after the Arab kid and the others went for the Chink kids at that new hotel up on Queen."

He recited the details like he was talking about a round of drinks. I was role hardened but this disgusted me beyond normal limits.

"When was the exchange going to happen?"

Just as he was about to respond there was a knock on the interview room door. Angry at the intrusion I stood up so quickly my chair fell over. Sergeant Douglas remained seated staring at the prisoner to maintain the pressure we had built up. I walked to the door and unlocked it.

Superintendent Fisher smiled because he knew I was about to rip someone's head off for interrupting my interview. It was an unwritten rule that only the extremely brave would contravene this canon. He waved me to come into the hall. "Ben, sorry to pull you out of there, but we need to catch up ASAP. It's been a huge day."

"Is Molly OK Sir?"

"Absolutely her operation went pretty well, that's part of what we need to talk about."

"OK, I'm nearly done, I'll wrap up and see you shortly."

I re-entered the interview room and Sergeant Douglas started the recording again. "OK, I had just asked you when the children were to be delivered?"

"This afternoon or tonight, we weren't sure when we would have all the kids we needed so we didn't fix a time, just a day. The arrangement was that I would phone a number when we passed

Dream World. Then we would be given a location to deliver." I could see that Robert was trying hard to be seen to cooperate.

"What do you think will happen if they don't get a call?" I asked.

"They'll chase me, because the Russians will chase them, they probably have customers booked into the brothel for tomorrow night."

I had the Intel I needed but I certainly wasn't sure what I would do with it.

"Alright Robert old mate, you'll be placed in a holding cell until we know what we want to do. Don't worry your cooperation won't be forgotten. I'll be in touch. The Constable outside will give you five minutes with your Solicitor." Douglas and I picked up our files and left them sitting in the cold interview room.

Sticking my head into the Boss's office I was pleased to see Molly and her new sidekick Margaret Worthington.

"I'll just going to grab a coffee and be there."

They were sitting in silence when I returned.

"Sorry but I'd be snoring without this." I said holding up my coffee mug.

For the next hour we debriefed on the separate missions. We had a lot to celebrate but the death of the young Constable Matt at Damien's hand, and the death of Paul run down by his own man outside the California Towers disallowed it at least for now. After so much work the outcome was nothing short of spectacular. Taking that many paedophiles off the streets would in a cascade affect protect a lot of children. Senior Constable Worthington contributed to the debrief but was wise enough to just listen and learn for the rest of the meeting.

Superintendent Fisher was beaming. "My shout for a dinner of your choice as long it's either Indian or Chinese. First we grieve for that young copper Matt O'Dwyer, I don't apologise for not giving a flying fuck about that old Paul Smith late of the Grub Club."

Molly and I were a little surprised by this outburst, but we were all tired. The adrenalin that had been surging through our bodies all day had started to leach out of our systems.

Fisher continued. "OK. Good news is we have the Grub Club either deceased or in custody. Charles Winchester, looks like his parents were M.A.S.H. fans hey?." Molly and I thought yeah. we're all tired.

The Boss continued. "Robert Walsh, Richard Cook, Michael (Mike) Jarrat. Damien Edwards is hopefully paying for his sins over and over again, and Paul Smith might be sitting on the same hot rock, shouldn't rate another mention. Now let's see what we have to tidy up before we can go home. Molly you got anything we need to do?"

"No not really, I was thinking about the best way to have them detained overnight. I think they should be held together for a while under covert supervision until later tonight. Then kept in single cells until morning."

I nodded. "Boss I think that's a great idea. We can throw them in a general cell, and slip a couple of U/Cs (under/Cover Police Officers), in with them to listen to their conversations. Who knows what we might over hear. It works in the per-court rooms, it always amazes me how dumb and how talkative people are when they think they are with people in the same boat as they are."

"Alright, I'll get Senior Sergeant Hansen to hurry up a couple of U/Cs that don't look like cops. OK, what else?"

"My concern is probably more immediate. Based on Intel I gathered from Robert Walsh, those kids were to be delivered to the Hunters Motorcycle Club by tonight. What are our options? It's a pity not to widen our net and catch those mongrels. They might not be paedos but they are making money on kid's suffering."

Nodding Fisher agreed."I would like nothing better than to close that part of it down but Ben what have we really got?"

"I know. I was thinking about it as I was walking up from the interview rooms. I can't see what we can do. Say we drive down there even if Robert was willing to make the call what happens then. We meet the Hunters and as disappointed as they may be there not going to admit it. All they would claim is they were looking forward to seeing their old Sergeant at Arms so sad too bad. We've got nothing."

"I hate to admit it but your assessment is spot on. Unless we took a bus load of Grub Club members and children down there we couldn't catch the Bikies with anything. Of course we aren't about to to do either so the Hunters will have to wait." Superintendent Fisher asserted.

"OK. It's a shame, but we have to live with what is possible not necessarily what we would like, or what is best." I said.

I was too tired to give this unexpected scenario a lot of thought but I smiled inwardly as my plans starting to climb out of the mire; *In the very near future, I will pay the Hunters a visit that they will never recover from. I was nearly relieved that the Boss had not ordered an official action because these Bikies deserved more than the Queensland Courts would ever deliver.*

The Boss looked at us both like a parent would rather than our Superintendent.

"OK, the uniforms will sort the prisoners and tomorrow is another day. Molly, Ben you have done an outstanding job in the last few weeks and especially today. Go home have a few drinks and get some sleep." He said stifling a yawn.

"Sir, one last thing. About that waiter's murder I'm convinced that it was Damien Edwards, but was he ordered to do it by Charles Winchester the Grub Club's leader. Even if he wasn't, it would be sweet to nail Winchester for sanctioning the murder, allowing it to go ahead."

"I totally agree, can it wait until tomorrow? We will all be sharper in the morning." Fisher said, concern showing on his face.

"Sure, and I'm so tired I can't remember did I tell you that none of the Club know Damien is dead including his partner today Robert Walsh."

Molly smiled. "Now that could be helpful when we come at them again tomorrow. Before we go I just want to say how well Margaret handled today."

Superintendent Fisher looked embarrassed and stated. "Of course, I'm sorry Margaret, I didn't mean to leave you out before. From all reports that was awesome work today. Well done."

Smiles all round, but we were too tired for any more speeches.

With that, once again the four of us congratulated ourselves on a job well done and headed home.

When I got home I made myself a large JD and sat out on the back patio to take in the last of the view of the Glasshouse Mountains before it got too dark to see anything. I had a lot of thinking to do but now was not the time. I got up to get another drink and decided I needed sleep more, and headed for bed. As exhausted as I was my rest didn't last long. Awake again, soaked in sweat and angry at who had hurt me so long ago. I was angry, just like every time my recurring dream woke me. I was angry every day, pretty well every minute. Nothing rational, not justifiable in the context of that moment, but just angry. I had matured with this anger and now managed it far better than I did especially as a teenager. High school years saw me in conflict with my environment and anyone or anything in it. I would over-react to the most benign statement or comment. My dominating paradigm was anger it didn't really matter about the other person's reality. I was angry and need someone to take it out on.

As the sun poked it's head above the horizon the sand seemed softer than usual as I poured on some pace to finish off the eight Ks I'd just run. I was hot, wet and sandy but I felt great, better than I had for a long time. I finished a steaming shower with a minute of cold and was ready to fight the world once again.

Molly hadn't arrived yet, but Margaret Worthington was in front of a terminal tapping away. "Morning Margaret, did you sleep OK after your big day?"

"Hi Ben, yeah I slept like the proverbial baby, how about you?" She asked.

I lied as usual about my sleep or my feelings. "Fine, any word from those U/Cs, has someone done a transcript of what they recorded?"

"Yeah, I was just starting to plough through it when you arrived."

"Because we know these creeps pretty well, let's listen to the audio first. Then we can analyse the transcript, OK?" I said taking a pull from my coffee.

Molly had arrived ten minutes into it. "Hey mate, we thought we'd make a start. You haven't missed anything, the U/Cs are just making their intros."

So for the next hour plus we listened, pausing it when one of us had a question or a thought. On the tape we heard one of the under-cover cops ask the first question prisoners always ask. "What have the pigs got you for?" Or something along those lines. Then the three of us settled in to listen for anything of interest.

"Robert do you know if Damo got away?" Charles asked.

"I'm not sure, they caught me on the beach but he took off up the stairs to the walkway. That was the last I saw of him before the pigs buried my face in the sand."

I had authorised the under-cover cop to inform them being alert to reactions and what was said. Molly had briefed the U/Cs that we were looking for anyone who knew about Damien's tendency towards violence or the waiter's murder. Because Robert and Damien seemed to work together I especially wanted to cross check whether Robert knew about Stan the waiter's murder. The U/C had to be careful not to name Damien as this hadn't been released to the public at this stage.

We heard the U/C set the trap. "Well, I don't know the guy's name but some bloke was shot just up from Kings Beach this morning."

We heard Robert react, slip and then catch himself. "Bullshit, he can't be dead, then how was he doin a deal with.... So, he's dead, do you guys know how it happened?"

"Sure, he killed one of the cops trying to arrest him. Then he went for another one and got nailed."

We could identify Charles's voice. "No surprise he was a crazy prick, just like he jumped at the chance to solve that waiter prob....." He realised what he had said and was angry at this slip.

That went well. It may have been a bit obvious if one of the U/Cs had asked, but they didn't need to.

Richard asked. "What do you mean? Was young Stan's accident not an....?" His question lost momentum as he realised what had happened to the eavesdropping waiter.

Charles's voice again. "Anyway enough of that talk, maybe these pigs have the cell bugged who knows?" We could hear some anonymous grunts of agreement and some swearing.

The U/Cs waited a while and started again. "So you guys don't know about the other shootings this morning? A cop killed, two of your crew killed. They've even named the mob involved the Grub Club. Fucked if I know why."

We could hear several moans and swearing in response to that.

Charles must have figured the more he knew the more prepared he was for what was to come. "What do you mean, we haven't seen or heard a thing?"

"Well, I don't know what was goin on but the Sunshine Coast was like friggin Chicago for a while. Like Dave said cops and your mate killed at Kings. Then outside that new hotel California all hell brakes loose. Anyway, whatever you guys were doing you're lucky you weren't anywhere near there." The deeper voice of the two stated.

Mike's voice was now heard, fear shaking every word. "So what happened?"

"Well, we don't know what started it all but apparently two guys, I don't know they might have tried to rob the hotel. Anyway, they run out onto Queens Road. Then one of those racers what are they called WRXs launches. Knocks one of them arse over tit and somehow the place is crawling with coppers. The guy I s'pose he was the get away driver he's fucked up. Then the reports said after a chase down to the beach some other guy was nabbed."

Silence filled the cell and our speakers. "These U/Cs deserve an Oscar, they're sharp." Molly commented.

Whether it was shock or concern that the cell was in fact bugged it all stayed silent except for some fragmented conversations that in some cases was unintelligible due to whispering and probably the distance from the under-cover cop's wires.

Superintendent Fisher looked pleased. "What have you guys got from the U/Cs was it worthwhile?"

"Mostly confirmed stuff we already knew but it all helps. The bonus came when Charles let it slip he knew about Damien Edwards 'solving the waiter problem'. I gestured the parentheses with my fingers. "The boys in Homicide will be happy, they've got their confirmation that Damien Edwards did in fact murder Stan the waiter. I think it also proves that Charles had fore-knowledge of Damien's actions and may infer he either directed them or at least approved of them."

Our Boss looked enquiringly at Molly who slid forward on her chair. "Yeah, I agree with Ben for what it's worth."

"OK, what do we do with it?" The Superintendent asked.

"I think we owe it to Jack Nolan over at Homicide to flick pass him this one. He can sweat Charles into a Conspiracy to commit murder, maybe even better. Is that OK with you Boss?"

Nodding his agreement Fisher continued."Sure, makes sense, we've got so much on our plate. We can get Charles back for our charges, after he's charged by Homicide, he's not going anywhere. Let's see him get his just desserts for the murder charges first. One thing we are sure of from the tapes is that he's the only one involved in the waiter's murder. You're right about us being busy, it'll take the three of us days to finish the interviews, then the follow ups. There's an incredible amount of evidence to line up so the Crown Prosecutor can safely proceed. This will clog up the Prosecutor's Office and the Courts for the next couple of months. They'll have their hands full with so many charges and multiple defendants. Ain't it terrific." He said with a satisfied smile.

Superintendent Fisher was a good leader and knew where he could take some of the load. He understood he could do whatever he liked but out of respect made it sound like our choice. "You guys concentrate on the interviews and evidence we already have. I'll get some clerical support. You OK if I organise the Search Warrants on the scum-bag's residences? I'll be amazed if that doesn't turn into more charges and more work."

Molly appreciated his input. "Sure Boss, that would be great, and I think you're right. Margaret's busy helping us but it would be great experience for her to be involved in that process. How about she assists you?"

Fisher nodded. "That's a terrific idea, the help would be appreciated and like you said a bit of deep end training would do her some good." He said with a fatherly smile.

It actually took us closer to two weeks, with Molly and I dotting all the Is and crossing the Ts. We tested the Chain of Custody on the evidence to ensure it was strong enough to withstand some Defence

Barrister's criticism. Molly and I had seen too many scum-bags get off on a legal technicality. For us to slacken off now, we weren't going to chance it. We'd let them have the few hours together with the U/Cs harvesting more Intel. But straight after that they were sent to Remand and went into single cell isolation and had been that way ever since. The interviews after that had been fruitful with us playing one paedo against the other. Experience had taught us long ago not to trust what these scum-bags told us. They would sell their grandmother for a chance at a reduced charge or sentence. The way they described their part in events butter wouldn't melt in their mouths. However, if we could confirm the veracity of this new Intel by cross referencing other evidence we used it to the max. Sometimes we would simply confront the individual. In most cases they fell in the trap of denying an accusation or falsely answering a question only to give in when confronted with our supporting evidence.

We had them as long as the legal eagles didn't stuff it up.

The Grub Club was out of business and for keeps.

CHAPTER 20

Any other time our arrests, although local would have made national and maybe International news. However, except for the briefest mention on one news cycle it didn't get a run. The media were still far more interested in the high profile arrests that had resulted from revelations found in the Bishop's laptop. Politicians, Judges, Clergy and Senior Public Servants including a few high ranking Police falling from grace and power made for far more juicy items for the news hounds than solid police work like ours. In some cases scores were being settled, agendas pursued. In the main it was just a great opportunity to attack authority. This near anonymity suited me down to the ground. I wasn't in this job for headlines and I knew our hard work and poor Constable Matt's life had been worth it on many levels.

It also suited me because I was hoping the lack of media coverage meant that the Hunters mightn't be too spooked. Not being able to contact Robert Walsh and obviously the fact that the 'delivery' didn't happen must have worried them. However, we had not made any of the paedophile's names public. This was common in abuse cases as a guard against the victims being identified, so the media didn't query it. So I had been thinking about how to bring the Hunters Motorcycle Club to justice. Real justice they would understand.

I was staring at my monitor and if anyone had asked what was on it I couldn't have told them. Eliminating an entire Bikie Club was a massive leap from dropping one grubby paedophile at a time. Two things were worrying the most. Firstly, how was I going to wipe out what, thirty or forty tough and armed outlaws without getting myself killed? Secondly, as far I knew, my Superintendent, nor any of the Homicide Detectives investigating the deaths of the scum-bags I had dispatched had thought about the assailant being a fellow cop. Especially not me. Of course, my Boss knew the Hunters Motorcycle

Club was involved in our recent operation, but they had eluded justice due to a lack of proof connecting them to child trafficking. If the Hunters MC Club was wiped out, would he wonder whether one of his team was involved? Normally, probably not. However, he was no fool. He would remember the other paedophile deaths and possibly put this all together. Was this a risk worth taking?

I looked up from the mound of paperwork and evidence boxes that smothered the meeting table. "Boss, you weren't wrong about those house searches. If we just had this stuff those paedos would be going away for a long time. Plus the abduction and all they won't see the sunshine for a long time."

"Yeah, no surprise, although they were clever in hiding it, the boys had found enough physical evidence including kiddie porn DVDs and digital files on their computers to supply the whole evil world. I know I keep saying it but, but closing this Grub Club down is like cutting out a festering filthy cancer that had operated here on the Sunshine Coast for way too long." We could all here the passion in the Superintendent's voice.

I was still exhausted and needed to vent. "Absolutely, it just brings home the fact that these sickos are everywhere and like weeds they seem to flourish. Some days I feel like we're shovelling sand on the beach. I come in the next day and the tide has washed all yesterday's work away, so I start again. We can never stop, never give in though. Even when supposed health experts and academics are trying lull the public and the government into saying paedophilia is acceptable, or a mental illness, or a person's right to have that preference. Well, we have to keep fighting, we owe it to the children what about their rights." My frustration and passion was palpable, even though I was preaching to the choir.

Molly, just as tired and just as passionate about abuse joined in. "Yeah, did you see that stupid bitch in the news today saying there was no proof having sex with a child harmed that child. Well she should look at all the grown up victims who have mental issues, and half the violent prisoners in the system who were abused as children. Seriously, it's just total selfishness, the sickos right to satisfy their preferences, what about the children's right to being allowed to be a kid?"

Superintendent Fisher, who knew we had to let off some steam to stay sane held up both hands. "Guys, I completely agree, and we all know working in this cesspit we must occasionally sound like we do. However, let's re-focus, and in the only way we can celebrate this massive victory we've had this time. Hey, let's nail these prick's hides to the wall and get 'em for everything we possibly can.?"

He stood up to leave and then turned as an after thought.

"I'll need you to take turns, but when we pass all this to the Crown Prosecutor's I want you each take your normal RDOs plus an extra three days off. You guys are in need it and God knows you've earned it."

My blood was still boiling, but on the surface I looked calm. That was because I had made a decision I was thinking; *Thank you Boss. That's five days. I'm going to the Gold Coast for a break. You never know I might bump into a few of the Hunters if I'm lucky.*

A large evidence bag that had been brought lay on the desk in front of me. Through the thick plastic a Hunters Motorcycle Club colours could be see, a leather jacket with cut off sleeves the club emblem facing upwards. There was a patch sown on the left breast 'Sergeant at Arms'. I picked up the bag and read the label. There was a Search Warrant reference number, an address, a specific location, in this case it was the main bedroom wardrobe. The house of course was owned by one Robert Walsh who was currently in Remand along with his other Grub Club members. The famous Walter Scott quote 'Oh, what a wicked web we weave when we first we practice to deceive.' was weighing heavily on my conscience. A spirit stronger than my morals and beliefs overpowered everything

I valued. Revenge perhaps, Anger definitely, clothed in righteous justice. It was still wrong and every fibre of my being knew it. Looking around I shoved the evidence bag containing the leather vest in my work bag. I justified my stealing evidence by being confident that in no way my actions would affect the outcome of the charges brought against the ex-Bikie Robert Walsh. It was still just a justification. His criminal record showed clearly his past history as an outlaw Bikie, and he had mentioned it during the interviews. Understanding Bikie culture, I was amazed that he had been allowed to leave the club with his colours still in his possession. I wasn't sure how, but I figured having them with me might come in handy.

Looking over from her desk, Molly interrupted my thoughts.

"I must have done somethin wrong. Old Charlie boy wants to talk to me again. Margaret and I will go see him down at sunny Woodford Prison tomorrow. It's probably a waste of time and petrol but as you know mate, you just cant take that chance."

"Oh, that's a major bummer. you're right though and especially Charles, he gets off on being their leader but he may well have maintained that by being the one who has all the contacts. Feed his ego Molly and he'll sing like Toby Keith." I said encouragingly.

"That's the bad news Ben, for me and Margy anyway. The good news is for you. The Boss said for you to take that leave he was offering. We'll get our turn when you get back all bright eyed and bushy tailed after your break." Molly said smiling.

At the end of the day I knocked on Superintendent Fisher's door. "Well I'm off Boss, thanks again for the extra days, I'm sure they'll do me some good." I said knowing that what I was planning to do would do just that at least for a little while. Simultaneously I was feeling bad about deceiving my mentor and Boss.

The unmarked Police car slowed as they neared the sign reading Welcome to Woodford Prison. Parking in the bay marked Police Molly and Constable Worthington walked towards reception.

About halfway from the car Molly stopped the young Senior Constable.

"Marg, you'll be fine, but these places can be a bit daunting the first time, cold, dark and the inmates love nothing more than scaring a female visitor, or saying something crude. Just look straight ahead and keep moving. At Reception they handed in their weapons and phones. Once signed in the two Sunshine Coast cops were sent through a high security door into a long hallway. Here they were met by a P.O. who clearly took pride in his uniform and appearance. Unlike the majority of Prison officers they had seen as they walked into the prison his light blue shirt had creases so straight and crisp they made you want to pinch them. He had to be fifty something, his grey hair and crow's feet around the eyes betraying his age. This was in spite of him having a body twenty years younger, exercise was obviously a big part of his life.

Following the Prison Officer Molly elbowed Margaret and smiled as she quickly pointed at his muscled buttocks. Margaret Worthington blushed and gently punched her colleague's shoulder as she shook her head from side to side. Talking over his shoulder the guard addressed them. "Now Winchester isn't dangerous but still be a bit careful. It doesn't take long for some them to turn nasty once they realise they're not goin to see the outside for a long time. He's been well behaved so far. Molly didn't want to sound too macho, but wondered if this guy would have offered male coppers the same warning. "We put the sick prick in here, so he's more afraid of us than the other way around. We'll still watch him though."

The Prison Officer nodded, but knew when he'd been put in his place. "I put you in Interview Room four, I figured you might want to record the lies he's going tell ya." He laughed feeling he had regained the ground he had lost by the Detective's comments.

Once the P.O. had left the room Molly whispered.

"Nice butt still thinks women are the weaker sex obviously. I forgot to mention the POs love scaring female coppers as much as the prisoners." Molly said and they both had a laugh while they waited for Charles Winchester to be brought in.

The old man they brought in was like a shadow of the confident, even arrogant man that had always sat at the head of the Grub Club table. The man before them dressed in prison garb seemed older, his shoulders stooped and his gait wobbly and slow.

"Do you want him chained to the table love?" Asked Nice Butt with a smile.

"Firstly, it's Detective Herbert, and no leave him be please." Molly asserted.

"Suit ya self lo.., I mean Detective, I'll be just outside if you need me." The P.O. hissed through his teeth as he left the room.

"Mr Winchester how are you today?" Asked Molly brightly.

"Well how the fuck do you think I am?" His words were forceful but not his delivery, he sounded angry but defeated. They knew he only swore when he was trying to act tough, it hadn't worked back at the coffee shop, and it didn't fly this time either.

"Yeah, well jail will do that to you every time, I guess." Molly replied her comment dripping with sarcasm.

As arranged Margaret started the questioning. "Now Charlie." She had read in his file that the use of Charlie infuriated him. Their strategy was to anger him, to keep him on the back foot.

He interrupted her. "Please call me Charles, please the humiliation of me suffering this hell is bad enough without being demeaned further. You know they've taken my underwear, who knows why. These denim shorts rub me raw." He pleaded.

It took all of Molly's self control not to laugh or say something sarcastic. "OK Charles, I don't mean to rub salt into your wounds but you being here is no one else's fault but your own."

"Yes, yes, enough already. Don't you think that's why I asked for you to talk to me? Desperation in every word.

Pulling her note book across the scarred metal table, Molly opened it and asked.

"Ok, so what did you want to talk about Charles?" Margaret wanted to demonstrate interest to the prisoner and slid forward in anticipation on the chair because it was bolted to he floor.

"OK, I know something, something none of the other guys know. I need a deal, I can't survive long or do hard time. I'm not like these other cretins." Charles pleaded.

The two Police Officers looked at each other expectantly.

"Charles it's impossible for me to broker a worthwhile deal without knowing what your Intel is worth to us. We're interested but we need to know what's involved, alright?" She made it a question rather than a statement.

Sounding like his throat was too dry to talk. "Give me some time to think about that." He mumbled

Molly hated being in the same room with this sicko and wasn't enjoying being polite.

"Whatever Charlie. The road out to here is littered with dead animals that couldn't decide which way to jump."

Turning to Margaret Worthington Molly said.

"I think we've wasted our time Senior, let's head back up the coast."

Charlie made his decision. "Ok, Ok, I have two things, if I give you one and it plays out will you get someone to get involved who has the authority to make a deal?" Charles asked sounding a little stronger.

He continued without waiting for the Detective to reply.

"OK, well I know a bloke who lives just outside Warwick. This guy is officially a chicken farmer but he has another cash business that he works from home. He rents out his kids to locals and special tourists if you get my drift. He's been operating for well over a year as far as I know. Out on his own farm, no one notices the coming and goings, he's got it all organised like a friggin B&B."

Molly lead the questioning from there on. "So how do you know him Charlie?"

She questioned the imprisoned paedophile for the next hour. Molly was satisfied that she had enough details to get a Bench warrant raised. She nodded to Margaret who had been silently taking the notes since Charles had started talking about Warwick.

"OK, Charles we have enough Intel about Warwick. We will check it out and if you have been telling us the truth Senior Constable Worthington and I will be back. Stay out of trouble hey?"

With that, the two Police Officers turned their legs left and right on the secured chairs and stood up. Molly knocked on the door and Nice Butt opened it with a flourish.

"You can take him back now please." Asked Molly.

Detective Herbert and Senior Constable Worthington retraced their steps and found their own way back to Reception. The Prison Officer looked up from her desk and smiled."How d'ya go ladies, exciting visit?"

"Don't know yet, it might be, you know what they're like. They'd tell you anything to cut a bit of time off their sentence." Molly replied.

"That dinosaur with the parade ground shirts that brought you in said you wanted to record the interview. Here's the audio. He's alright, he's just been here too long, and fancies himself a bit because he's a gym junkie. You know low self esteem, compensated by muscles and an inflated ego with no cause." The female P.O. confided to the two Detectives.

"Yeah, thanks we noticed he was special. You gotta work with him. Good luck with that." Molly and Margaret laughed.

By the following afternoon, the Warwick Police Station had confirmed that there was indeed a family of that name at the address Winchester had supplied. They were slightly aware of the family and had visited the farm on two occasions chasing up truancy complaints from the children's school. On both visits promises were made that the kids would attend school, however they never fronted. Somehow, the school gave up and therefore the Police had no further cause to contact them. The local cops had heard the faintest of rumours of Paedophiles coming into town for some reason and were attempting to keep an eye on those individuals on the Child Protection Offender Register. However, if they weren't on parole people could come and go as they wanted with no obligation to report.

Superintendent Fisher was over the moon. "This Grub Club is great, it's the gift that keeps on giving hey?"

Nodding Molly replied."Yeah, I think you're right Boss. I wasn't real confident about Charlie's latest offering but it sounds good so far. How do we play it, let the locals have it all?"

Superintendent Barry Fisher ex Military, seen it all, hadn't slept as much as he needed and it was showing.

"That whole Warwick business." He paused straining to control his emotions. "You know just when I think I've seen every perversion, debauchery and depravity. I was so friggin close to launching across that table and throttling that sicko. When we were interviewing him here and he started in on that rationalising when Charles espoused; 'You see Superintendent I believe in Moral Relativism- What is true for you may not be true for me.' Dead set, he didn't know just how close his reality nearly ended there and then." Fisher said passionately. Then sadness flooded the hard man's face and eyes. He continued, emotion on every word. "How can a man, a father trade his own children for money. He's not a father. he's a fuckin animal, not even animals would do what he did."

Molly too, had seen so much that could never be unseen. She was revolted by the Intel harvested from Winchester. In hurt her on yet another level to see her Boss this way. In was a new thing, something that she wasn't confident about ever coming back from. Only time would tell. She knew that seeing some high ranking cops he had known and worked with being caught up in the Bishop's laptop arrests had shaken him to his core.

"Molly am I weak to think it's best for the Warwick boys take it all over?" Fisher asked, becoming quieter with each word he uttered.

Molly resisted a desire just to hug this bear of a man in front of her.

"Boss you ain't weak in any way. You know how it works, it doesn't matter how hot the water we all know that feeling. This shit just won't wash off. Sometimes no amount of JD can make you forget what we deal with every day. But, we keep doing it, because we have to."

Molly said holding back tears. Noticing her female co-worker's countenance, Margaret Worthington, new to the unit, stayed very, very quiet. Gently, she put a comforting arm around Molly's shoulders.

He rationalised out loud. "Sure, let Warwick handle it. Yeah, why not, it's another seventy odd Ks the other side of Warwick anyway, and we've got enough goin on. If this plays out how it's looking so far, you and I will need to go to Woodford Prison for another chat with our old mate Charlie. Then we might have even more to do."

Pushing down this pent up emotion Molly encouraged Fisher's decision.

"That all makes sense and we'd have to have the local yokels involved anyway. Let have a big win on their home turf."

"Yeah, if Warwick plays out, who knows what a grub like him might come up with? Have you spoken to the Crown Prosecutor about some sort of a deal?" She asked in as light a tone as she could muster.

Looking exhausted the older man replied. "Molly, not that I've done many, but these are tricky. We don't know what to offer because we don't know what we are getting. The other part is deep down I want to see these scum-bags go away for ever and a day, not discount his sentence. Another paedo off the map is good, but these filth don't deserve to escape a minute of their maximum jail time. You see what I mean. You know how this works. I have to sell the deal to the Crown Prosecutor who just wants headlines and stats." Superintendent Fisher explained, even though Molly already understood the intricacies of such a set up.

Earlier that day I had driven towards the Gold Coast, the M1 was pretty good after I had waited for the commuters to finish their journeys. I had a sort of plan. The sort that normally blew up in your face but you lost your balls. I remembered that there was a Council Quarry just north of Nerang so I set out for that. Being a Saturday I was hoping that the Council workers were all enjoying their weekend and it would be unattended. I hid my bike behind a couple of mounds of crushed granite and jumped the chain across the driveway. I was banking on a mobile security service visiting the site on a regular basis rather than a static sentry on site. I hopped the chain across the track in, thankfully there were no cars parked near the work sheds. So I figured my theory about security was sound. Anyway that was how I was going to play it.

I was wearing the Outlaw Motor Cycle Club colours, shades and long bill cap in case I was Monday morning movie star on any CCTV. I looked for the explosives warning signs on a shed and found what I was looking for. Thankfully, unlike the old days of Nitro and Dynamite the modern cheaper mining alternative, Ammonium Nitrate / Fuel Oil (ANFO) wasn't locked up as securely. It came in twenty Kilo bags that discouraged high tech secure storage. I grabbed two bags and some blasting caps. I would have like more but two twenty kilo bags on my bike were going to be enough trouble. I found some bush just near the industrial estate and hid the bags of explosives under some bushes.

I changed down my Harley Iron 883, and turned off the Gold Coast Highway heading for Nerang. The Hunters Motorcycle Club had their clubhouse there, they didn't know it but I was planning to visit with them with a surprise. Turning into Smith Crescent I kept on going with my revs low so as not to attract any attention as I passed the industrial shed that they had made home. There was a six foot high chain wire fence, but the double gates were wide open. Two or three of the outlaw Bikies were standing near the entrance to the shed. I roughly counted twenty-five or more Harleys and Indians parked outside. None of that 'Jap Crap' for these boys. It looked like there was a back fence into a junk yard so I headed over there figuring I'd wait until dark and come in that way. I parked outside and walked into the greasy wrecker's office. "Hey mate you got a passenger mirror for a 2010 Hilux?" I asked.

"Only about a thousand of em mate, you Ok to pull one off yourself it'll safe you ten bucks."

"Sounds like a plan, can I borrow some tools?" I asked.

As I walked around supposedly looking for a Hilux 4WD to take the mirror from I noted all the CCTVs. I circled the yard to the fence shared by the Hunters Clubhouse and worked out the entry point. Then I went back to the office.

"How d'ya go did you get one?" The greasy wrecker manager asked.

"I did and then I fuckin remembered I've left my wallet at home, dumb ass hey? I'll come back later." I answered.

The last part about me coming back later being the truth.

Being a man of my word I rode back three hours later when I was sure all the local businesses would be closed. I had an errand to do in preparation for my visit that evening. I stopped two doors down from the Hunters clubhouse and walked back. Using the fence to block their view of the road and therefore me I stopped at the corner of the Bikie's front fence. The twenty kilo bags were heavy as they slid from my shoulder onto the footpath. I didn't expect the club to post guards. Who would have the balls to burgle or attack an Outlaw Motorcycle Club? I still had to be careful so as not to be seen from some Bikie having a leak or quicky with his girlfriend on the front lawn. I looked around the now padlocked gate towards the shed where all the music was coming from. All clear. I stood on top of the green power box and dropped the bags over the fence into the dark corner between the two fences.

CHAPTER 21

It was dark and I was lucky the moon was just a slither. It shone on the iron corpses of cars who now reached for the sky like an altar to man's throwaway culture. I had removed the Sergeant at Arms patch from chest of the stolen colours vest, to become a little less identifiable. Now, although I gave the appearance of attempting to move stealthily through the wrecker's yard I was making sure every CCTV I had located earlier caught me at several places. I had a ski mask on and long bill baseball cap, so the leather vest was the only identifying feature. Playing the part, the camera would have seen me stop and turn to check my six, making sure the Hunters colours would star on the video when the cops investigated the scene. I reached the back fence and stood in the shadows between the rows of wrecks. Nearly three hours later, it was finally time.

I knew Saturday nights were usually party nights for Bikies and figured the majority of the guys would camp in the clubhouse until they sobered up the next day. When the music and laughter died down I used the bumper bars and roofs of three wrecks to get high enough to overlook the Clubhouse yard. Avoiding three loose strands of barb wire I climbed over the steel sheet fence and silently dropped into the concrete yard. By the high pitch screams and laughter I had heard the girlfriends and or hookers had stayed for the duration. I sincerely regretted that, but my plan hadn't allowed for visitors. I had no choice now. I was committed. I stuck to the shadows and worked my way to the front corner where I had dropped the bags of ANFO explosives and diesel.

I had just put my hand on it and a gravelly voice asked. "What ya doin mate, are you so pissed you can find the fuckin shed?"

My initial thought was; *How come this challenge is so friendly. Then I remembered I was in club colours and it pretty dark this side of the yard.*

Slurring my words I answered. "I mush be, I can't walk straight and I think I just pished my pants."

"Ya dumbass, hang on I'll come down and give you a hand." The unknown Bikie replied.

I kept my back turned to him as I swayed like I was drunk. The instant his hands touched my arms I pivoted and hit him as hard as I could between the eyes. He looked bewildered for a moment then his legs sagged and he fell into my arms. I always carry some zippy-ties just in case so I secured his wrists and ankles and shoved a rag into his mouth to keep him quiet. This was incredibly fortunate because I had thought about interrogating one of the Bikies but couldn't see a way to isolate one before I managed the rest of them.

This guy was an absolute gift. I put him in a Fireman's carry and headed back to the shadows where I had entered the Clubhouse yard. I only had a couple of questions to ask him so I figured with only two questions to ask I might just get away with torturing the answers out of him. I left him trussed up in the shadows and returned to the front fence. I grabbed the bags of explosives and set about rigging the clubhouse.

There were two doors to the Hunters Clubhouse, the front one a vehicle access roller door, the other a person door at the rear of the shed. I was only guessing but I figured most of the Bikies would be in the rear of the building. I believed that the front would be used more for recreation and accessing the BBQ on the front lawn, part of the front might also be for motorcycle repairs. Accordingly, I set the majority of the charges around the three sides at the back of the building and two across the front. The shed was steel framed cover by thin gauge steel sheeting. I was sure this would allow the full force of the explosions to enter the building and kill everyone inside. Once the charges were in place I returned to the rear of the yard and the Bikie waiting for me near the fence shared by the Wreckers.

He had re-gained consciousness and was writhing around attempting to free himself. I slapped him hard across his face and he immediately settled into glaring at me.

"Now mate I'm going to ask you a few questions. You will only answer the questions, nothing more. OK?"

Gag out.

"You're fuckin dead you dumb pri.."

Gag in. Slap, his nose bleeds.

"Now I explained the rules. The rules are very simple. I ask. You answer."

Gag out.

"If I don't my brothers will cut you bal..."

Gag in. Slap, back-hander nose bleeds more, lip is split.

"You have a disability, or you just grumpy? Now, let's try again. If you don't catch on soon, I'm going to have to take this to a whole new level. Got it?"

Gag out. Raised my fist as an encouragement.

"OK, what do ya want?"

"Now that's more like it. I know you guys are sellin kids. I want to know who's the buyer?"

"You're fuckin joking mate, I'm a dead man if I tell you."

Gag in. I withdrew my knife from the sheath strapped to my left wrist. It isn't a huge knife, but it the curve of its razor sharp blade speaks volumes.

"Like I said, I tell you anything like that and I'm dea..."

Gag in.

I slashed his chest leaving a six inch gash. He screamed into the gag.

Gag out.

"Oh man, that really sucks." He spat.

His hard eyes had lost all their aggro. He was close to cracking.

"I'll ask one more time. Who are you selling kids to?"

Another slash a little lower on his chest.

Gag out.

"OK, OK man, I'll tell ya. The Russians, OK the fuckin Russians."

Gag in.

"Nice work, now you keep sticking to the rules and I'll put the knife away."

He nodded furiously.

"What do you mean the Russian? Which Russian, I need a name."

Gag out.

"Not Russian you dumb shit. The Russians, as in the Russian Mafia."

Gag in.

I didn't see that coming.

"Ok, old mate were are nearly done. I need and address, where the kids are delivered, I need to know."

"OK, Burleigh Heads, there's an old Movie Theatre. They've set up a brothel, spa and bar all legal as a bank."

"Don't try and con me, I can find out their legit businesses on google. Where do the kids go?"

He'd had enough and figured I was probably going to kill him when I had run out of questions. He began to scream. I hit him hard on the right jaw bone and he stopped trying to alert his fellow Bikies.

Gag in.

I held up the knife again.

Gag out.

He looked scared.

"No, no. I'm being straight with you. If you know where to go, and can say the password there's a connecting door between the legal brothel and the back section of the next door Pizza Shop. That's where the sick fucks who like children go for fun."

I hoped that I'd got the right answers, I was pretty sure but you never know. I'd pushed my luck far enough and had a good run questioning the Bikie. It was time to go. Although he had provided the answers, that was way off cleaning his slate with me. He was still a club member, a part of selling innocent children to perverts. It was pretty callous. I dragged my new best friend closer to the back of the Clubhouse, but not so close that he could kick the walls and alert his brothers inside. His eyes widened when he saw the bag of of fertiliser not more than a mitre away from where he now lay. I set the timers for twenty minutes and climbed back into the Wreckers Yard. Retracing my steps this time nearly running to reinforce that I had done something bad and wanted to leave in a hurry. The cops would love it. Once out of the Wreckers I walked back to my bike and rode out of the industrial area. I found a good place off the road to park, and waited astride my bike.

Precisely twelve minutes later the timers I had set connected igniting the blasting caps in each location. Technically, the explosive charges of Ammonium Nitrate mixed with Diesel caused a high-velocity shock wave and a tremendous release of gas. The shock waves ripped and crushed the iron wall sheeting near the explosives driven by the rapidly expanding gases. The gases continue to fill and expand. In a normal mining application these gases are confined in a rock tube or crevice. The Bikie Clubhouse being much weaker than rock imploded. The full force of each directional charge converged inside the shed causing millions of shredded metal fragment travelling at hundreds of miles an hour to fill the entire Clubhouse. The Bikies and their female visitors near the walls were vaporised by the initial blast. Those further away were mauled by the molten shrapnel and extremely high temperatures, bleeding and melting the now lifeless forms slid to the concrete floor. Those few poor souls that were still alive were mercifully smothered by a cloud of toxic fumes manufactured when the combustibles combined with excess oxygen in the explosion.

I had considered staying near enough to see the destruction confirming how successful my bombs had been, but figured the risk far outweighed the rewards. I could read about it tomorrow. Looking back towards the industrial area I was rewarded with several huge bangs so close together they nearly sounded like one. The ground under my Harley shook and the sky was filled with birds. A plume of dirty black smoke ballooned in the air over the industrial estate I had just left. It was Sunday morning but the sun didn't know it yet. I was exhausted so I found a motel just over the New South Wales border so my presence wouldn't show up anywhere on the Gold Coast. I paid cash and used an alias to help that.

I was no expert on the Russian Mafia, but everyone knows the word Mafia means crims, soldiers and weapons and lots of them. And with the Russians having such a huge Army you knew that they had probably all been Military. Hard and experienced fighters. I gave it a lot of thought and came up with a workable solution. I only had today and tomorrow to get this done so it would take some luck. I was wondering if I had used my quota of that lady, it felt a bit like that. I slept for a few hours and then rode back to Burleigh Heads. I found a spot in a park across from the theatre and waited. I had decided I would settle for the big boss, the rest I would give to the police who would be able to arrest the Russians and hopefully some of their customers. The concern I had was after the bombing of the clubhouse that the Second in Charge thinking their enterprise was compromised or under attack. He may consider moving the operation overnight. The only way to overcome this would be to nearly have the Police execute their search warrants and make arrests while my shots were still echoing.

Of course was an impossibility attempting to orchestrate all these different groups to suit the opportunity I was now facing. The last thing I wanted was to place the arrests of the Russian crew and any customers in jeopardy. However, on consideration I decided that the likelihood of the decision to move the entire operation was very small. Hiding this evil paedophile brothel next to a legal 'ordinary' brothel had so many advantages. The customers were constantly being dropped off by taxi and arriving and going. The punter could walk in the front door and disappear, no one would realise they had actually gone next door to the paedophile brothel. Surely, the new leader would be loath to lose these advantages. No, I could eliminate the Mafia Boss and then pass the Intel on to the Police a few hours later, while the 2IC was re-organising his promotion. At least that's what I was hoping and praying for. Would God bless this? I doubted it.

I couldn't see a Russian Boss getting out of bed too early, his various Operations were twenty-four seven, so he could be up all night. I sat on the Burleigh theatre brothel from about dawn onward. I planned to wait for him to arrive, make the shot and be gone before the smoke from my rifle's muzzle was all blown away. At around midday I started to wonder about my plan. I could tell by their choice of wheels these comrades had obviously been watching the same movies as me. During the morning a few black SUVs rolled up carrying some muscle. There were boxes carried in and boxes carried out again. It was nearly four in the afternoon and except for wondering about what was in the boxes I had nothing going.

Apparently Russian Mafia Bosses didn't go for black SUVs. A white Ferrari 488 Spider pulled into a private parking spot, immediately two of the muscles flew out from the side door. One of them opened the door even where I was I could tell he was being extremely careful not to look at the incredibly beautiful blond who climbed from the low sports car. I couldn't hear of course.

"Yeah, Yuri you better be careful, I catch you looking up my skirt again I cut your balls off and feed them to my dog." The blonde said in Russian, she smiled but everyone nearby knew she wasn't joking.

"Sacha, I know you wouldn't look up my dress because you sick fuck, at a beautiful thirty-nine I am already thirty years too old for your tastes." She said with another venomous smile.

Sacha grimaced and took the yellow bag from the passenger seat and headed for the side door into the brothel. While Yuri with a sheepish look on his pale face followed his Boss Tiana Lebedev through the thick steel braced doorway.

Inside was ex KGB/FSV Viktor Morozov, he had transitioned into the criminal sector effortlessly. As he often joked, he was now doing the same work but getting paid about ten times as much, plus bonuses. After showing so much promise he was asked to support the Russian Mafia's push into the Gold Coast. Swapping the ice and snow of his homeland for the hot sand full of bikini clad women was an easy choice. Perhaps even more so now he was second in charge and had played a big role in taking over the bulk of the Gold Coast criminal enterprises. At first this was strongly and violently resisted by the incumbent criminals. However, being a gaggle of independent ma and pa operations they couldn't hold back the Russian tide that engulfed them. Morozov had lived up to the meaning of his name; Frost, and quickly gained a reputation for resolving conflict in a permanent manner. Soon those not chained on the bottom of the ocean off the Gold Coast beaches had moved to easier pickings further north. The Russians controlled the drugs, prostitution and illegal gambling businesses up and down the strip.

Having a woman as a Boss especially in this macho culture caused him grief at times, but she was bright and had connections all the way back to Moscow. She could be as ruthless as he had ever been, as long as he did the dirty work.

Tiana Lebedev was dressed in skin tight jeans tucked into red RM Williams Boots and a white Loewe Flower tee-shirt. When her 2IC Morozov walked into the room she smiled, this time it went all the way to her sparkling blue eyes."Dobryy den' Viktor, have you heard the news?"

"Good afternoon to you Tiana, remember no Russian, I'm trying to practice my English. Yes, I did hear the news, any ideas on who has killed all our Hunter friends? Like always, we should ask ourselves who would this benefit? No one comes to mind as this time." Morozov asked seriously.

Smiling again she replied. "Sorry mate." Her attempt at an Australian accent sounded terrible. "It's 'nekhorosho', not good. The cops on our payroll haven't got a clue. There's a bit of a rumour that it was one of their own, that seems a bit strange to me."

"Why would a fellow Bikie kill them all? I suppose from a rival gang maybe? Who would have that level of skill in their mob? That bombing was done by someone trained and highly committed. I've been thinking about what it means to us and as you say 'nekhorosho' allfuckin right, not good at all. Where are we going to get kids now, that was a good system we had developed now it's gone." He was pragmatic if nothing else.

"Nearly as importantly, it took all that time to trust them to courier our drugs from the wharves to Brisbane, here and Sydney. All that work, now wasted, gone up in smoke hey? Have you got any ideas about who can replace them?"

They discussed the new challenges and possible solutions for the next hour or so until they had nothing new to say.

The Mafia Boss had already spent longer in this luxurious cesspit than she usually allowed.

"Viktor, there's no reason to think the attack on the Hunters has any link to us, but..."

Viktor Morozov interrupted. "But, you can never be too careful. Tiana, I've already doubled security at all our places. Hopefully, you won't notice it but I've also beefed up your bodyguard. Just for a few weeks or so, until we know what's going on."

Tiana knew her job was so much easier because this tough enforcer had her back. He was different as ice cold as his frosty name but more intelligent than many in higher positions. Little wonder the KGB and then the new FSV didn't want him he would have scared most of them and made the rest feel insecure.

"Vik, thank you for looking after things so well and for making sure I'm safe."

"My pleasure and my job Boss." He replied.

"Paka Paka moya lyubov'. Ah! I am so sorry Vik, in English. Bye Bye my love, is that better Viktor?"

Smiling her 2 IC laughed at her teasing. "Da, Da moya koroleva."

"I'll give you; my queen bullshit smart arse." She replied with a laugh.

With that she spun and exited the office. As soon as she entered the outer room Yuri and Feodore became alert like a pair of gun dogs when their master picks up his gun. Yuri was holding Tiana's yellow bag got the door, Feodore was carrying a box of her favourite Vodka for home.

Even though I had ridden my Harley, the 308 Remington Rifle was a take down, disassembling to a size that fitted neatly into one of my bike's panniers. Under the branches of the eighty- year-old Burleigh Heads avenue of Norfolk Pines I had climbed onto the roof of the public toilets. Due to the darkness caused by the pine's shade and the fact I was off the ground I was invisible. I was alert, but lying there my mind was racing around a random track. A female Mafia Boss was a massive surprise especially a Russian one, however everything I had seen made me sure that the attractive blond I had seen was exactly that. Her aura of authority, the way people jumped in her presence supported my supposition.

Wet and dirty, holding my rifle lightly my mind drifted to my childhood. The only time I was close to happy was when dad took me hunting, he seemed to change into a great father as our house filled the rear vision mirror on our way out of town. The other reason I loved going hunting was I could kill stuff. At that age my insight was negligible but I was aware the constant red cloud of anger was replaced by a cold calmness. Stalking and killing was the only thing that had this affect. Unlike the movies a sniper's life isn't shot after shot. It's mostly lying in cold, wet and dirty holes, or scalding hot and dry ones waiting with the hope of getting an opportunity for that one clean shot. This was my lot. After years of rain, falling leaves became rotting vegetable material that had built up where I was lying. My front was saturated by the stinking ooze sitting on top of the cold concrete roof.

I was focused on the alley where I'd seen the blond disappear, at this stage there had been nothing except a scantily clad girl standing in the sun for a few minutes holding out her fingers to dry her nails. I nearly missed it because as the red head went back inside the door stayed open and out came my one of the muscles that had been with my target when she arrived. He was carrying that big yellow bag again. Rule 1, broken; Bodyguards are not baggage handlers. Carrying her bags slowed a man's ability to draw a weapon down by a second or two. However, it wasn't going to make any difference this time. By the time he had walked around the Ferrari, the Mafia Boss had exited the building and was waiting for the second bodyguard to open the sports car's door.

He too was carrying something. Through the hi-def telescopic sight I could see it was a box of Baccarat Beluga, Russia's best Vodka. I could also see his slow mind trying to decide which to do first. Open the door for his Principal or put the box in the trunk. Through the Bushnell TAC 4.5 – 30×50 Mil Dot Rifle Scope I saw her say something and the guy carrying the box flinched. Being a Ferrari he then walked to the front to put the box of Vodka in the trunk.

Sighting through the scope the Mil Dot settled on her left ear as she waited stamping her expensive Western Boot in impatience. I took up the first amount of pressure on the trigger, breathed in, allowed some to escape and held. Taking up the rest of the trigger I gently squeezed sending the one-hundred and eighty grain projectile on it's perfect flight. A fraction of a second later after it had travelled its two hundred and seven metres. Instantaneously, Tiana Lebedev's brain matter was liquidised, expanded and then pushed by the mushrooming bullet until the mess flew through the huge exit wound on the far side of her skull. A lot of it hit the open trunk saving the bodyguard from a bloody shower.

Each of the bodyguards drew their MP-443 Grach 'Pistolet Yarygina' the handgun favoured by the Russian Military. They had heard the shot but weren't in positions to locate the shooter by the sound as reverberated off the brick wall and steel fence either side of the sports car. Even though their reason to exist now lay twisted and sprawled over her beloved Ferrari as Bodyguards the two men needed to do something. They took up the classic pistol shooting stance, glaring impotently as they traversed around, scanning for an enemy to shoot. I quickly dismantled my rifle and dropped unseen to the ground. Being careful not to suggest any concern I slowly walked toward the Surf life Saving Clubhouse. I entered the change rooms and seconds later with my smelly cam overalls in a beach bag walked out into the sunlight dressed in a Hawaiian shirt over a pair of brightly striped boardies. Within two steps I looked like twenty other guys going to or leaving the beach. Just like many of the beach goers I was carrying a floral cotton bag in the other hand a longer thin brown case, perhaps a small shade.

CHAPTER 22

Molly, this time accompanied by Superintendent Fisher was back at Woodford Prison. As they walked to Reception Superintendent Fisher said to Molly.

"Now I think we are OK, but as Churchill said; 'However beautiful the strategy, you should occasionally look for results.' So we will proceed as planned, but Mol keep up if I have to change tack."

After the usual hand over of weapons and signing in they were awaiting a Prison Officer to take them to an interview room. The security doors swung toward them and there was Nice Butt in his parade ground immaculate uniform.

"Good morning Mam, good morning Sir. Please follow me." He said as he pivoted and lead them down the hall.

Molly thought; *Friggin annoying, what a change butter wouldn't melt in his smirking mouth now I have a male Detective with me. All crisp, nice butt still but no balls.* Then she was angry at herself for letting someone like him get under her skin. Then she thought; *I suppose I'm just as bad leering at his tight shorts and naming him Nice Butt.*

His voice interrupted her thoughts.

"Now I've put you in Four again so you can get a recording like last time. You make yourselves comfortable and I'll go and get Charles Winchester the Third hey? He said with a laugh, and walked away whistling the theme song from MASH.

"He's sharp for a PO." Fisher said to Molly who grimaced at her Boss's assessment of Nice Butt.

On the drive down to Woodford they had decided that the key to Charles was always going to be his ego followed now by survival. To feed this arrogance, as the Senior Officer the Superintendent would do most of the talking. He had the authority to make statements that while not binding were at least possible regarding sentence reductions, or improved conditions.

Molly had to place her hand over her mouth to stifle her shock at the state of the man who came into the room and sat at the scratched steel table. Winchester looked even older than he had at the last visit. His nose meandered across his face in at least two different directions and was a vivid dark purple like a plum or a grape. His left eye was closed and swollen, his right eye while open was bloody inside and had a crescent cut on the eyebrow with two butterfly bandages holding it together.

Looking at the Prison Officer Superintendent Fisher demanded.

"What on earth has happened to this prisoner?"

"Well Sir, Mr Winchester here until very recently at least, didn't understand that he wasn't in charge any longer. In here if you through your weight around, well you have to be able to back it up. As you can see Mr Winchester here couldn't and didn't. I think he'll be fine now though."

Fisher was hiding the fact that deep down he couldn't care less that this paedophile had copped a hiding, both the Police Officers believed that he deserved that and more.

"Alright, uncuff him, you can leave us now thank you."

The Superintendent said still acting outraged by Winchester's treatment. He waited until the PO had shut the door behind him.

"Charles, can I call you Charles?" He waited for permission, a massive strategy giving a prisoner that power when they really had none in the jail environment.

"Yes, you can." Winchester replied as though that really was the least of his concerns.

"Thank you Charles I am Superintendent Barry Fisher, we haven't met before because I am in charge of the Section that Detective Herbert works within."

He let this assertion of authority sink in for a minute and then continued.

"Now Charles looking at your appearance, I would think resolving the length and style of your stay in prison may be even more critical than when Molly spoke to you last time." Once again he waited for Charles to understand what was just said.

Molly nodding slid forward on the cold metal chair.

"Now Charles, when Constable Worthington and I were here last time you mentioned that you knew important things that no one else could tell us. The Intel about Warwick proved to be sound and so as I promised I've brought my Boss along to talk to you. He can weigh up the new information and maybe help you with sentencing time and also which prison you go to. We all know some are easier than others, don't we?" Molly asked encouragingly.

Turning on an angle a little so he faced more towards Fisher, and with an edge of desperation in his shaky voice he responded.

"Yes, yes, that's what I need, less time and a safe place. Now what I know has to be of value to your mob, what can you offer me?" The prisoner asked turning his one blood shot eye further in Fisher's direction. It was clear that he had dismissed Molly in his mind and was only interested in the Superintendent, the man who could fix things.

He continued in a rambling sort of vague manner.

"Before we get onto that, what happened at Nerang Saturday night? Going on not waiting or needing an answer. "Someone took out the entire Hunters Motorcycle Club, the body toll is rising by the minute. Who would do that, who could do that?" He asked rhetorically.

The Superintendent choked his first response, that it was none of Charles' business and stroked his now fragile ego.

"You can be sure there's a truck load of Gold Coast and Brisbane coppers asking those same questions all over town. Now Charles, we know Scientia Potestas is even more true in here. We're not here to empower you by giving you outside information. If you want a deal it's the other way around OK?" Fisher used the Latin knowing it would stroke his ego believing he was better educated than most of the inmates here at Woodford.

"Superintendent you are right, Scientia Potestas, Knowledge is Power and not just here but in my experience everywhere." Winchester couldn't resist demonstrating his understanding of the term by interpreting out loud. However, it really had the opposite affect. Fisher was enjoying this. Both Detectives although still highly interested feigned the beginnings of boredom or frustration.

Winchester was enjoying this interaction on multiple levels, however reading their body language he began to panic a little that he was in danger of jeopardising his goal here. He re-focused.

Trying to sound confident and stronger he sat straight up in his chair.

"Alright Superintendent, now what I am about to tell you I can back up with addresses, emails and phone numbers OK? The destruction of the Bikies is interesting for another reason. The thing is it's like a chain with all these different links. We were a link, then the Hunters MC another."

Superintendent Fisher needed to move this along, the danger of playing to a crims ego was always that they loved the sound of their own voice commanding attention they strung it out into a mini-series. "We know that Winchester, we need new Intel." Fisher stated strongly.

"OK, OK, I'm getting there. I was explaining the chain to you. The link after the Bikies is Russian Gold, as in the Russian Mafia on the Gold Coast." The battered prisoner claimed.

Molly and Fisher were stunned, neither showed it but that Intel hit both of them between the eyes like a huge wet fish. They had pushed, cajoled and threatened every member of the Grub Club, wanting to know where the children went after being delivered to the Bikies. Not one of them buckled, and the Detectives were beginning to think that maybe they didn't know. Well except for their intrepid leader currently sitting before them. Controlling any sign of excitement the Superintendent looked up a lack of interest clear on his face.

"Come on Charles this isn't some Jason Statham movie, you think we are stupid or something?"

Charles bit down on the obvious sarcastic answer to that question.

"No not at all, it's the absolute truth, and I've got more."

"OK, for now we believe you, the Russian Mafia are involved in this supply 'chain'. Tell me more."

"Well, probably with some help from Queensland's finest they have taken over the Gold Coast. Not just the businesses in the shadows but plenty of the legal stuff too. Most of the legal brothels are licensed to 'comrades' who are clean as the driven Siberian snow. That's worth a look but what I've got for you is even more interesting to you mob in Child Protection. The Ruskies operate a paedophile brothel, that's where the kids were headed." Even though the two Detectives had their poker faces on Charles didn't miss the furtive look that passed between them as he dropped that last bombshell. He had been careful to keep the location of the kid's brothel back until they made their offer.

Fisher controlling his voice to sound a hell of a lot calmer than he felt responded.

"Charles, I just thought of something I need to discuss with my colleague, just sit tight for a minute will you?" The two detectives stood up, Fisher being taller struggling to free himself from the steel table and chair both bolted to the concrete floor. They calmly left the interview room, closing the door behind them.

Nice Butt was standing a little down the hall reading his phone, ready to take the prisoner back to his cell. Molly and Fisher took a few steps up the hall away from the Prison Officer.

"Shit Boss, I had no idea, and it sounds like there's more to come. We'll be putting this scum-bag on a Princess Cruise at this rate. She laughed but nervously.

"Yeah, not quite but I hear ya. You know what really yanked my chain in there was what happened Sunday afternoon. There's gotta be a connection there. The media didn't quite call it Russian Mafia but the hint was there. Some one blew the head of that pretty Russian doll at Burleigh Heads, and talk around HQ is that she was the Boss." Superintendent Fisher stated.

Molly nodded and turned with her back to the P.O. when she realised he was trying to listen to their discussion.

"And I'm sure you see the different angle on that hit. Was it a Bikie hit, revenge for the bombing? Was it a rival hit from some Aussie crim who doesn't like Borscht taking over their business. And my least favourite option, was it this vigilante again whose been killing paedophiles all over Australia but especially Queensland? The timing is all a bit too coincidental for it not to be related in some way."

Shaking his head. "We're not going to answer that question here at the moment, let's get back in there."

Fisher headed towards the interview room, as he placed his huge hand on the door handle he said.

"Molly this is getting bigger by the minute just play along with whatever way it goes."

"Charles, we are interested in hearing more about the Russian connection." The Superintendent enquired.

The attention had given a new lease of arrogance.

"Well I've shown you mine, pardon the crudeness Mam, but I'm in jail, and its pretty big. I think it's your turn to show me yours now." Charles said with a satisfied look on his battered face.

"Now Charles I want to make this very clear. This is not a friggin auction. I will say what I think and you know that's what I can and am offering."

"Alright get on with it, but have this in mind, I still have another card up my sleeve and the quality of the deal you offer may or may not encourage me to part with that Intel. I can't miss this boat, you understand that Superintendent?" He said fear making him bold.

"Sure, I'm putting three years off your sentence on the table, plus Palen Creek Prison Farm, like a country B&B. OK?" Fisher stated firmly.

Charles new that was a good offer and that he wasn't really in a terrific bargaining position. He also knew that the cops working with what he had given them would have eventually stumble on the Russian paedophile brothel without his tip. Arrogantly he thought; *Yeah, even a broken clock gets it right twice a day.* He may as well tell them the location to demonstrate he was willing to cooperate even more.

"That sounds good, for another year I'll tell you where the kiddie brothel is."

Fisher interrupted hard. "Charles I told you this wasn't an auction or a fish market. The deal I've offered is today only based on you telling us everything you know about the kid's brothel. Unless you think you'll be OK in General Population at Sir David Longlands.

I hear there are few of the boys who welcome paedos at SDL if you know what I mean." Molly said with the lightest brush of menace.

"OK, it was worth a try one less day is worth a go in here. OK, facing the legal straight brothel, if there is such a thing as straight these days. Anyway the kid's brothel is on the left behind the Pizza Shop next door. One entry no other exits but through the main brothel and then through a connecting door." He said like it hurt.

Waving his hands around to encompass his surroundings. "I'm sorry Superintendent, in here trust is a non-existent commodity. What guarantees do I have you'll keep your word and not get back to your safe warm office and forget about me?"

In a tone a school teacher might use on a wayward student Superintendent Fisher replied. "Charles, don't be sorry. However, you have me confused with a Used Car Dealer there are no guarantees Charlie boy. You're in here because you did a lot of things that hurt a lot of children. That doesn't buy you any guarantees. You have my word, take it or leave it and if the Intel you gave us doesn't check out my recommendations to Crown Prosecution will be the maximum sentence possible."

Charles appeared as though the Superintendent had physically hit him several times, he realised that he had overstepped his mark.

"Sorry, I might deserve to be here but that doesn't make it any more tolerable does it."

Friendly again now. "Alright, I understand from your point of view. Thanks Charles, once we have checked out that Intel the Crown Prosecutor will put the deal in writing and you will await trial knowing that sentencing will include the discount plus you get to become a farmer." The Superintendent stated in conclusion.

As they drove out of the prison car park Molly clicked in her seat belt. "Sir, I hope that's the end of that. I hate prisons, and I get to leave. It'd do my head in locked away like that."

"Yeah Molly different parts of it get to you but I'm the same helps us stay honest hey? He laughed.

"Sorry to tell you but you will be coming back here sooner rather than later. He still knows things that we need to get hold of. I don't have a clue what it is but he's holding back some more bargaining chips. My bet is we will here from him in the next few days."

Changing the subject Molly enquired. "How we handling that paedophile brothel, same as Warwick, let the locals get all the glory?" She said smiling because glory wasn't what drove her dedication.

"I think so, they've been waiting for this for years, I know talking to my counter-part down there he can feel it, he knows something is going on and his team have been so close a few times but he just can't grab them. He's pretty sure some of the Uniforms and Detectives are on the take. The crims spread around enough to let a little fish get caught while the whales and sharks swim with impunity. The Superintendent said sadly.

"What about that hit, have you given it any more thought?" She asked taking a Mars Bar from her purse and offering half to her Boss.

Declining the chocolate. "I have and I'm convinced that the timing is too perfect. The Hunters Clubhouse is bombed and literally hours later the Mafia Boss of the crew working with the same outlaw Bikies has her head blown off. Nah, too much of a coincidence. You were the first to use the word vigilante and I hate the thought of it. I think you right though, we've been even busier than usual and murder is a Homicide case of course."

Pausing as he chose his words Fisher continued.

"That scum-bag who was getting early release shot from a distance like the Burleigh Heads shooting. Then the Homicide boys looking into the wheelchair death, surprise, surprise he's a paedo as well, but they couldn't be sure it was murder. Well, I think I am."

Molly was thinking about all these seemingly unrelated events that all of a sudden seemed so connected.

"Ok, we'll go with that, so Boss is there just one murderer or a group? I mean that hit on the Bishop in Brisbane, was that our guy too?" She asked.

"All I know Molly is he was killed and then his laptop appears miraculously on the steps of Roma Street HQ and all hell brakes loose. Don't get me wrong, the worlds a better place without these paedophiles. The fact that whoever this vigilante is he hands in the Intel he gathers is an absolute bonus. In a way this guy or girl, I guess it could be a girl, is a friggin Superhero. But the law is the law and we can't have some zealot catching, judging and executing these paedophiles even if they deserve it." The Superintendent stated as they arrived at their offices on the Sunshine Coast.

Wearily made their way inside and signed the log they overheard the desk Sergeant talking to a young copper.

"Sergeant I swear, that's the absolute truth. That new Detective catches this young fella climbing out of the window dead to rights. So he hauls in old mate and he calls me in to witness the questioning in Room 3. It goes like this." The young Officer can hardly talk because he is laughing so much.

Detective. "So Mr Brasch did you see anything unusual?

Mr. Brasch. "Yeah, once I saw a dolphin wearing a hat."

Detective. "No I meant around here."

Mr Brasch. Not a smile or a smirk says. "Well no they live in the ocean."

Everyone within earshot exploded into laughter, the young copper tears rolling down his cheeks.

Not waiting for the end of the story but still laughing, the Superintendent and Molly headed for the lifts only to be met by an excited Margaret Worthington.

"Sir, Molly, I'm so glad you two are back incredible things are happening on the gold Coast. I can't be sure but I'm wondering if it has anything to do with our Grub Club."

"What's happened Margaret?" Molly asked

"Well you knew about the shooting at Burleigh Heads Sunday arvo. Anyway, there's been a massive raid on a brothel where the hit took place. Beside the legal brothel they found a brothel full of kids. A paedophile brothel behind a Pizza Shop. You just missed the press conference on TV. Their Superintendent said they had received an anonymous tip sometime Sunday night. They executed the search warrants while you guys were on your way out at Woodford. They rescued fourteen boys and girls ranging from four-years-old up to a thirteen year-old girl. It was horrible, but wonderful at the same time."

Molly and the Superintendent looked at each other dazed.

"If that doesn't confirm my theory about this vigilante nothing will." Claimed Fisher to the two women.

"I'll fill you in later Margaret." Molly said to the bewildered Senior Constable.

I made good time back to the Sunshine Coast. Once I got home I thoroughly cleaned my the Remington, although ballistics may be able to match the projectile to my rifle, it was still good practice not to have a recently fired rifle in your possession. Two quick JDs and I crashed on the sofa exhausted, it had been a huge weekend. I slept soundly all night perhaps my nightmares satiated by the destruction I had wrought on the Bikies and the Mafia. Having finished my leave I returned to work the next morning to find Molly and Margaret had gone on leave. I was wondering about some sort of handover when my office phone chirped.

"Hey Ben, Jack Nolan I was wondering if you had a few minutes for a quick catch up some time this morning?" The Homicide Detective asked cordially.

"Sure I'm home alone here mate, if anything happens or even the phone I'll have to grab it if that's OK?" I asked hoping to put him off. A small part of me not really wanting to spend time with the man investigating one of my executions.

"Know how it goes mate, maybe just after ten sound OK?"

"See you then." I hung up and wondered why he really want to see me. I was fairly sure I hadn't left any tracks when the paedo's wheelchair had gone amphibious. But you just never knew. A lot of our cases were broken by the smallest thing, a great example was our curious waiter in a coffee shop.

Jack Nolan arrived carting a dozen hot doughnuts. "If we were Yankee Detectives these would be a bit of a cliché, but I just love them." Said the fit looking Homicide Detective, who didn't look like he ate them too often. I thought; *Seriously, bringing food to make me relax...... Don't be stupid, I'm being paranoid.*

"Yeah, same here, I'll get us a coffee, how do you like it?" I said and headed for the kitchenette.

As I passed the Boss's office. "Ben, I was just going to come and see you, you gotta minute?" Superintendent Fisher asked.

"Jack Nolan just arrived Boss, I'll come see you when he goes, if that's alright with you? Shouldn't be too long. Hey, you want a hot doughnut, Jack brought them and I'm sure he wouldn't mind sharing."

I heard the Boss's chair scrape on the vinyl floor and smiling he came out of his cave like a grizzly smelling food. "That sounds good."

After grabbing a couple of doughnuts he disappeared leaving me alone with Jack. I noted he was alone, and it encouraged me. If he had anything on me about the murder his partner would have been there as well.

"OK what can I do for you?" I asked in as relaxed tone as I could muster.

"I wanted to let you know the outcome about that waiter's murder and connecting Charles Winchester to it. We visited him out at Woodford, the P.O. said he may as well leave him in the interview room he has so many coppers visiting these days." We both laughed and he grabbed another doughnut.

"Yeah, I had some time off but I think we have been out there two or three times." I added.

"Anyway, we approached it like Damien Edwards was the devil incarnate and Charlie fell for it and joined in speaking ill of his dead colleague. Only thing was he said so much that it demonstrated that he had for-knowledge of the murder. Now even though you have told his he was a sort of a leader of that group we didn't get the feeling he had initiated the idea of getting rid of young Stan Croft. He was trying hard to align with us against Damien Edwards by blackening his character as much as he could. We still think Damo who was obviously the aggro one in the sicko club came up with the idea. Our supposition is that Charles went along with it to gain a bit of kudos with the strong member of his group. We also reckon he realised that he couldn't stop Damo anyway so he re-gained some esteem by making out he was in the midst of it." The Detective paused as though he needed sustenance to continue and jammed a whole doughnut in his mouth. The bottom line is if he'd wanted to Winchester could have stopped Edwards killing the boy by coming to us. I realise that was impossible but that provides our foundation against him."

As he mangled the last cake with cinnamon sugar spraying everywhere he continued. "Anyway, we are about to charge him with Conspiracy to Commit Murder, it's with the Crown Prosecutor as we speak." He said brushing the crumbs off his lap.

"That's great work, with our assessment of Charles the individual and his roll in the group I think you are spot on. We think he may come over like somebodies Grandpa or Professor but he is dead set evil. Cold as ice and totally self centred without an atom of empathy for these kids they have harmed so badly." I said, aware that my passionate hatred for paedophiles had shone through a little. I hoped that the Homicide Detective would just think of me being in the right job and not anything to do with the vigilante currently stalking paedophiles in our State.

"Man, you really hate them don't you? I suppose it's only natural because of your victim group, what you see. In my work I sometimes charge people I feel sorry for because I understand why they killed someone. Not the stone cold killers or of course the pros but the spur of the moments, the bar fights and so on, they've killed but their not killers.

"Yeah, I see what you mean, nah, with us these are scum-bags that have chosen the road and deserve the end they end up with. I thought; *Shut up, is he doing this on purpose, just shut up and let him leave.*

"Mate, I better go the Boss wanted to see me just as you arrived. Thanks for the update and the doughnuts. We'll have lunch when the girls get back from leave, yeah?"

"Sounds good Ben. Keep in touch." And he was gone.

I felt mentally and emotionally wrung out, most of all guilty. He was a good Detective and bloke. I hated being on the wrong side of all this.

CHAPTER 23

I made another coffee, and was walking back to my office thinking about my meeting with the friendly Homicide Detective. *I was annoyed with myself at being so stupid as to express my hatred of paedophile when he may have been in my office to confirm just that. Was he driving back to his HQ wondering if I hated them enough to be killing them on a regular basis? I knew he was smart, willing to push and prepared to look for solutions in other locations even when others accept the evidence that was easier to collect, and before them. Countless times before I had put subtle pressure on a suspect to see how they reacted or to see what they would do after I left them. Had Jack Nolan just done that to me? Did he suspect me, and if so, why? Maybe I'm being stupid and he was just there out of professional courtesy because we had given him the tip on the coffee shop murder.*

"Ben has the doughnut king left? If you're OK, come in and sit down will you?"

Carrying my coffee mug I sat down opposite the Boss and willed myself to concentrate on what he was saying rather than continuing to worry about the Homicide Detective's visit.

"Sorry Boss I was getting my head straight after being away." I said honestly.

"You had a chance to catch up on what's been going on at the Gold Coast?" Superintendent Fisher enquired.

"Only what I saw on the news, obviously my ears pricked up when they named the Bikie

Clubhouse as the Hunters. At first they were reporting it as some sort of gas explosion, like an accident. Then they changed it to a bombing, I mean it's Nerang Gold Coast not Belfast during the troubles. Were there any survivors? The Channel 9 vision looked like a war zone."

"Mate, this does not leave this room, OK?"

"Of course Boss, what is it?"

"Yes, there was a survivor. As best as they can work out there was this Bikie in the back yard. Don't know why. Theory is he went out for a leak, or something anyway lucky prick the blast catapults him away from the shed, that means the shrapnel. He got hit by the heat of course but the power pushed him rather than peppered him with steel like his mates inside. Sure he smelt like a BBQ when they found him but he's alive. Alive but in a coma at the ICU Gold Coast Hospital."

I was thinking to myself; *that small distance between his trussed up body and the shed wall made all the difference. As the Boss had said it blew him out of the kill zone. What did that mean to me. Could he do a Comfit picture of me? Doubtful considering my clothing and how dark it had been.*

"Wow, he's lucky that's for sure." Only I knew just how incredibly lucky. It was worth a try to misdirect the enquiry, after all I had worn the Club Colours for that precise reason.

"Boss, I'm sure smarter coppers than me are on this, but is there any chance that he's the bomber and that's why he was outside? I asked sounding as innocent as possible.

The Boss smiled.

"That's a great thought Ben, they're probably on it as we speak. Anyway, onto our piece of the pie hey? Someone gave Gold Coast Child Protection a tip off about a paedophile brothel at Burleigh Heads, run by the Russian Mafia no less. Molly and I had just returned from talking with Charlie Winchester out at Woodford Holiday Resort. He had just told us about the very same Burleigh Heads brothel, and we were looking forward to letting the Gold Coast boys know. Turns out they didn't need us, the Gold Coast Child Protection already knew from a tip off and had raided the Russians while we were still visiting the prison."

"Incredible Sir, the connection between our group of paedos here on the Sunshine Coast, the Hunters Motorcycle Club in Nerang and now the Russian Mafia at Burleigh. It's like a hydra, it's got so many heads." I said because for me not to show surprise followed by a deduction such as I had just stated would have been suspect.

"You're right, and these are strong connections too. Even though we weren't needed to pass on the Intel we got from Winchester, it was still sound. For an ego-tripper he definitely knows stuff." Superintendent Fisher paused to take a sip of what by now must have freezing coffee.

"Anyway, that didn't really matter, we had decided to flick pass the Intel to them with no more involvement on our part. The main thing is it proved Charlie Winchester knows things that other people don't. He phoned me this morning claiming he has more." The anticipation and excitement was sizzling in his tone. How do you feel about sunny Woodford?"

As we parked in the secure parking area of Woodford Prison Superintendent Fisher turned to me and said. "OK, Ben you concentrate on reading him, ask questions when you think he's lying or when he's holding back on me. After the Boss mentioned Winchester's request for a visit I wanted us to rush out here before Homicide charged him. He might not be too happy or cooperative once he knows he's probably never going to see the outside world again. Between our charges and the conspiracy to commit and his age if he ever makes it out he'll be a very old man. So a couple more years discount off his sentence won't mean much all of a sudden. He could well clam up."

"Yeah, you're right, I'm glad Jack from Homicide gave us a heads up." I added.

Fisher nodded. "Charles knows how it works. It's me he has to sell this to, only then can I take it higher and get him some form of dispensation. So far his Intel has been gold, let's see what treasure he has for us today, hey?" Superintendent Fisher asked more rhetorically.

I grunted in agreement to our mutual hope that what he had summoned us for would be valuable. We went through the entry security process and were sitting waiting for Winchester to be brought into the interview room.

The hard metal chairs and the cold scarred walls made us both uncomfortable, but it made for a fertile environment to question a prisoner.

A tough looking female Prison Officer followed Winchester in and lightly touched his shoulder to sit him opposite us. Without a word she nodded and left the room and closing the door as she went.

"Ah, a new face I see." Winchester said looking at me."

"Yes, Charles this is Detective-Sergeant McQueen, I forgot that you two have never met." Superintendent Fisher said, the reciprocal introduction unnecessary. I was surprised by the man before me he only slightly resembled the Charles Winchester that I had seen on the coffee shop videos. This version was dishevelled, his face wore recent scars and his hair seemed a lot greyer, his shoulders stooped and he was studiously avoiding eye contact.

"Well Charles what new revelation have you got for us today?" Asked Fisher sincerely.

"Superintendent I still know things here in Queensland, but this is big, this is overseas info. I mean some bloke up at Warwick, yeah that was interesting but this. Well this is big." Winchester said sounding very like a salesman desperate to make his monthly target. Gently Fisher encouraged him to continue. I appreciated my Boss's willingness to accommodate Winchester's needs and ego. Many Detectives I had known over the years were one trick ponies, just bullies so that was their only club in the bag. I'm the big cop with all the power you better tell me what I want to hear. To be fair that works on some. However, it would have closed this guy up tighter than a fish's arse. Different horses for different courses as they say.

"OK Charles, you have our attention, what have you got?"

"I remember that female Detective questioning me about all of us going to Thailand?" He asked.

The Boss looked a bit vague because it was a minor enquiry, any the Superintendent wasn't involved at that level. The question had risen from the mountain of audio and video evidence collected at the coffee shop in any case.

Knowing we didn't want to discourage Winchester from continuing, and he may have been offended to know the Superintendent had studies every word he had uttered. I jumped in "Sure we do Mr Winchester go on." I could see my use of Mr made his shoulders straighten a little. The Boss looked relieved at my knowing what the prisoner was talking about.

"Ok, well we are in here so it won't hurt to tell you this. We were booked on a sex tour, a special one to accommodate our specific needs and desires if you get my drift." he said casually.

"OK, but this isn't earth shattering, we pretty well guessed that much when we saw you were all going to Thailand around the same dates but travelling separately." The Superintendent prodded.

A little crestfallen Charles pressed on.

"Sure you did, but that didn't give you the tour operator, or the method of payment for our group booking. And you don't know who the tour operator is, I don't mean his name or address, I'm talking about the link he has back all the way to Nerang. That's what I think you'll be keen for. Am I right?" Winchester continued a little more confidently.

"OK, keep talking, Charles we'll need a lot of detail for this to be workable."

Charles smiled knowing he had our undivided attention. We didn't show it but we both knew what he was bringing to the table was gold.

"Firstly, we never paid any money. We received credits for the delivery of children to Wellington New South Wales. We would have got the same for the shipment you guys raided and caught us collecting." The imprisoned paedophile stated unashamedly as calmly as if he were talking about a shipment of stolen iPhones.

Winchester paused and then asked. "Could I get a Coke or something, all this talk is making me a bit scratchy?"

I looked at my Boss and he nodded his approval. Walking to the door I was thinking; *Instead of a Coke I'd like to give you a bullet just behind your right ear you sick bastard.* I went into the hall and up to the vending machine I had seen as we came in. Grabbing a Coke I went back into the interview room and after opening it placed it on the table in front of Winchester. He gloated at being able to have a Detective buy and serve him a drink. Different strokes for different blokes. After he took a big pull from the can we resumed, his voice sounding smoother and more assertive. The arrogant edge we had grown so accustomed to on the surveillance tapes was back. He figured he had a ticket that might not buy him freedom, but he wouldn't have to put up with this indignation too long.

"Well anyway, like I was saying. No money, have you been wondering how that would work. I mean two operations in Australia and an all expenses paid sex tour in Thailand? Well I'll tell you." He paused and took a smaller drink of Coke.

"The contact in Bangkok is the Ex President of the late and great Hunters Motorcycle Club." He hesitated waiting for that to sink in.

Superintendent Fisher chipped in.

"So Charles, are you telling us you sold the children to the Hunter Bikies and this guy in Thailand is still connected to them?"

"That's exactly what I'm saying. He runs a bar, a heap of girls, grown ups that still look young but cater for the 'ordinary' male tourists. You know how those Thai girls all look like they are twelve even when they are thirty. The guys who probably want to be like us but haven't got the guts to be honest. This guy even has lady-boys. Of course that's no big deal, all legit over there, any Aussie tourist can get some of that."

He paused to take another swig of Coke, and belched loudly. He was clearly embarrassed by this breakdown in his manners.

"Pardon me. Anyway, he also runs a stable of kids, any age, gender or colour. He's into vertical integration. He can even supply babies because some of his other babies and older girls get knocked up. You see he's involved on every level of the trade. You know what I mean it's like KFC owning a wheat growing property, a chicken farm, a slaughter house and selling it by the bucket load through the businesses he owns." Winchester was getting excited and we didn't like it a bit. He was getting off on this stuff, but we didn't want to stop the flow of Intel so we both nodded silently encouraging him to continue. I was thinking; *if I could get away with it I would shove the whole Coke can into his filthy mouth and throttle him slowly.*

Totally ignorant of the hatred and revulsion we both felt towards this animal he continued in bliss. "Anyway, that's how it works, that's what I have to give to you. Names, encrypted email addresses, and physical street addresses in Thailand. This like I promised is big so I expect a lot of years sliced off the going price I was headed for." He added arrogantly.

"Charles that is good Intel, we are just going to grab a drink ourselves and then we'll talk some more. Yes?" Fisher said and the two of us headed out of the room into the hall, neither of us made a move towards the drink machine.

"Shit Ben, that guy makes me want to jump over that table and ring his scrawny neck. It's a horrible thing to confess but we're used to the depravity and inhuman attitudes these paedos have but this guy is a king amongst them, he's an absolute model psychopath. Maybe not actually killing someone but not an ounce of empathy or thought that the little boy or girl he is destroying is a human being who used to have a future."

"Yeah, I couldn't agree more. The only consolation is he I sitting up all clever now, and we know he's about to go for a row of shit-houses for his roll in Stan Croft's murder. I'd love to be there when Jack Nolan delivers that news to Mr Winchester. That Intel he's giving us, that's way out of our jurisdiction isn't it?" I asked pushing down my anger like a geyser trying not to blow.

Fisher nodded. "Yeah, for sure, I'll hand it over to the Feds, but it's awesome Intel that is for certain. OK, back we go. It's not my usual style to be deceitful, but he deserves worse, so just go along with me." Fisher said, looking weary all of a sudden.

I thought; The Australian Federal Police are going to love this. And you didn't have to be Sherlock Holmes to assume this sex tour operator had probably exiled himself to Thailand because he had a truck load of outstanding State Warrants waiting for him if he ever returned home.

"OK Charles, I've spoken to the Crown prosecutor and we are willing to take another three off, that's more than he wanted but we talked him round. Now we need all those Thai contacts."

My mind was rushing at a hundred miles an hour as we sped our way home. Thoughts of whether I could go to Thailand and finish off what I had started by bombing the Bikie's Clubhouse flew in and out of my mind. *No it would be suicide.*

"Ben, you're quiet?" Asked my Boss.

"Just thinking about all of it Sir, what an evil web between the local Grub Club, the Gold Coast Bikies, the Russian Mafia and now back again to the Bikies but in Thailand. Seriously you couldn't make this stuff up." I said sincerely, although my thoughts were a lot more proactive than I'd just sounded. I didn't want to create any mental links for Superintendent Fisher, he was no fool. However, if I was going to finish all this off in Thailand I needed to get there fast, before anyone else. The AFP (Australian Federal Police) would take a while to mobilise, that is if they didn't just hand the Intel over to the Bangkok Police. Which ever way it went, I wasn't prepared to trust that this Bikie would get what he deserved. The AFP were top class and it was my understanding that corruption within their ranks was virtually non-existent. The Bangkok Police were OK as well, but like every Police Force it had its share of corruption. The amount of money involved in the dark sex trade and trafficking children seduced even the best of them.

As we headed for Caloundra I casually said to the Boss. "Those couple of days off showed me just how tired I am, I slept for most of it. What are your thoughts about me taking another week once Molly gets back? I've got weeks of leave up my sleeve."

"Ben I think that's a great idea, this work wears you down and we need to clean off the filth and recharge our batteries. Yeah, I can't see any problem. From what Molly said about Margaret's part at the California Towers she is switched on and smart. The girls can hold the fort."

"Thanks Sir, even though we live on the coast I'm going to head somewhere with lots of sun and just chill out." I said truthfully, sort of. With that request for leave I had committed to go Thailand. Whether I would return was in God's hands, and although I believed he had looked after me at times, I seriously doubted he'd assign an angel for that trip.

CHAPTER 24

Two days later Molly and Margaret wandered into the office looking relaxed and rested. "Welcome back you two. Do anything exciting on your days off?"

Margaret replied first. "Not exciting but I went to Brisbane caught up with mum and my sister, it was nice to be around some normal people."

"Oh, so you're saying Molly and I aren't normal now?" I joked.

"Ignore him Marg, he's been here alone and the poor baby had no one to harass. So Ben, anything happening here?"

"Good news from Jack Nolan...."

Margaret interrupted. "Sorry whose Jack Nolan?"

Realising that she had no way of knowing who he was I explained. "He's a Homicide Detective we worked with on the Grub Club case. You were so busy going forward you might have missed it. Damien Edwards the guy who murdered that Constable and was then shot himself at Kings Beach. Well he murdered a young waiter from the coffee shop who we assume heard something he shouldn't have. Read the file it's worth it for your training to see how people assume things. It looked like an accident until Jack looked into it further." I said gently, I could see Molly was being patient, both of us willing to invest in the new team member's training.

"Anyway, your up to speed now. Jack came over the other day with some great news. They are going to charge Charlie Winchester with conspiracy to murder because he knew Damien was going to and didn't stop him, he sanctioned in a passive sort of way." I stated.

"That is good news more jail time for that horrible little man. Anything else?" Molly asked.

"Well you guys were still here when the Hunters Clubhouse was bombed and the Mafia Boss was hit so you know all about that."

I hated raising either of those events but I figured it would seem strange if I didn't.

"What's your take on all that Molly?" I asked fearing her answer.

"Well Marg and I talked about it while you were on leave. Killing all those Bikies that's big time. We wondered if someone was trying to tie off some loose ends to do with us, but that seems a bit random. Then that hit on the Mafia Boss whatever her name was. By the time the Boss and I get back from visiting Charlie the Gold Coast boys have raided the paedophile brothel we had only learned about two hours before. Now if they had known about it before that Monday they would have hit earlier." Molly said with an air of mystery.

"What we think is the bombing and the hit at Burleigh is the same person, that vigilante guy. Neither of us thought that until the raid."

Margaret added to Molly's comments, then looked a little sheepish because she had spoken.

I had no choice but to join the dots, I had to avoid looking like I was avoiding the obvious.

"So what you're saying is it's the same MO the vigilante seems to follow. Execute some paedo, and somehow get Intel from their home or computer to the cops. So he or she bombs the Clubhouse, shoots the Mafia Boss and gives the Gold Coast a tip about the paedophile brothel run by the Russians. I s'pose that all makes sense." I said confidently.

Both women nodded in agreement. "It's a bit out there, but it's definitely possible. I mean bombing and killing thirty-eight people is a big escalation for this guy. Do you really think it could be a female Ben, or were you just being PC?" Molly asked.

"Yeah, it could be someone of the weaker sex but I sure wouldn't call them that to their face." I joked to appear a little less invested in the topic.

"But the multiple vics is just from necessity, as in the MC Outlaw Group not a normal psychopath escalation or need for more to satisfy the person's cravings. This is nothing like that, this is justice on the person's terms. He or SHE probably don't even want to do these hits but something is driving them. So seeing we aren't Homicide what do we do from here?" I asked.

Molly smiled. "Wow, I thought I was watching Criminal Minds there for a minute. Yeah Marg and I have discussed that as well. We figure the Boss has already thought all this through. If he wants to kick it to Homicide so be it. It's only a theory, but it seems to make sense." Margaret Worthington nodded in silent agreement.

"Who would have dreamed that a young waiter with a curious mind at a coffee shop could start this avalanche hey?" I asked innocently.

I was toying with the idea of not mentioning Thailand to Molly and Margaret but once again realised that it may raise questions if I didn't and then something happened in Bangkok. I recounted the visit Superintendent Fisher and I had with Charles Winchester and passed on all the Intel he had given us. "Because it's overseas I'm pretty sure the Boss is handing it all over to the AFP. Now an international case, this just keeps getting bigger and bigger."

"You're right Ben, it's a weird question, but do you think the vigilante knows about Thailand?" Molly asked obviously inferring he would go there and execute the ex Bikie President.

I was probably flogging a dead horse but in a way I was trying to plant the seed that it may just be a female vigilante. I wasn't concerned about political correctness, our work was too important and we were supportive of each other on a level that negated those issues.

"He or she seems to have been ahead of us every time so far. I reckon there's every chance the vigilante knows about the Thai connection. Whether that is beyond their resources, who knows?

Superintendent Fisher looked around his small team. "Glad you are all here, welcome back Molly and Margaret. No rest for the wicked as they say. Ben, your leave has been approved and processed starting Saturday. Molly looked up surprised.

"We've been talking so much I hadn't had a chance to tell you, I'm taking a week off." I said smiling.

"Marg and I'll be fine, don't you worry mate, women can do anything right Margy?" Molly joked.

Not really understanding the banter and ignoring it anyway the Boss continued.

"Anyway, girls there's a violin teacher that's been fiddling a couple of his students can you guys look into ASAP." Fisher asked.

We all looked astounded. "I'm so sorry that was totally unintentional.

Molly attempting to minimise her Boss' embarrassment at his slip quickly responded as though nothing had occurred.

"Sure thing, you know there are all these people teaching dancing or a musical instrument who never get a Blue Card, they're s'posed to but never do." Margaret said as she picked up her bag ready to head out.

"Yeah, the back yarders slip though the cracks and some make the best of that." Molly said. "See you later Ben don't work too hard." She said sarcastically.

"I'm not sure that Worthington character is a good influence I said laughing. "I can remember when you used to be nice." Molly stuck up a friendly finger as they left.

Saturday couldn't come fast enough, it would be over-playing my hand to ask Fisher if he had passed through that Intel about Thailand. I just had to go do my thing and hope the AFP were as slow as most government agencies. By ten o'clock Saturday I was half way through the eight hour flight to Suvarnabhumi Airport Bangkok. My plan was simple confirm the target, take him out and then go on a holiday to cover my presence in Thailand. I got off the plane and picked up the hire car I had arranged, thankfully it had a Satnav and in English, all was good with the world. Three hours later I arrived at the entrance to where I would have my holiday. "Sawasdee kha. Hello Sir. Khop khun. Thank you for choosing Anantara Hua Hin Resort." I replied as best I could and went through the check in process. "Sawasdee khaa." Please climb aboard Sir. He placed my bags on the rear shelf and we climbed into a golf buggy that took me to my room. What a great place.

"Would you mind if I got a lift back to Reception? I asked the man as he placed my bags in my room. He looked terrified for a moment and asked if everything was alright.

"Sure, I just left something in the car, no this is wonderful." I quickly said to reassure him.

"Can you wait for me just for a minute please?" I asked.

As soon he was out of the room I raced over and made the bed look like I'd slept in it, I then put up the toilet seat. Then I went outside and jumped into the waiting golf buggy.

I drove back to Bangkok and now checked into the Best Western Premier Sukhumvit Hotel that I had also booked because it was within walking distance of the Bikie's Bar. I went through the same wonderful polite system that the Thai hotel and resort staff seem to have mastered if not invented. Once again I was accompanied to my room with the extra bag I had held back at the resort. I sat on the bed and caught my breath after the six odd hours of driving and a bit of jet lag thrown in. I had given myself twelve hours to find, identify and eliminate the Thai end of this evil chain started with the Grub Club back in Caloundra Sunshine Coast. I had no way of knowing if he would be in Bangkok at this precise moment but I had to start somewhere. I headed out, the air conditioned hotel soon forgotten in the oppressive wet heat on street level. Crossing the Sukhumvit 1 Alley, a once attractive but now drug ravaged girl approached me.

"I give you happy ending mista, just follow me please." My heart felt for her, she may well have been sold by her desperate father off a subsistence farm and was now too old and drug effected to work in one of the many bars.

Ignoring her I walked past the massive Bumrungrad International Hospital and turned onto the street that was clearly the Thai version of Sodom and Gomorrah. Food stalls, cafés and endless gory bars assaulting your eyes with flashing coloured lights. Outside every bar was either a man encouraging every passer-by that their every desire would be met within. Some were less subtle with scantily clad girls over oral sex if you bought them a drink.

Jack Dewar same as in whiskey, was the ex Hunters President's name and the irony of his name hadn't been missed by it's owner. Avoiding a screaming scooter rider by a breath I looked up to see the bawdy neon sign confirming that I had at least found where he might be. Jack Dewar's Whiskey Bar flashed in reds and blues like a demented police car. I walked in just another Aussie tourist looking for cheap drinks and girls in any order they came. I sat at the bar and wasn't alone long, the girls were well trained and managed to make sure a customer got instantaneous service. In a wonderful accent with an even better smile my girl asked what I would like in a voice that promised to take you places you had only dreamed about.

After we had a couple of drinks, mine double Jacks on the rocks, hers, three times the cost with fruit and umbrellas and probably alcohol free I started to ask questions.

"I've heard that the owner here is an Aussie like me?" I asked. Her answer while still friendly was a bit evasive but didn't slam the door in my face. However, her eyes had told me much more than her words. They had strayed away from my face to a staircase behind me. It was only a beginning but it was something. I started touching her hair and gently drawing imaginary animals on her leg occasionally letting my hand slip under her very short dress. I was hoping that those stairs led to her room and also to an office where I might find ex Bikie Jack Dewar. She got the hint that I was ready so hand in hand like old friends we headed upstairs.

When we got to the top there was a wall allowing us to go either left or right. I felt the tiny warm hand I was holding gently urging me left. However, as I glanced the other way I saw two big guys probably Australians but could be just about anything but local. I squeezed my new friends hand and dropped hers staggering to the right I drunkenly mumbled "In need a toilet." I repeated myself twice more and by then I had staggered between the two guards. I could hear the girl saying. "You no go that way, please"

They were used to drunks and unlike bouncers who enjoyed hurting easy targets on the way out, these guys knew the club hadn't got all my money yet. In a friendly tone Mr Left said. "Come on mate, you gotta go that way." As he spoke Mr Right gently took my arm to steer me back towards the stairs and my waiting girl. It was over in three moves. They were big, but slow, they were overconfident because they only dealt with drunks, and because of this they was stupid. I grabbed Mr Right's arm and slammed him into the wall so hard his head stayed there stuck in the plaster. Mr Left reacted quickly these weren't overweight board doormen but he was still too slow. I had staggered under their radar and they paid the price. I throat punched Mr Left so hard blood came out of his mouth before his knees gave way and he sunk to the polished wood floor.

I had noticed the bulges under each man's coat and was glad to find an Emperor Scorpion a classic 1911 version put out by Sig Sauer. I quietly cranked the slide back to ensure there was one in the chamber. Then I dropped the mag out to see how many I had to play with, locked and loaded ready to roll. I didn't expect the door to be locked and was right. I knocked like I would expect the bodyguards to do and entered when I heard an invitation. The office was large, but sparsely furnished sitting at a large black desk was a man who could only be Jack Dewar. He was holding a twin for the hand gun I had taken from Mr Left or was it Mr Right. I was impressed he either had CCTVs or maybe he heard Mr Right's head slam into the wall. It didn't really matter.

"How ya goin mate, what can I do for ya?" He asked without fear or anger. He was forty something, totally bald his shiny smooth skull reflecting the down-light above him. He had clearly moved on from his Bikie days and was dressed in an expensive looking dark suit with a black silk shirt and no tie. He looked like he'd come straight from a Godfather movie but his voice betrayed his roots.

"I'll ask again, what the fuck do you want?" He was glaring at me, unused to not being in total control. His gun was as steady as mine and I was aware that he had stopped me silhouetted by the open doorway.

He asked calmly. "You look like a cop but you're not acting like one, so I think I know who you might be. I'm honoured if I'm right. Are you the guy that closed down that mob of old wankers on the Sunshine Coast, no that was the pigs? I'm still not sure if I can smell pork or not." He laughed with his mouth but his reptilian eyes did get the joke.

I hadn't spoken at this stage, but I didn't want to be here too much longer. He wasn't showing any fear at all, and we were equal gun wise.

"Jack, can I call you Jack?" I waited for him to nod his permission.

"Well anyway Jack, I'm here to see you and now I have. And your nose is working fine because I'm a cop but I'm on holidays so I can do stuff I wouldn't normally do back home. You're right I was involved in the arrests of those Grub Club guys that's what we call them because they used to meet every morning for coffee. And guess what Jack I was the one who blew up your old clubhouse and killed all those brothers in arms." I could see this got a reaction.

"You prick, you got some balls coming here and telling me this stuff. What do you want, how much?"

I laughed and said, I even shot that Russian Doll that was running the Gold Coast operations. Did you know her?"

"Nah, she arrived after my time. But you killed her, just one guy all my Hunter mates."

He was street smart and a leader, he knew I was there for only one purpose.

"You know, it's just money, business, I hate the sickos but they just keep comin, and their money is good."

I'd had enough and I was thinking he probably had as well. He'd also come to the realisation that as soon as his confession was over I would have to kill him.

He smiled like a lion about to chew down on an antelope.

"So that's a lovely story but why are you here?....." I shot him just above his right eye and again in the middle of his forehead. His ready gun slipping to his desk.

ISAIAH 59:18

According to their deeds, accordingly He will repay, fury to his adversaries, recompense to his enemies; to the islands he will repay recompense.

Talking to myself now."Well if you really have to know I came here to kill you." I said through closed teeth as the adrenalin that had been surging through me started to leech out of my bloodstream. Just in case I needed it to get out of the club I shoved the Sig Sauer into my jeans and covered it with my shirt. I walked around to the other side of the desk where I could see the video recorders attached to the numerous CCTVs secreted around the offices and club. I grabbed all five of the DVDs not knowing which ones I needed to remain unseen and shoved them in a shopping bag that I found in the bin. Poking my head out of the office doorway I was glad to see the hallway and steps were all empty. I took the stairs three steps at a time and was thankful that the music had covered the gun shots and now the darkness of the bar allowed me to moved invisibly to the front door.

As I was leaving the club two men I picked as Australian cops walked by me. They were slightly better dressed than Aussie Detectives so I was thinking Australian Federal Police (AFP). I was careful not to show any recognition of them at all. Like I did to them, they looked at me like cops always look at everybody, noting appearance, guessing attitudes checking for that tell tale bulge that said the person was armed. We all kept moving. I was glad I'd shoved the gun down the back of my jeans. I headed in the opposite direction of my hotel. If those two AFP guys had someone outside, which would have been Standard Operating Procedure (SOP) they may have decided that I was worth following. I would have been amazed if anyone was coming after me but it was better to be cautious. I kept a reasonable pace as I headed into yet one of Bangkok's famous malls. The Emporium five floors of luxury clothing and items a great place to lose someone.

I took a quick look at the Directory board and headed for the first of many escalators. I stood near the side so anyone following me would see me effortlessly, I repeated this exercise five times. As I walked off the last escalator I headed for the EMPRIVE CINECLUB. I quickly purchased a ticket to a Thai speaking movie that the operator suggested, or at least I think that's what she was saying. She kept pointing to the a board showing film start times and then to the wall clock. The theatre worker couldn't understand why I wanted to pay for a movie that had already been going for an hour. I had my reasons, buying and keeping the ticket provided me a soft alibi that wasn't bad. I walked up the foyer with several theatres doors branching off either side. Thinking how smart I was I looked around one more time.

There, next to the ticket booth buying a ticket was the man I had seen outside Jack Dewar's Club. He had to be Federal Police. Hiding out in the open and drawing him on the escalator and follow me more closely had worked. Until I spotted him all my anti-surveillance tricks were only a precaution. I had doubted whether the AFP Officers had any reason to think I was worth following. However, like any good cop he must have IDed me as an Aussie, and alerted by some primitive hunter's gut feeling that told him I was somehow involved, and worth following me to this theatre. They didn't know who I was so my new concern was that this switched on Officer may have taken photos of me before I had seen him.

By looking at the advertising poster outside I deduced I had a ticket for theatre four. I walked in casually, not showing any awareness that I was being followed. I waited in the dark allowing my eyes to adapt to the darkness. I preserved my newly acquired night-vision by closing my eyes. Secreted in the darkest shadow of the dark entry to the theatre I waited. I heard the door open and waited for it shut knowing I would be invisible to the man who had just left the brightly lit hallway. Before his eyes could adjust I sprang on him, grabbing his arm I slammed my fist into his Solar Plexus following up with a solid hit to the back of his head. I wanted him unconscious not seriously injured or dead. He was after all a fellow cop, not a crim or a paedophile. He crumpled and I picked him up under his arms and dragged him the darkest part of the entry.

By his presence my alibi and therefore the ticket were now shot to shreds, but I was aware that we were standing in the doorway to the theatre. But it served another way, and I was now grateful the film was half way through as it meant that no one would probably come through that door. I had already decided taking him into the seating area would be exposing myself to those patrons already in there. Alternatively, dragging him into the hall was out of the question because it was too well lit and had CCTVs everywhere. It was here or no where. By feel in the dark I quickly searched his pockets, not taking the time to look at anything I simply emptied them and took everything with me including his phone in case it held photos of me. The only thing I left was his AFP Glock, I didn't want it and I didn't want to ditch it for some Bangkok crim to pick up. Making sure he was OK I checked the pulse on his neck and his breathing and rolled him into the recovery position. The skilful AFP Officer would probably have a headache, but he'd live.

Circling round the dead Bikie's Bar I returned to my hotel room. It was too late to check out without being remembered by the hotel staff. In the unlikely event that the cops visited all the hotels the next day looking for a western male leaving unexpectedly I wanted to avoid being that obvious. I wasn't Jason Bourne with multiple Pass Ports so I had to be careful relying on just common sense and acting just like the tourist I was supposed to be. I was starving and it would add to an alibi if I needed one. I phoned Room Service and ordered a steak sandwich and two Jack Daniels on the rocks. I couldn't relax until I was back at the Anantara Hua Hin Resort. However the JDs calmed me down as the adrenalin slowly dissipated out of my system, and the sandwich was outstanding. Setting my bedside alarm for seven AM I put the TV on and was asleep within a few minutes. It was common for people to spend a few days in Bangkok and then go elsewhere so the next morning when I checked out from the hotel it was as normal as breathing to all concerned.

The four hour trip back to Anantara Hua Hin Beach flew by. Stopping for fuel I slipped into the bathroom and changed into a pair of boardies and a local tee-shirt I had bought in the resort gift shop. As I drove through all the little beach villages along the coast my mind juggled its way through the last few days. What it meant, what I'd done right and wrong. I understood how my revenge against paedophiles worked. It didn't matter how many I executed, how many I officially arrested there would always be more. There would be more individuals, more paedo rings and more criminals involved or supporting them by supplying victims or distributing their poison. It was shovelling sand on the beach, every day. I couldn't kill them all. But every one must have had a child saving effect somehow.

I had thought about holding off killing Jack Dewar the Bikie-cum-paedophile tour organiser and discovering his contacts and organisation. However, this might take more time that I had in country and a foreign country at that. Just as importantly, I had no jurisdiction and enquiries or interrogations are hard without me speaking Thai. And now clearly I knew from the previous night's encounter that the Australian Federal police had mobilised incredibly fast. I knew I had only just got out of there, and wasn't real sure I was in the clear even now. So I settled for the head of the snake, often that head person would be replaced quickly. However I didn't think Dewar had set up his organisation that way. Hopefully, his death would spell disaster with no contender to take over. I didn't know that, but I couldn't solve every issue in the world.

Only the ones that came across my dirty radar screen. As usual the guilts arrived, seeing the AFP boys had arrived showed me that I could have left all the Thai connection for them to clean up. Knowing how thorough they were I was confident that they would investigate every angle of the dead Bikie's organisation. That may have lead to a heap of names and arrests both in Thailand and back home in Australia. But who knows?

I drove into the outdoor car park of the Anantara Hua Hin Resort and casually walked through Reception and up to my room. I was going to stay the rest of the week as I had booked. Although the first few days had been hectic especially with the AFP boys showing up I was really looking forward to the break. Jack Dewar's death didn't even make the TV News. There was a small piece on a middle page of the Bangkok Post and that was the late Mr Dewar forgotten.

Unsurprisingly there was no news anywhere regarding the presence of the Australian Federal Police in Thailand. A week wasn't going to be enough but it was sure nice. Daily massages, cheap drinks and plenty of sun and I was feeling great. It was nearly enough of a distraction for me to forget about my constant pain and the battle that raged within me.

CHAPTER 25

Maroochydore Airport and I was just about through Passport Control. There were the usual mix of AFP Officers, Queensland Police Officers and Customs standing around or checking the passengers or bags coming in. All was going well, having nothing to declare I was directed down that lane to exit the airport when an Australian Federal Police Officer approached me. My heart nearly stopped when I realised that it was one of the men I had seen briefly at the darkened entry to the Bikie's bar in Thailand. This was either a crazy coincidence or they were waiting for me.

"Welcome back to Australia Sir." He said in a friendly manner.

Smiling, I couldn't trust my voice not to betray my nervousness so I just nodded and made to keep walking.

"Just hang on a minute please. Can I see your paperwork please?" He requested.

I handed my Passport and Boarding Pass stub over to him with a smile. He looked at both documents and at me and then asked. "Where did you stay in Thailand Mr McQueen?"

I knew as a cop alarm bells rang if someone I was questioning ask me why I had required that information. I had also decided that I wouldn't reveal that I was a Detective unless I was asked what my occupation was. Flashing one's badge when being questions can also appear guilty or raise alarms.

"Sure, Sir I stayed at the Anantara Hua Hin Resort, it's a bit of a drive out of Bangkok but what a place, amazing." I called him Sir because respect usually helped but I wondered if that might have over done it a little.

"I can look it up on Goggle, but just how far is it?" he asked still in a friendly tone.

Knowing what was behind the question I replied. "Well, it took me about four hours but maybe a local can do it a bit quicker."

"So just briefly tell me what you did from the moment you flew into Bangkok to now, will you?" He asked.

"Oh, you serious, I'm really beat after that flight." I said hoping to discourage him.

"I can understand Sir, but just quickly tell me about your holiday." He asked just a hint of demand creeping in.

I was so happy I'd been given the chance to lay out my alibi but I hid it and answered. "Well, I flew into Bangkok, hired the car and drove straight to the resort. You want a daily activity sort of report?" I asked trying to appear like I was willing to cooperate.

"So you were at the resort the whole time, all of your holiday?" He asked a little cloud of disappointment shading his face.

That was the question I had been waiting for, I had made sure I didn't offer the answer before he asked. "Yeah, I hate big cities and I've been to Bangkok before." I left out the connecting lines and let him work it out. I could see more disappointment cover his face and then he said.

"I'll just take some notes Sir, and you can be on your way."

He asked me the details of the resort I'd stayed in. He was looking for a physical description of things, he even asked what were some of the meals I had enjoyed while I was there. Of course this was easy as in a way my answers were true. He wrote down my flight times in and out of Thailand, although both of us knew that he probably had that information already. All things that he would check and I hoped he would because they should provide me with a rock solid alibi. I talked about the last few days at the resort as though the whole week was the same. Plenty of sleep, walks, massages, pool bar drinks.

"I'm going to miss those cheap Mai Tais standing in the pool every arvo. I mean, that's why I went there, I didn't want a lot running around, just a rest and everything I needed was right there at the resort."

I had to assume that the AFP were cross-checking every Australian male of my description arriving home from Thailand in a hope to ID the man who had killed Jack Dewar and they had seen leaving the bar. He may have initially thought I was the man they had fleetingly seen leaving the dead Bikie's Bar in Bangkok, but the lighting and the short time we passed each other didn't give them much to go on. I was darker from days of sun and hadn't been near a razor a week. The AFP Officer was probably asking himself; he doesn't really look like the guy we saw, and anyway, *how could it be me if I had been some four hours drive away at the time?*

"Thank you Sir, what were you looking for?" I asked to complete the charade.

"Just routine enquiries Sir, thank you for your cooperation." The AFP Officer responding brusquely, clearly disappointed I wasn't his target.

I turned towards the exit and wheeled my suitcase towards the taxi rank. I had another day before I was expected back at work so I headed home ready to settle back into normal routine. Looking at my watch I smiled and thought; *Must be time for a Mai Tai and a massage.*

Entering the familiar surroundings of my offices I found Molly and Margaret hard at it. "Welcome back Ben, hey even around here on the coast that tan is pretty damn cool." Molly said smiling as she looked up from her monitor. I had shaved but I was darker than I had been since I was a teen.

"Sorry to rub it in girls, but what a place? It was amazing, massages, Pina Coladas and Mai Tais all day long, surf is crap but it's nice to swim in." I replied looking between Molly and Margaret.

"The Boss will be glad you're back there's a bit goin on as usual." Molly added.

"What did the final wash up on the Grub Club look like?" I asked expectantly.

Molly replied with a smile. "I hope those coffee lovers like instant coffee because that's all they'll be getting where they're going. You already know all the charges they'll go for. Then of course we re-visited Richard Cook for buying that kid in Melbourne. The other one named for that we would have charged was Paul Simpson but obviously he's dead." She paused and took a swig from a can of Red Bull.

"The Homicide boys got Charles for Conspiracy to Murder Stan Croft the coffee shop waiter. That was great because it more than negated the sentence discount he had wrangled. That allowed us to keep our promises and he still got plenty of time behind bars." Molly said still smiling.

"Good, he deserves to die an old man in there." I added, thinking I'd prefer to see him through my telescopic sight instead.

"Because he heard Charles had been arrested his mate in Warwick figured out it was Charles who had dobbed him in for selling his children for sex. So anyway the Warwick guy knows there is no denying his part. Anyway it gets better he's got a video of Charles and his coffee mates abusing this scum-bag's kids. So they all got that added onto their scores. Charles got even more time because the Warwick paedo told the local cops that Charles had organised it all." Molly stated triumphantly.

"That's great to hear, you guys have been busy while I was away. Any news on the Hunters Motorcycle Club? Did anyone find a connection with the Russian Mafia Boss who got killed?"

"Yeah, do you remember there was just the one survivor from the bombing. Anyway he's still alive and Bikie style he hasn't been very forthcoming. He wouldn't tell them any details but he did confirm that the Hunters had a business relationship with the Russians on the Gold Coast.

We still aren't sure of every detail, but we have confirmed what we thought. The Grub Club grabbed the kids to supply the Bikies who then passed them onto the Russian paedophile brothel." Molly stated easily.

I was happy all round, it was great to hear these sickos had gotten charged with so many crimes, and I couldn't see them avoiding long term sentences. The other thing that was making me happy was that I was obviously in the clear. The Bikie hadn't been able to describe me enough for anyone to identify me, it was dark, and I had bashed him the whole time so he didn't really maintain eye contact enough to look past the sunnies and the long bill cap. And after my questioning at the airport it looked pretty certain that I had carried out the Thai operation successfully and was home free. The next week or so was fairly usual stuff, complaints to follow up, I had my annual Range Certification. I always enjoyed shooting my hand gun and always exceeded the Police service requirements. Superintendent Fisher stayed around that first week I was back and then took some leave himself. The Unit pretty well ran itself as long as there wasn't any political requirements or inter-state liaison going on. Being the Senior Officer I was in charge but Molly was so experienced we all just worked together. We were all mindful to take every opportunity to include Margaret as the new team member to continue her training. She would eventually be referred to the 'Charm School' where she would go in an above average Constable and graduate as a Detective. Hopefully, maintaining the qualities we had seen so far. The Grub Club member's trials came and went with all three of us called upon to confirm our notes and clarify any queries. As usual the Defence Barristers attacked us trying to find a flaw in the evidence or if that failed the processes employed to collect that evidence. Thankfully, our statements and the evidence was deemed admissible.

An email came through to Superintendent Fisher, but because I was standing in for his role he had redirected his emails to me. I had arrested Arthur/ Arty Campbell twice before and he had served a combined sentence of eight years. On his release from Sir David

Longlands Prison about two years ago and as soon as his Parole had been completed, wisely he had moved to Victoria. Being on the Federal Sex Offenders Register the various State bodies kept track of his where abouts. The email before me was from the Victorian Police Service advising all Child Protection and Investigation Units that he had left Victoria. It was believed that he planned to move back onto the Sunshine Coast. His speciality was grabbing kids in parks and picnic areas. Taking girls no older than five into public toilets, if challenged by an onlooker he would pretend to be their father. He would then sexually abuse them and leave them in the toilet stall terrified and crying. I knew this vermin so well I was confident that he would move back to be close to where he had lived before.

The next day another email came this time from the Child Protection and Investigation Unit at Roma St Headquarters. It confirmed that he had moved to Queensland and had applied to the Housing Commission for a unit in or around Caloundra. If nothing else he was predictable, and not just where he would live. I knew he would re-offend it was the nature of the beast. I made a mental note to go for a drive and see if I could find him. Standard Operating Procedure was that I inform my team of this new threat to our patch, it was obvious, it made great sense. But I chose not to tell Molly and Margaret about Artie's arrival. I suppose by doing that I knew in the very depth of my being I had already started to think about his need to face even more justice than the courts had imposed. More importantly, there was no way he was going to hurt a little girl again, here or anywhere. And that was why he had moved back, it was only a matter of time and opportunity.

"Anything exciting going on Molly?" I asked knowing that if there was she would have already told me.

"Nah mate, it's great seems quiet for a while, that can't be a bad thing?" She answered.

"That's for sure, we might re-direct the phones and grab some lunch what do you think?" I asked.

"Sounds great, Kawana pub might be nice, I like their food and being on the water. Any particular reason or you just missing your massages and cocktails?" Laughing she stood up.

"A little bit. Molly I want to go somewhere afterwards so I'll meet you and Margaret there."

I said casually, and the three of us headed off.

Lunch was nice, I enjoyed sitting in the sun enjoying the sights and sounds of the little marina that surrounded the hotel. Not rushing off too quickly I said my goodbyes and headed towards where Arthur Campbell had last lived. There was a park with play ground equipment and BBQs nearby so I started my hunt there. Like I said a lot of these guy's downfall was they were so predictable. I found him in under twenty minutes sitting under a huge Pandanus Tree trying to look like he was reading a news paper. There were five families picnicking or playing on the swings and slippery slides. Campbell must have been so busy watching the kids that he didn't see me approaching him.

"Well Arty isn't this a big surprise. Seen anything unusual?" Sarcasm dripping from every word.

In his shock he raised the paper and I was so relieved that he hadn't been 'helping himself' under the newspaper, because although that wasn't his MO, it certainly wouldn't be past him.

"Ahhhhhhh, Mr McQueen fancy seeing you here. To answer your question, yes I have, I once saw a two headed calf. Can you believe it?" He responded just as sarcastically. Then he realised it would do him no good to cross swords with a Detective who who knew all about him. "Just enjoying this Sunshine Coast sun after that cold Victoria Sir." He said convincingly.

Laughing I played with sand using the toe of my boot.

"You guys must read the same books or something, the last time I heard that it was a dolphin wearing a hat and not a two headed calf. Makes sense Arty, it's a lovely day to be out in the sun." He was looking uncomfortable and that made my day.

"Where you living Arty?" I asked in a friendly voice.

"Just around the corner." He said jerking his thumb over his left shoulder.

"Great, do you have to advise the register?" I asked knowing full well that he had to inform the Sex Offenders Register of any change of address.

"You know, as soon as I got home this morning that was top of my things to do list, Mr McQueen." He said like it was the truth. Nodding, he stood up as if he was rushing off right now to do just that.

Taking out my notebook and pen. "Just in case you forget again Arty can I just grab it while we think of it?" I asked with a tone that he knew left him no choice.

"Unit 5 Bulimba Court on Sunset Drive." He recited unhappily.

"OK, well maybe you should head home now, and Arty stay away from parks and swings hey?" I said threateningly as I walked away. "And don't forget to register."

He came over as a sort of harmless person who wouldn't hurt anyone especially a child. He was soft talking in his mid-thirties with a slight build and sparse mousy coloured hair. He dressed a bit like an old surfie but the only board he had ever been on was a floor board. Part of his 'uniform' always included a Tee-shirt with a big Disney cartoon character whose bright colours and fun would attract a five-year-old. However his benign looks aside, he was a proven paedophile who had hurt so many children that we knew of. We always believed there were more victims that never reported or that the paedophile we charged had abused but was never caught. Even his presence in this park demonstrated that nothing had changed. I was positive that he wasn't about to grab a little girl that very moment, however he was getting some sort of sick satisfaction just watching them at play. We call it 'getting a glimpse', sadly the definition doesn't demand too much imagination. Eventually, as it had in the past the efficacy of this looking and getting on the net would lose its diminish. Then fantasy would become action and another little one would be changed, damaged for life. As I drove back to the office I had already decided that old mate Arty Campbell was next.

Back at the office all was still pretty quite. There had been a report of a man with an intellectual disability who claimed to have been abused by his carer. While the victim was at nearly fifty-years-old and no child it came under our purview. These cases were extremely difficult because the victim was not a child but had diminished ability to understand what had occurred. Understandably, they struggled with the processes involving us and in some cases had limited communication skills or ability to recall with any confidence. I asked Molly and Margaret to investigate it and let me know how it went. There were organisational procedures including the carer possessing a Blue Card issued by the Commission for Children. These were better than nothing although they lacked photo ID which always concerned us.

However, they represented a more detailed Police pre-employment check, and that was a good thing. In reality this meant that even if the applicant was a paedophile they could gain a card because they had never been caught. We knew it, the Commission for Children knew it, and of course the paedos were aware of this gap as well. The lack of photo ID permitted the cards to be traded, stolen or bought by paedophiles seeking access to their victims. Molly and Margaret would investigate the complaint as well as they could. They would collect victim statements, Supervisors or Management, and co-workers would be interviewed. If it was shared accommodation co-tenants would be as well as of course the victim and the alleged perpetrator. Sometimes the person with the disability was just savvy enough to know they could hurt the carer by making an accusation. Although this was not how we ever approached such cases it did happen. However, all these challenges would never stop our team investigating the claims thoroughly. Sometimes we couldn't proceed due to lack of evidence, but often the process caused the support worker to leave both that organisation and the sector. Nothing's perfect.

That night I parked well away from Arty Campbell's address, walking on the shadow side of the street I approached Bulimba Court a six pack of units probably built in the sixties. Campbell's Unit 5 was a back one, this suited me as it meant I would be off the street. There was no need for confirmation or talk this time, straight in execute the paedophile and home for a late dinner. I knocked on the door and put my finger over the spy hole so he couldn't see who it was. He opened the door a fraction, and I noticed he wasn't surprised to see me.

"Ah, Mr McQueen I wondered if you might visit, but I didn't expect you at this late hour." he said a little louder than I had ever heard him speak.

"Well Arty I thought I'd come and see how you were." I pushed passed him and walked into his lounge, the lights were off and the TV was flickering, reflecting on the walls of his unit. I unholstered my gun and turned to shoot the skinny little paedophile.

"Evening Detective-Sergeant McQueen, we've talked but never really introduced each other did we? I'm Sergeant Ron Jessop, I knew we'd get to know each other" Said the Australian Federal Police Officer I had seen in Bangkok and at Maroochydore Airport.

I was thinking; *Well now I know it was no coincidence him being at the Maroochydore Airport, he had been waiting for me.*

Recovering quickly I put my hand out to shake his. "Yeah, you're right I'm Ben." I said knowing I couldn't explain why I had a gun in my hand. I couldn't, but I had to give it a try. I noticed Arty Campbell was no where to be seen. A thought one that terrified me flew into my mind; *They had used Arty as bait and I had the hook in my mouth.*

"Oh man I'm glad that was you. I somehow sensed that there was someone behind me that's why I turned with my gun out. You ought to be a bit careful surprising people that way." I said hoping I sounded better than I felt.

"Oh yeah you're probably right, but I did want to surprise you after all. Now this can go one of two ways." As he spoke he raised his hand gun from beside his leg where he had been hiding it mostly hidden.

"We both put our guns down and talk a bit. Or, you get excited and who knows what will happen?" He spoke calmly but confidently.

He continued. "Now Ben I s'pose we have a lot to talk about, but you comin here gun out and everything has told me we are right about you. You were planning on killing Arty weren't you Ben? Now I know you will probably deny it, and short of letting you shoot that little scum-bag this was about as close as I could get at being sure." He paused for a moment looking at me I could feel his eyes boring into mine, trying to figure what I would do.

"I'm not real sure what you mean Ron, can I call you Ron? I came here tonight to check on a known paedophile whose on the National Sexual Offenders Register. I'm just doin my my job." I bluffed.

"Sure call me Ron, I mean we are on the same side aren't we? Now we still haven't worked out how you managed Thailand, but what we do know is you killed Jack Dewar. If there are a big hunk of sub-humans who profit in depravity and deserve killing he was right high on that tree. I agree." The AFP investigator knew he was dealing with a well trained and experienced Detective, but it was worth a try.

The old Empathy card, sort of 'yeah she deserved to be raped wearing that skimpy dress' attempting to get a rapist to talk.

I needed to get into a position where I could avoid any gun play but escape, after that I would work out what I was going to do. The last thing I wanted was to shoot a fellow cop doing his job, he didn't deserve it like all the sickos I had done in the past.

"Ron what are you talking about, mate, I'm pretty tired I think I might call it a night." I said ignoring all of his Thailand accusation as though he hadn't spoken.

He acted the same way. "But all these local ones well it just can't happen Ben. It can't keep going, mate you might think you are some righteous avenger but we have courts and jails, not self appointed vigilantes. We've had a team investigating you. Mate what happened? you're a damn good cop, a hard working, honest detective. But, it wasn't enough."

My resolve crumpled, just like I'd seen it lots of times when crims were questioned it was nearly a relief to be caught. To finally not be looking over their shoulder. For me it was more the constant battle between knowing what I was doing and knowing it was wrong both in the eyes of the law and God.

Speaking softly at first I confessed. "Ron, I've never taken a bribe or let someone go that was guilty. I've never crossed the lines, you know planting evidence when other guys, so many times they are beginning to blur. I've seen these Judges let paedophiles go completely, or a suspended sentence, or an early parole. What about the victims, the kids of course but their families. This abuse keeps hurting until you die." I said the passion rising in my voice.

Sergeant Jessop was very experienced and knew I was working myself up to something, he hoped not to a point of no return. The AFP Sergeant thought to himself; *This Detective in front of me is by definition a serial killer, but one I understand. Here, or in the AFP offices I will walk this walk. However, if you wanted a personal opinion buy me a drink after work and I might just as easily agree with the bloke. A man who had probably seen so many children and families destroyed by abuse and then to be let down by the system that he was eventually crushed.*

I was committed to not shooting this AFP investigator, but I had to get away. Of course I would lose everything, but I could start afresh in the Northern Territory or somewhere, if I could just escape. I took the three steps towards him and he raised his gun. "Ben don't do anything silly, the last thing I want to have to do is shoot you."

"That's reassuring, and for what it's worth the feeling is mutual." As I spoke the last word I launched the last few feet and clocked him hard on the side of the head with my gun. He looked like he was going to recover so I swung back for another hit. Thankfully, his eyes glazed over, his knees buckled and he collapsed onto the threadbare carpet. "Sorry mate." I whispered as I stepped over his supine body and headed for the door. My only thought was escape and I was still shaken by the trap I had so easily fallen for. I opened the door and exited the unit running down the ten steps three at a time and landed on the scarred concrete path. There was a light at the front gate that I wanted to avoid so I jumped a bedraggled flower bed and stepped onto the lawn. Mercifully, the yard was dark and I let out a breath Stress had been holding. I was free.

"That's far enough Detective-Sergeant McQueen." A voice from the shadows caused me to freeze. My thoughts were like popcorn ricocheting anywhere and everywhere; *Who was it, had the AFP Sergeant regained consciousness and caught up with me? No he couldn't have. Whoever this is I can't let him arrest me. In my confusion of being trapped I had forgotten the basics, you don't go to arrest someone by yourself. This must be his partner who was watching the exit.*

I turned towards the voice. I forgot something else as well. I still had my gun in my hand. In the dark it must have looked like I was making a move on him. Bang. I felt like a truck had hit me in the chest. I fell backwards into some bush, spread-eagles my eyes filled with light and my last breath hissed through my closed mouth.

"You fucking idiot, why did you do that." Asked AFP Constable First Class Jake Borderman speaking to himself because he was sure the man lying in front of him was dead.

"Jake what happened?" The voice was familiar to the AFP Officer, but weaker than usual.

Turning towards the unit steps. "Sergeant Jessop, you're wounded, you're covered in blood. Are you OK?" Asked Jake Borderman clearly worried about his partner.

Falling to his knees on the tiny landing he used his hand to make sure he didn't fall any further Jessop responded quietly.

"What happened mate, are you OK, what happened?"

AFP Constable First Class Jake Borderman explained the events that had resulted in him shooting Detective Ben McQueen. He knew that he would have to repeat his report several times when the Investigation Standards (AFP) and the Coroner's Enquiry investigated the shooting.

"Sergeant he turned so quickly, his gun came up like he was going to shoot, I figured it was either him or me." He said, confidence coming back into his voice, but still a cloud of sadness.

"Jake, it's a real pity but I wouldn't be surprised if deep down he wanted it this way. You and I know from looking hard at this bloke he was a top class Detective. But to do the stuff he did he was broken inside. I don't know what broke him, or what it was all about, but I nearly feel like you did him a favour mate. It's a pity, but you did what you had to do." Sergeant Jessop said to make both of the law enforcement officers feel better about killing one of their own.

THE END

About the Author

ABOUT THE AUTHOR David Adams spends as much time as possible in the Australian bush, honing survival skills, gold, treasure fossicking, and hunting feral animals throughout Australia. He served as an Officer in the Australian Army Reserve during the post-Vietnam era. Dave has trained alongside members of the United States Marine Corps and Special Air Services SAS personnel. Serving his last two years in the A.D.F as a Platoon Commander Military Police provided him with exposure to law enforcement working closely with his civilian counterparts in the Queensland Police Service. Dave relies on this real-life experience to provide him with authentic characters, settings, and a knowledge of military equipment and procedures. He continues to travel the world in search of exciting settings and characters that he hopes will transport his readers to these exotic places while adding a reality to his books.

www.ingramcontent.com/pod-product-compliance
Lightning Source LLC
Chambersburg PA
CBHW020612260626
47157CB00003B/983